A WOMAN TORN IN TWO

Katie had to find out if the hands that caressed her had also held the gun in a shocking assassination.

She had to find out if the lips that kissed her and whispered words of love also could snarl epithets of hate.

She had to find out if the man who was her lover was also her country's most dangerous enemy.

And if she found out that the truth was what she feared, she had to decide which side she was on— and whom she would betray . . .

BETRAYED

BASED ON THE FILM WRITTEN BY

JOE ESZTERHAS

A novel by Leonore Fleischer

A SIGNET BOOK

NEW AMERICAN LIBRARY

PUBLISHER'S NOTE

This book is a work of fiction. Names, characters, places, and incidents either are the product of the author's imagination or are used fictitiously, and any resemblance to actual persons, living or dead, events, or locales is entirely coincidental.

Copyright © 1988 by United Artists Pictures, Inc.

SIGNET, SIGNET CLASSIC, MENTOR, ONYX, PLUME, MERIDIAN and NAL BOOKS are published by NAL PENGUIN INC., 1633 Broadway, New York, New York 10019

First Printing, August, 1988

1 2 3 4 5 6 7 8 9

PRINTED IN THE UNITED STATES OF AMERICA

It begins with a death. Not the usual kind of old-age tailing off and fading away that nature provides in the fullness of time, but an unnatural, man-made, violent, and treacherous death, death from behind, conceived in secret and carried out in stealth.

A planned, deliberate murder, with no allowance for mercy or pity. And there's more. More to come. The death of this one man is only the bloody beginning, because, once shed, blood leads with inexorable steps to more blood . . . and still more.

As though violence were an addiction, a hunger that knows no appeasement, an angry hunger that demands to be fed . . . again . . . and yet again. With human food.

Chapter One

Kraus

The air in the broadcast booth was stagnant with stale cigarette smoke and the stink of overflowing ashtrays. No amount of artificial coolant pumped in by the overworked air conditioning could overcome Chicago's blistering early-summer heat and the smoke that wreathed in the humidity around Kraus's balding head. At the microphone, Kraus was sweating, his jacket off, no tie, his collar open, his voice rasping with exhaustion as his four-hour shift at the mike wound down to another day's finale.

The calls kept coming in, although they'd tailed off a little in the last hour. The customary handful of saucer-spotters; one woman who swore she'd been kidnapped by beings from the outer edge of the galaxy and was now carrying a Plutonian's baby; a man who wanted to tell the world that the phone company was after him and had planted a bug in his toilet. The hopeful, lonely callers, men and women reaching out, wanting to be heard, listening to their radios at work, or driving home from work, or just sitting with idle hands. Men and women with problems, with bizarre beliefs, with stubborn opinions—mostly misinformed—who wanted to hear themselves talk over the radio. And a lot of them were just plain kooks.

Dan Kraus attracted kooks—it was his stock in trade.

"Controversy" the station called it when they bragged about him in the promos. "For controversy, for the fastest, freshest, feistiest talk in town, tune in Dan Kraus over WLD Chicago, the voice of the Midwest." The station encouraged Kraus to be foulmouthed and argumentative; he had become a "personality," and the personality paid off. People tuned in just to hear what outrageous thing he was going to say next; he insulted his listeners and they came back begging for more. Most of Kraus's listeners were ordinary men and women, normal, intelligent people, but they rarely phoned in to express their normal, intelligent opinions. Nor would anybody be interested if they did.

For every sane, sensible, and boring phone call, there were at least six wackos from the so-called lunatic fringe, that hostile and belligerent mother lode whose fingers were always on the phone dial, who loved to participate in talk radio, and who didn't mind being held up to ridicule by Dan Kraus as long as they could hear the sound of their own voices booming out over the airwaves.

Kraus drew deeply on a Camel, stubbed it out into the ashtray, and mopped the sweat out of his eyes. In a Chicago summer, headphones are torture, trapping heat to the broadcaster's head and neck. Even his scraggly, salt-and-pepper beard was sweating. Perspiration flowed from his brow into the deep lines and folds of his furrowed, middle-aged face. Yet, oddly, he didn't much mind the heat or the humidity. After all, only an irritated oyster can produce a pearl. And Kraus considered his words pearls, if not solid gold. His irritation was worth big bucks in station advertising, and he had the weekly income and the ratings to prove it.

"We've got twenty-one minutes remaining in the hour, it's eighty-two degrees," he growled at his listeners. "Hey, people, you know what we're talkin' about tonight? Jewboys!" His gravelly voice gave the words an explosive twist. "Anti-Semitism! Hate! I know there's lots of kike haters out there among all you nice and friendly Gentiles. You got the guts to talk about it, don't you? You're not ashamed of what you believe in, are you?" His taunts were deliberate, designed to provide a flood of furious incoming calls.

Grinning contemptuously at the microphone, Kraus pictured his lowest-common-denominator listeners bristling with anger and a hatred barely kept in check. He loved yanking their moronic, bigoted chains.

"This is Kraus on WLD, the voice of the Midwest, ninety thousand watts from Chicago, Sickago, whatever you wanna call it. And you know what, partner? I'm an ol' Jew myself. Come on, show me how brave you are. Call this Jewboy and we'll talk turkey, right after this message."

As the taped commercial hit the airwaves, Kraus turned off his mike and reached into his shirt pocket for an unfiltered Camel. Lighting up, he drew a long drag on the cigarette and rubbed at the back of his neck through his sweat-soaked shirt collar. He was always knotted with tension when he was on the air; twenty-two years of broadcasting had never seen his muscles in a relaxed state.

From the other side of the glassed-in broadcast booth, Bob Reilley, the studio sound engineer, swung around to the control panel.

"You're asking for it tonight, Dan," he said, only half joking, his voice coming through the speaker.

Kraus grinned sourly. "Yeah? Fuck 'em if they can't take it." He pointed to his phone. All the buttons were lit. "See. I knew that would bring 'em out. It's the heat. Chicago summer and a chance to Jew-bait; you can't beat the combination."

The commercial was over. Kraus switched the microphone to live and his finger punched the first phone button. "Talk to me!" he demanded.

"Well, what you said about the Jews . . ." began the first phone call, a feeble, scratchy, old voice, with the clatter of brittle bones behind it.

"Yeah? So what?"

"They carry diseases, that's what. And they spread 'em around. They've all got syphilis."

A snort of astonished laughter escaped Dan Kraus's lips. "You're kidding, right?"

"No, sir! I wouldn't never joke about a thing like that!" Aggrieved, the feeble voice took on color and strength.

"Let me get this straight," said Kraus, not bothering to hide the ridicule in his tone. "You hate Jews because they've all got syphilis?"

"That's right."

"How do you know all Jews have syphilis?"

"It's in the Bible," answered the caller with growing confidence. "It says it right there in Genesis—"

"Don't tell me about the Bible, dum-dum," interrupted Kraus. "It's just a best-seller. So was *Peyton Place*." He hit the next lit button, cutting the first caller off.

The next voice belonged to a teenaged boy. He started a long, rambling, indignant story about a Jewish girl he wanted to date but "the whore" had turned him down. Kraus let him get about three sentences into it before he cut the boy off, but he was less insulting than he'd been to the Bible thumper. The kid sounded pathetic enough; Kraus could picture him—dirty fingernails and pimply skin and a chip on his shoulder that weighed a thousand pounds.

The next caller was exactly his meat. One of the vast nation of ignorant yet opinionated people whose ideas were so absurd when they were voiced over the air that they hardly needed editorial comment from Dan Kraus. This woman was exactly what his listeners turned in to hear—dumb to the point of hilarity. Kraus lived for callers like her. They were like wealthy tourists from another galaxy.

"Jews is devils, you know—with horns and tails and everything."

"You've seen one? A devil, I mean? A Jew with horns?"

"Well, no, but them fellers is dead clever. They know how to hide their tails, and they wears them funny little round hats to cover up their horns. But they got 'em, you can count on it."

"I'm a Jew, but I don't wear a funny hat. Where are *my* horns?"

"Well, I reckon you must've shaved 'em off or something, because you was borned with 'em, that's fer sure."

"Are you calling me a devil?" Kraus smiled, tickled. "Aren't you afraid I'm gonna come there where you live and grab you up and carry you off to hell?"

A little scream of terror and a click as the woman hastily slammed down her phone.

"Just wait until Halloween." Kraus chortled. "I'm gonna dress up in my red devil suit and find out where that woman lives when I go trick or treating. When she opens the door to me and my pitchfork, she's gonna need bypass surgery! Don't go away now, people. We got another couple of messages for you, and then we'll open the switchboard again and hear how some more of you geniuses feel about the Chosen People. Of whom, let me remind you, I am one."

He glanced at the big clock on the studio wall. Only five minutes to go. Not too bad. The calls were coming in steadily; it was one of his livelier broadcasts. It never failed to amaze him how many misconceptions and outright destructive lies were accepted as gospel by so many people, no questions asked.

"Talk to me!"

"I just wanted to say that the Holocaust, that was a big exaggeration," began the woman on the other end of the line.

"An *exaggeration*?" Kraus's eyes met Reilley's and the two men shook their heads in mimed disbelief.

"Uh-huh," the caller continued blithely. "I mean, there *were* some Jews killed. But that was just war. There were a lot of GIs killed, too."

Kraus took a second to swallow this chunk of revisionist history. "What about the gas chambers?" he asked softly.

The question didn't faze her. "All that was, was those Jews had to get their lice taken off. It was like takin' 'em to the dry cleaners."

That such ignorance walks around in shoes, marveled Kraus to himself with infinite sadness. That a history lesson of such enormity, such monstrous magnitude can have completely escaped vast segments of the world's population! No matter how often he dealt with fools— and he earned a six-figure income dealing with fools— their complacent self-righteousness never ceased to astound him. Insulting them, chewing them out, calling them names, cutting them off in midsentence—these were satisfactions, granted, but satisfactions often blunted by sorrow and even bewilderment. *Gottenyu*, he thought bitterly. Where do stupid people like these *come* from? What kind of world is this?

"Did I hear you right? You did say 'dry cleaners,' didn't you?"

"Uh-huh. You take somethin' to the dry cleaners, it don't hurt it any. Sometimes it shrinks a little but you can still wear it."

"Lady, do me a favor and hang up, please. You are so damn dumb it boggles the mind. I have nothing to say to you, nothing. There is no power on earth that can convince you that you are dead wrong about everything you just said, *every single thing*! I wouldn't believe so much as a weather report from you if you came in here covered head to foot in new-fallen snow!" He cut the call off angrily.

With an expression of disgust, Dan Kraus switched off his mike and removed his earphones. There were times when people like this got to him—smug and opinionated and utterly ignorant. Times when the job wasn't fun anymore, but pathetic and harsh. His two decades of broadcasting experience, his five decades of life experience, weren't enough to protect his weary soul from moments like this one, when defeat and despair mingled with the disgust. He was glad the shift had finally come to an end. His neck and shoulders were aching like hell.

The engineer was playing the taped signature that ended the show. Kraus pulled his rumpled seersucker jacket off the back of his chair, checked his board to see that all the "on" lights were out, and took a lit cigarette out of the ashtray. He felt suddenly drained. God, was he ever ready to go home, to a shower, a quiet drink, some music on the stereo, a sandwich, and a good book. He was halfway through a biography of President Truman, and he was eager to get back to it, and to the sanity of his private world.

"We just about blew the damn board." Reilley grinned.

"What've we got tomorrow, Bob?" Kraus asked wearily.

"Transsexuals," the engineer told him.

Kraus smiled thinly. "God bless America."

It was already dark when he left the studio, but it was still hot. Not a breath of air came stirring over Lake Michigan; the humidity pressed down on Kraus's shoulders, making them sag. Chicago. Cold as a bitch in the winter; hot as a bitch in the summer. The wind off the lake cut right through you like a knife anytime of the year. He was crazy about the place, wouldn't live anywhere else if you paid him.

Dan Kraus crossed the studio parking lot. It was a badly lit lot, but he knew exactly where he was parked. His precious jewel shone in the darkness. His baby, his darling. A sparkling white cream puff of a Cadillac, vintage 1969. Kraus loved that car; the affection he withheld from human beings was lavished on the caddy. It had red leather upholstery; it had wide, comfortable bucket seats and whitewall tires; it could do ninety without shaking a fender; and it got between eight and nine miles to the gallon. Nothing made him happy like his Cadillac. What more could a man ask for?

Intent on his car, how could Dan Kraus know that he wasn't alone in the parking lot? How could his tired, fifty-year-old eyes, stinging from cigarette smoke, aching

with unshed tears at the world's foolishness and deprav-
ity, penetrate the darkness of the lot to see the four-
wheel-drive vehicle parked near the exit gate?

Intent only on getting home, how could Dan Kraus
know that, just seconds after the Caddy left the lot, the
4×4 would spark into life and follow him? Who the hell
bothers to stalk a radio personality, even a controversial,
abrasive radio personality? Who would give that much of
a damn? Who would take him and his words so seriously?

Kraus drove the three miles between the studio and his
apartment without checking his rearview mirror. And
even if he had, he wouldn't have noticed that the same
car was tagging two cars behind for the whole three
miles.

Dan Kraus lived in a brand-new, luxury, high-security
condo building. The lobby boasted a staff of uniformed
private security guards and a huge central console that
monitored every floor by closed-circuit television. Kraus
was no fool; these were parlous times. Robberies and
muggings were commonplace in Chicago and the rest of
the world. You couldn't be too careful.

A little more paranoia on his part might have helped.
But probably not. Nothing could have saved him, not the
security staff or the lobby cameras, not his big mouth,
not his six-figure income, not the weary disgust he felt
for the world, not his sudden, brief, rare flashes of
empathy. With all of these, he was still doomed.

Kraus pulled the gleaming car into the underground
parking garage and slid it sweetly into its own numbered
space, a space that cost a full fifty percent more than
what he paid in rent every month. As he stepped out of
the Caddy, he heard a click. Just that. A click.

Not being weapons minded, Dan Kraus had no way of
knowing that the click was the sound of the first bullet of
a thirty-two-bullet clip being chambered into the two-
inch barrel of an Ingram Mac-10 assault submachine gun.
A lightweight short-range automatic weapon, it was 8.8
pounds of vicious, black metallic power. Dan Kraus also

had no way of knowing that the little click would be the last sound he would hear.

Kraus didn't hear the quiet chuffing of the nine-millimeter bullets as they tore his body apart; the weapon had a noise suppressor designed to mute its barking. One moment he was alive; the next moment quivering and jerking under the impact of the bullets, and the next he was dead, sprayed by a deadly rain of a full clip of ammunition—thirty-two bullets, as least twenty of which had found their target.

Kraus didn't see the face of the man who shot him down, and maybe that was a mercy, because the man was grinning as he kept his finger on the trigger, and his grin alone was enough to congeal the blood in anybody's veins.

Kraus never got the chance to confront his killer, to ask why or to tremble at the answer. Because the answer was "hate." Standing here was the hatred made flesh, the very hatred that Dan Kraus was paid to evoke, needling it, prodding at it, poking the embers into flame, all to earn his six figures.

Kraus didn't see his beloved white Cadillac sprayed red with his blood. He never would get that shower, or that last drink, or a chance to finish his book. He never knew just how seriously his words had been taken. Ironically, that might have pleased him.

As the Mac-10's clip coughed empty and the tattered body lay sprawled in blood on the garage floor, the silent shooter lowered his gun hand. He patted the silencer, as though congratulating it on a job well done. A small smile played over his lips. Fine hunting, a good stalk, and a clean kill. The animal was dead, his carcass shot full of holes, blood oozing from them, staining the concrete of the garage floor.

Walking on booted feet toward the remains of Dan Kraus, the shooter lifted his left hand. In it he held a can of spray paint, ordinary red hardware-store spray paint, blood-colored spray paint.

The last insult, the final desecration. On the roof of the perfect white Cadillac, now spattered foully with its owner's blood, the shooter wrote three letters in red spray paint. His arm, in its camouflage jacket sleeve, was strong and steady, the letters clear, six inches high for the uncaring world to read and wonder at. A three-letter message, laconically defining the sudden, savage ending of a man's life.

ZOG, it read.

Z O G.

That was the first death. Only the first.

Chapter Two

Katie

The George Jones classic, "Aching, Breaking Heart," came pouring in over the cab's radio, so meltingly warm and sweet you could pour it on a waffle. Katie Phillips wrinkled her nose and shook her dark head. Between the nagging whine of country music and Betty Jo Babcock's unceasing chatter, a small but insistent headache was starting up behind her dark eyebrows. She tightened her grip on the steering wheel of the pickup truck she was driving.

The heat and dust kicked up by the slow, clumsy procession of farm vehicles—huge combines, machines designed to gather the wheat, thresh it and clean it, and the rattling of the convoy, a half-dozen or so flatbeds and pickup trucks—down the winding two-lane blacktop "highway" weren't helping her headache much. The red bandana knotted around Katie's slender throat was just about soaked through with perspiration; there was a thin film of sweat along her bare arms below the rolled-up sleeves of her blue chambray workshirt. And the working day hadn't even begun yet.

On both sides of the road, fields of ripe wheat stood tall in the postdawn breeze. It was early July in the Middle West. By ten o'clock the harvest would be well under way, the morning breeze would have died down

under the merciless sun, and the heat would be ferocious. By noon the cloudless sky would be a caldron.

Even now, at six in the morning, the sun sent its fiery
tentacles snaking through the open windows of the pickup,
carrying with it particles of road dust and grain chaff that
made Katie's eyes itch and burn and crunched between
her teeth like sand.

"Ah'm a good cook! Ain't ah a good cook?" demanded Betty Jo, aggrieved. The two young women—
"combine girls," as they were called—were temporary
workers, part of a skilled combine crew hired annually to
bring in the harvest. They worked from farm to farm,
and were paid by the day. Katie and Betty Jo had met
only a couple of days before, but they were staying at the
same motel, the Lazy-Vu.

Despite the differences in their personalities, they'd
already struck up one of those quick friendships that
come and go so easily, part of the life of "movin' on."

Now they were rolling out through the country to the
wheat fields, where they'd drive the huge combines and
bring in the harvest. Betty Jo had been complaining
about her boyfriend for the last ten miles. "He says to
me, he says, 'This ain't as good as my mama makes.'
Well, shit! You know what ah'm gonna do? Tomorrow
ah'm gonna make him nothin' but a peanut butter sandwich, that's what!"

Katie laughed and glanced over at her friend. With her
mad face on, her short brow furrowed indignantly, and
the corners of her red lips turning down in a pout, pretty
little Betty Jo resembled nothing so much as a snub-
nosed Persian kitten being force-fed Brand X cat food.
She was forever facing every minor crisis in her life as
though thermonuclear war had just broken out.

The grating country song was proving too much for
Katie's nerves. Exasperated, she took one hand off the
wheel, stripped off the heavy work glove, and punched at
the buttons on the radio. "Gimme some rock 'n' roll!"

As if on cue, Black Sabbath's "Bark at the Moon"
blasted out of the tinny speaker at top volume, raucous,

angry, defiant, and evil. A scowling Katie hastily reached
for the buttons again. "Heavy metal! I hate heavy metal!"
Whatever happened to good ol' rock? Where the hell
was U-2 or Bruce Springsteen, or even the great oldies—
Creedence or Blind Faith or Cream?

"He *hates* peanut butter!" Betty Jo Babcock had a
one-track mind, and right now hurt feelings and peanut
butter were riding that track.

Just then the trained and impersonal voice of a news
reader cut through the sweltering air inside the pickup's
cab.

"—in the garage of his parking lot two weeks ago. FBI
officials said they have no new leads, but—"

Another punch of the buttons on the dial, switching off
the follow-up account of Dan Kraus's murder, and more
country music—Porter and Dolly wailing about Jesus in
one of their relentlessly eternal duets—made Katie utter
a little bark of frustration.

"Shit on a stick!"

"That's what peanut butter *is*," chimed in Betty Jo,
and the two girls broke up laughing.

Not a single cloud in the bright blue midmorning sky
took the edge off the sun's remorseless oppression. Sweat
had soaked right through Katie Phillips's bandana, which
she'd taken off her neck and tied around her brow under
the hairline. She rubbed her arm across her forehead and
licked her lips, tasting salt. There was no shade, no tree
cover or cloud cover—nothing to protect her from the
merciless sun. July in wheat country, shit!

Katie sat high up off the ground, in the cab of the huge
combine. As it moved slowly through the furrows of
the wheat field, large revolving rotors, extending on either
side of the vehicle like the metallic whiskers of a giant
mechanical cat, pushed the ripe grain toward the cutter
bar, where an oscillating knife lopped off the stalks at
close to ground level.

The harvested wheat would then be conveyed up into a
feeder mechanism, where it would be threshed by a

threshing cylinder, to separate the kernels of wheat from the straw. Then the grain was processed a second time, in a cleaning shoe. There the useless chaff would be removed by an air blast and sieves, while the straw was dropped out the back, to fall behind into a windrow for baling later.

The combine harvester was a complicated machine. A number of manually worked gears in the driver's cab determined the air blast that cleaned and salvaged the kernels of wheat, and moved the rotors. Also, Katie had to keep one eye on the rotating oscillator while the rest of her concentrated on moving the combine down a straight path through the field. A hard job for anybody, let alone a hundred-and-ten-pound young woman. It was hot and noisy work; the grinding and clanking did nothing to relieve the pain in Katie's head.

Had the sweat in her eyes blurred her vision? There was something . . . just up ahead . . . lying in the path of the combine's cutter bar. Something . . . familiar, menacingly familiar and chilling. Katie slammed the gears forward, switching off the motor. Lightly, she leaped down from the high cab and began to move cautiously toward the crumpled figure lying in the rows of wheat.

Figures. There were two of them, two bodies, and they weren't moving. Katie swallowed hard, and moved closer, tension showing in the angle of her jaw. Dead men?

No, not corpses, scarecrows. But very peculiar-looking scarecrows. Katie picked one up and looked it over.

The scarecrow was dressed all in black, and was riddled with bullet holes, especially down its left side, where the fabric had been either ripped away or shot away. The other figure was exactly the same. Scarecrows, shit! Katie let out a snort of relief mingled with irritation. Damnfool kids playing cops and robbers with guns, leaving their target garbage behind to scare a person half to death!

Even though the scarecrows were harmless, something sinister about them made Katie's skin crawl. With a small exclamation she dropped the one she'd been holding. But damn if he still didn't look like a dead body, lying crumpled there among the tall stalks of grain.

A low growl behind her made Katie's neck prickle. There was no mistaking the menace in it. She wheeled around. A large, black German shepherd, the biggest she'd ever seen, was behind her, its legs braced as though for attack, its lips drawn back over its big white teeth, fangs bared, a deep, snarling growl emerging from its throat. This was one mean dog.

Katie's eyes widened in fear. But her mother hadn't raised any cowardly children. Besides, dogs smell fear on a person and it encourages them to attack. You had to show them who was boss, who was in control, even if you were scared shitless. She took a deep breath and hung tough.

"You get away from me, you ugly son-of-a-bitch," she yelled at the dog. "Or I'm going to kick the living shit outta you!" Even to herself, the words sounded futile, but, surprisingly, the big dog stopped growling, sat down, and looked at her with huge doggy eyes. His tail began to thump the ground, and the snarl turned into a canine smile.

Well, damn *me*! thought Katie in surprise. It worked!

"You sure got a mouth on *you*," a man's deep voice spoke suddenly behind her.

Katie whirled and found herself confronting a shirtless man in jeans. Tall, with dark, curly hair cut short and a dirty old John Deere Tractor cap jammed on the back of his head. He was deeply tanned, with the color that comes only from working hard out of doors. In his young but weathered face, a pair of wide, dark blue eyes regarded Katie with amusement, and the corners of his mouth turned up in a smile. The mouth itself was beautifully sculpted, with curved, full lips like those on a Greek statue.

His body was lean, Katie noticed, but strong, with powerful chest muscles, sinewy forearms, and wide shoulders. He was maybe thirty-five years old and handsome

as hell, and Katie noticed that, too, but it didn't make
her any less angry.

"You know what somethin' like this could do to my
rotors?" she demanded, jerking her chin at the offending
scarecrows.

Gary Simmons nodded slowly, then smiled an apology.
"Yeah, I know," he admitted. "I did some target shootin'
out here with my boy. I guess we forgot about these."

But Katie wasn't in a smiling mood; she was pissed off
and showing it. The anxiety she'd felt when she saw what
she thought were bodies, and then faced down that mutt
with the fangs, had been translated into fury. "You're
supposed to clear these fields!" she barked at him angrily.

The man's smile widened, and crinkly lines curled from
the outer corners of his eyes. "You got a real *temper* on
you, too," he observed cheerfully. "Where you from?"

Katie stomped back to the combine in her heavy work
boots and swung herself angrily into the high cab. "Texas!"
she flung over her shoulder, biting the word off as shortly
as she could.

Gary chuckled. "You're a real cowgirl, huh?"

It wasn't a remark worth answering, and Katie didn't
deign to answer it. But almost without her being aware
of it, her eyes were drawn to his naked chest and the thin
coating of sweat that gleamed across the muscles. Her
gaze flickered there only a fraction of a second before
she tore it away, but it was long enough for Gary to see
that she was looking, and for Katie to see that he'd seen.
Embarrassment stained her cheeks bright red, and she
slammed the combine into gear.

"I don't need any shit from you," she growled. "I'm
just tryin' to do my job here."

Gary raised his hand to his shoulders, palms outward,
in the universal gesture of conciliation. "I'm sorry." It
was plain that he was interested in her, but Katie wanted
no truck with him.

He bent down to move the scarecrows out of the way
of the combine, and as he did, Katie drove the huge
machine forward, passing him only by inches, almost

scraping the Levi's label off his behind. It was a smooth, if vindictive, piece of driving, and it took the man completely by surprise, as Katie intended it to.

She didn't look back, but she did steal a peek at her rearview mirror, which showed Gary Simmons jump damn near a foot in the air, and come down scowling. Good, served him right for letting that damn dog scare her half to death, not to mention the scarecrow targets.

What Katie didn't see was his scowl changing into a wide, slow smile as he watched her drive off down the field.

In every small midwestern or near-western town like Denison, there's always one bar and grill more popular than the others. It's the place where everybody goes to relax after a long hard working day. It's hard to know why one bar stands out from others just like it. They all sell the same brands of beer—Miller Lite, Coors, Rolling Rock, Lone Star, Michelob. They all have the same songs and singers on the juke—Hank Williams, Patsy Cline, Loretta Lynn, Willie Nelson, George and Tammy, Dolly, Kenny Rogers, Roy Clark, Johnny Cash.

They all have the identical small bandstand and antiquated sound system for the local pickers and singers to put on an occasional live performance. Every one of them has the same handkerchief-sized dance floor where men in western shirts and girls in jeans or petticoats can sashay around to the Texas two-step. They all smell the same—a pungent mix of stale beer, sweat, sawdust, and dried-out, aging redwood.

Yet, on any given night the other bars will be half empty, while a bar like Alice's will have them hanging off the rafters. Now, why is that?

Philosophical considerations aside, Alice was as jampacked as it always was; Betty Jo and Katie almost had to claw their way to the bar and wait nearly ten minutes for seats. But once they had them, they settled in gratefully and ordered drinks. A bar like Alice's was the only entertainment a farming community like Denison afforded.

Earlier, at the motel, Betty Jo had primped and fussed for hours, curling her yellow hair with hot rollers and applying three coats of mascara, with drying time between the coats. All Katie had done was take a long, hot shower and wash her hair. She didn't even bother to dry it, but rubbed it damp with a towel and pinned it back, where it fell sweetly and darkly to her shoulder blades. Clean jeans, a pretty blouse, western boots, and a dab of lipstick and she was ready to go, while Betty Jo Babcock was still agonizing over what shade of nail polish to wear on her toes.

Yet, as the two girls sat side by side at the bar, Katie with her bottle of beer and Betty Jo with a fancy mixed drink, the differences between them didn't reflect the amount of time they'd spent on themselves. Where Betty Jo Babcock was pretty in an overly fussy way, Katie Phillips was like a polished gemstone, spare and gleaming.

Her translucent white skin was shadowed by a faint sunburn and enhanced the soft darkness of her hair. Her enormous hazel eyes, innocent of makeup, glowed from behind long, naturally curling eyelashes. Rising from the collar of her simple blouse, Katie's throat was a graceful, unbroken line.

"You want another Fuzzy Navel?" asked the bartender, mopping at the counter with a soiled rag.

Betty Jo wrinkled up her tiny nose and shook her fluffy head. She bit her red lip delicately as she tried to decide. "No . . . I want . . . a . . . I know! Gimme a Colorado Motherfucker!" She turned to Katie as she heard her friend laughing in astonishment. "You ain't never had of a Colorado Motherfucker?"

Katie took another slug of her Lone Star and shook her head.

"He's cuuuute," breathed Betty Jo, already distracted. Katie turned around on her bar stool to see where Betty Jo was looking. A young man, tall, thin, and no more than seventeen or eighteen years old, was staring openly at Betty Jo, who giggled and batted her mascaraed lashes at him. "I'm real glad I went back on the Pill," she confided to Katie, giggling again.

"Here's your Motherfucker, ma'am," the bartender said politely as he set the drink down on the bar. Katie's eyes opened wider at the sight of it.

There was a layer of pink in it, topped by another layer of purple—Katie couldn't begin to imagine what it was—and the whole thing was topped off by a froth of beaten sugar and egg white. It looked unfit for human consumption, but Betty Jo raised it to her lips enthusiastically and took a long, thirsty sip through both straws.

"Mmmmm, yum! Taste it, Katie, you gotta taste it!" she urged, pressing the noxious concoction on her friend.

Katie was trying to find the words that would convince Betty Joe she'd rather eat lunch with a family of rabid hogs, when she was saved. The tall, thin young man had approached and was standing behind them, blushing.

"You wanna dance?" he asked Betty Jo.

"Sure do," she replied eagerly, jumping off the bar stool. The pair of them swung onto the floor and began two-stepping to a Carl Perkins tune. They made an amusing pair, him so tall and Betty Jo so small; he was bent over almost double, listening to her chatter away. Katie watched them as Betty Jo began dancing closer, until the two of them were pressed tightly together as if they were glued.

Katie took another sip of her beer and looked casually around the bar. Sitting at a table nearby, with two other men, was the man from the fields that morning, the handsome one with the bare chest. Now he was fully dressed, wearing a striped western shirt with pearl snap buttons, jeans, a silver-eagle belt buckle, and a large western hat, made of felt instead of the usual straw. He was clean and freshly shaven, and better-looking than ever. And he was looking straight at Katie Phillips.

"Hey, cowgirl," he called. "Buy you a beer."

"Got a beer," replied Katie shortly.

"Buy you another beer," Gary suggested, unfazed.

She shook her dark head slightly. "No, thanks."

Gary put his head to one side and regarded her with a grin. "You always like this or do some folks just bring it out in you?" he asked.

Katie hesitated, wondering if she was angry or what, but it was what, and a small secret smile escaped her, a smile Gary saw. He stood up.

"Come on, Texas, we can go out there and dance one dance, can't we? I'll keep my hands in my pockets, and I won't bust your feet. I promise." He cocked one quizzical eyebrow at her, waiting for her response.

When she said nothing, Gary stuck his hands into his back pockets and walked to the little dance floor, standing there waiting for Katie's next move. Around him, couples were two-stepping, bumping into him, looking at him curiously, but he didn't budge. He just stood there, grinning hopefully, continuing to wait until Katie made her mind up.

Suddenly Katie felt foolish. All this fuss about nothing more than a few minutes with some guy on a dance floor. Slipping off the bar stool, she strolled over to Gary, and they started to dance. Gary's hands were still tucked tightly into his back pockets, and other people stared at them in amusement.

Hearing the snickers and seeing the stares, Katie became self-conscious. She hated being gawked at. "You don't have to keep 'em there," she told Gary stiffly.

"I don't? Well, good." He put his arms around her casually and they danced, not close, but a little less far apart than they'd been. "What's your name?" he asked, looking down into her upturned face.

"Katie Phillips."

"I'm Gary Simmons. Hi."

"Hi. You dance with all the girls who work the combines?"

Gary threw his head back and laughed loudly. "Honey, you combine girls are the biggest thing to hit this town. These old boys here, every year about this time, they think it's Santy Claus!"

It was an unfortunate remark, and a crude one. He felt

her stiffen in his arms and pull away, and he saw the look of displeasure cross her lovely face. His grin faded.

"Tell you the truth," said Gary quietly, "this is the first time I've danced in three years." He stole a look at Katie to see how she was accepting this, and her raised eyebrow informed him that she wasn't, not at all.

"Since my wife died," he added softly.

Katie shot him a sharp assessing look. He was serious. His eyes and the sober expression on his face informed her that Gary was telling the truth, and her face softened. "I'm sorry," she said in a low voice, and they exchanged long looks. For a while they danced in silence, moving easily together.

The music came to an end. "You thirsty?" Gary asked her.

"I guess," Katie admitted, allowing him to steer her back to his table. She looked for Betty Jo, but Betty Jo was so deeply involved with her new young man that she wasn't missing Katie at all. In fact, she no longer even seemed to be aware of Katie's existence.

The two men sitting at the table made no effort to stand up as Katie approached. One appeared to be the same age as Gary, the other a good 25 years older.

"Katie, I want you to meet two friends of mine. This here's Shorty Richards and that there's Wes Bond. Shorty, Wes, say hello to Katie Phillips."

Shorty carried at least twenty extra pounds, a chubby-faced man in a cowboy hat, with a wide smile and a big beer belly. Wes was another piece of goods entirely. He was strongly built and not bad-looking, with even, regular features and close-cut blond hair. But it was the expression on his face, and most especially his eyes, that made him different from other men. Set deeply into his tanned face, Wes's eyes were of a blue so pale as to be almost invisible, and they were cold, icy cold, the deep cold of an arctic sea. You couldn't imagine eyes like that ever smiling or having anything to smile about.

Shorty said howdy and held his hand out for Katie to

shake, but Wes only gave a quick, silent glance in her direction and turned his face away.

Katie sat at the table, listening to the men talking, feeling like a fifth wheel. If Gary hadn't kept directing his words and smiles at her, she'd have thought she was invisible. It was obvious that men like Wes and Shorty didn't pay women much mind or care what they thought about anything. Mostly she sat silent, her eyes straying to Gary's full sculptured lips and strong chin, which jutted out when he laughed. He looked much younger when he smiled, and he smiled often. He was damn good-looking, no lie.

Shorty had embarked on a long, rambling narrative about an affliction of his; Katie hardly followed it, but Gary appeared interested, so she forced herself to listen. The music was loud, and she'd already had four beers, so it wasn't all that easy to concentrate.

"Doc Adams, shit," he complained, "he didn't know somethin', he'd tell you it was nerves. These young doctors settin' in their air conditioning, they use all these big words, tell you exactly what you got. I liked it better the other way."

"So what is it you got, Shorty?" asked Gary.

The older man hesitated, then admitted bashfully, "Hemorrhoids." Katie had to laugh, joined by Gary and Shorty himself. But Wes Bond barely smiled, a thin, sour stretching of the lips.

"Hey, I heard this one today." Shorty chortled, setting them up for the joke. "This old yeller-haired blue-gum nigger gets to heaven. Saint Pete's there, and ol' blue-gum says, 'Mr. Pete, suh, I is here for my just rewards.' Saint Pete says, 'Hell yes, boy, you go on in, but first, can you shine up my shoes?' "

The joke broke everybody up except Katie. Even Wes was laughing out loud.

"That's funny, don't you think that's funny?" demanded Shorty, seeing that Katie was showing little enthusiasm.

She shrugged uncomfortably. "I don't laugh a lot at jokes, I guess. I always been like—"

"You like niggers?" Wes interrupted abruptly, his pale eyes boring into her face.

Offended by the meanness of the joke, Katie felt herself flushing. "I don't really know any of 'em," she said defensively, not wishing to meet his icy stare.

It was an awkward situation. Katie could feel Gary watching her speculatively. Although he said nothing, she had the feeling that she was somehow being evaluated, weighed in some kind of balance. Was she measuring up? What did they expect of her? Katie searched for something to say.

A man in his fifties, dressed in farm clothes, walked by their table at that moment.

"Howdy, Hank," Gary called easily.

But the man moved on without a glance.

"I said, howdy, Hank." This time Gary's voice was louder and harder, a voice that commanded attention and, even more, obedience.

The man stopped but didn't look around. "Howdy," he said, in a low, grudging voice tinged with fear, then he walked away. It was the barest minimum of a greeting. Obviously, something had gone down in the past between the two men, something unpleasant.

Gary pushed his chair away from the table and stood up. "I gotta go," he announced. "I gotta put my kids to bed." He turned to Katie. "I'll give you a ride," he offered.

Katie shook her head. "No thanks, I'm ridin' with Betty Jo." She looked around for her friend. Betty Jo was still on the dance floor with her new friend, but they were no longer dancing. They stood swaying, pressed together, locked in a long, deep kiss.

Gary Simmons laughed. "Betty Jo's gonna need the car." He grinned. "That boy ain't even got a driver's license yet."

Katie hesitated, but she could see that Gary was right. It was plain to anybody who cared to look that Betty Jo Babcock didn't plan on sleeping alone that night. It was either hang around and get in her friend's way or take this blue-eyed man's offer of a ride. Well, hell, she was a big girl; she could take care of herself.

"Come on," he urged. "I'll keep my hands in my pockets. You ever see a man drive with his feet?"

"No," Katie confessed, and grinned. The image was a funny one.

She stood up and followed Gary out, feeling a little dizzy from the beer and the sudden chill of air on her skin after the overheated bar. She felt, too, the chill of Wes's obvious dislike cutting into her, like a knife between her shoulder blades.

Katie shivered.

Chapter Three

Gary

The evening was surprisingly cool. Summer was still too young to deliver up warm nights. The air was very dry and clear; in the black arch of the sky constellations spread themselves out as brightly as on a star map. Katie shivered a little in her thin blouse. Drawing her denim jacket tightly around her, she followed Gary to his pickup, a 1986 Chevrolet Scottsdale, mud-splashed and dusty from the fields, but in excellent shape otherwise.

The seat next to the driver was piled high with stuff—maps, the local newspaper, farm equipment and tool catalogs, sporting magazines, even a paper bag that had obviously once held a lunch. With a muttered apology, Gary Simmons grabbed all of it from the seat, threw it behind him into the pickup bed, and motioned Katie in.

As soon as he started the motor, Gary switched on the heater, and the cab began to warm up a little. Katie looked around. No doubt about it, this was your typical western pickup truck, driven by farmers and ranchers throughout the Midwest, filled with a strong masculine presence, from the smell of cigarettes and beer to the musky odor of dog.

A gun rack was mounted across the back window, holding a state-of-the-art new Englander muzzle loader with interchangeable barrels. The racked hunting firearm was fitted out as a twelve-gauge shotgun, but mounted

directly beneath it was the gleaming .50-caliber big-game
rifle barrel. Between the seats were a couple of fresh
boxes of shells and rifle bullets. On the floor under her
feet Katie spotted one old work glove, a screwdriver with
a broken handle, a couple of beer cans, and a crumpled,
empty Camels pack.

As they drove away, Katie looked over her shoulder.
Alice's giant neon sign lit up the night in gaudy splendor,
its glow outlining the dozens of sedans, 4 × 4s and pickup
trucks parked around the front and back doors. Otherwise, there was nothing on the flat landscape to capture
the eye.

Even Denison itself was next to nothing, Katie thought
as they drove through the town. A couple of gas stations
selling diesel fuel, a large, prosperous feed and grain
store, a veterinary office, one church, a handful of little
stores, and a city hall fronting the small town square with
its flagpole, war monuments, and antiquated band shell.
Most of the buildings clustered around the square had
been built around 1870. They still sported their ginger-
bread trim and mansard roofs, their turrets and towers
and other mid-Victorian architectural excesses.

Denison didn't even have a movie theater or a Stop 'n'
Shop; people had to drive close to thirty miles to the mall
to buy stuff at Sears or to see a film.

The railroad spur about five miles from town was the
real heart of Denison. There, as close to the tracks as
they could get, tall grain elevators pierced the skyline
like big-city skyscrapers. Around them were parked the
heavy machinery used in packing and loading grain for
market. The loading platform was always buzzing with
activity. Wheat was big business, agribusiness, and it left
no time for goofing off or fooling around.

Gary Simmons drove easily, with one hand resting
lightly on the wheel, the other elbow out the window.
The pickup headed west. In the far distance, towards
Wyoming, loomed the shadows of the buttes, where the
flatland began to yield gently to the foothills of the Great
Rockies. It was the same view the pioneer wagon trains

marveled at as they crossed over rutted wagon trails on their way to the promised lands of Oregon and California. It was a countryside fought for, died for, bitterly—and in the end, hopelessly—by the Pawnee, the Sioux, the Cheyenne. A century ago, the land they were driving over now had cost a lot of Indian and settler blood, but progress was inevitable. The railroads came and the Indians left, decimated, defeated, pushed off their ancient hunting grounds in the name of Manifest Destiny.

For a few minutes they drove along in silence, companionable on Gary's part, guarded on Katie's, then Gary asked, "You like workin' them combines?"

Katie didn't look at him. "I used to work at this little diner," she said quietly, "waitin' on tips, pushin' their hands away."

It was answer enough. It told the story. Gary nodded and switched on the radio, twisting the dial to find a station with a transmitter powerful enough to reach out to the countryside. There was a burst of country music, followed by a trickle of talk, followed by static, and some more music.

"You ever listen to that guy? I miss that guy."

Katie glanced at Gary, puzzled.

"That radio guy that got killed," he explained.

She nodded, understanding. Dan Kraus. The murder had made national headlines. "I just saw about it on TV."

He kept switching around the dial, trying to bring in a decent station, without success. "There ain't nothin' to listen to now." He scowled.

"Rock 'n' roll," suggested Katie.

"It gives me a headache." He looked hard at her, seeing the freshness of her skin and her clear bright eyes, realizing perhaps for the first time how very young Katie was, no more than twenty-five, for sure. "I'll bet you like rock 'n' roll." It was almost an accusation.

"I don't like heavy metal. It gives *me* a headache."

Gary brightened. "Hey, we got somethin' in common."

Katie peered out the cab window. Everything looked

the same out there, just acres and acres of standing wheat, the monotony broken only by an occasional farmhouse, with barns, sheds, outbuildings, and silos clustered around it. Even so, Katie knew with certainty that this *wasn't* the way back to the Lazy-Vu. She was speeding through the darkness to the ass-end of nowhere with a man she knew nothing about.

"Where we goin'?" she demanded, just a little scared. "You said you were gonna take me back."

Gary caught the husk of alarm in Katie's voice, and it made him grin. The lines around his eyes deepened in amusement. "Don't worry yourself," he told her cheerfully. "I ain't gonna hurt you."

A farmhouse was coming up on the left-hand side of the road, an old house surrounded by a picket fence. The big yard light was turned on, its heavy wattage illuminating the rough driveway, the weathered clapboard of the house, and the barn behind it. Gary drove in without a word. Turning off the ignition, he climbed out of the cab and started for the barn. Reluctantly, Katie followed him. What else was there to do? She was stuck with him, like it or not, miles away from anywhere, with no way to get anywhere.

The large German shepherd who'd growled so ferociously at her this morning now came bounding out of the shadows near the barn. He was barking loudly, and looked very black and threatening. Katie froze, her heart was in her mouth, as the dog displayed his sharp white teeth.

But Gary didn't turn a hair. "Aw, he's just an old candy-ass, ain't you, Ronnie?" he called out affectionately.

At the sound of his name, the big shepherd set his tail furiously in motion, jumping up on Gary and licking him joyfully on his face and hands, now including his new friend Katie in his slobbering display of affection. When Gary pushed him off, Ronnie jumped up on Katie. She staggered a little under the heavy weight of the dog and took a step or two backward.

"He acts real tough, though, just like the other Ron-

nie." Gary laughed, patting the dog and dragging him off
her. Katie realized that the dog was named for the president of the United States. Gary led Katie to the barn and
switched on the overhead lights.

The barn smelled comfortably of sweet hay and grassy
manure, but there was another scent, too, one that Katie
couldn't identify, the odor of mortal illness. In one of the
stalls, an aged chestnut mare was lying, sides heaving,
each laborious breath a fresh effort. It was obvious that
she was very old, very sick, and didn't have long to live.

Quietly, Gary Simmons entered the stall and knelt
beside the mare, stroking her ever so gently, embracing
her with a loving arm. The chestnut attempted to raise
her head, but she was too weak.

"There you go now, Beauty. It's all right," he told her
tenderly. Looking up at Katie, he explained, "I got her
when I was eleven years old. My dad taught me to ride
her. I'm gonna lose her, I know that." Tears stung his
eyelids and he blinked them back.

Despite herself, Katie found herself moved by the big
man's gentleness, and by the sorrow he displayed so
openly. "I used to have an old calico," she said softly.
"My daddy got it for me, too." Coming into the stall, she
sat down on the straw beside Gary, stroking Beauty with
a sympathetic hand.

"See there—we got somethin' else in common." Gary
smiled, and his face softened. In the shadows of the barn
the gentleness of his expression was so beautiful that
Katie found it difficult to take her eyes off him. She was
very drawn to him, more drawn that she wanted to admit
to herself. She could find nothing to say, but the palms of
her hands were damp, her pulse was running faster, and
she was having a little trouble breathing normally.

They stood up, brushing straw off their clothing, both
of them somewhat embarrassed by the intimacy of the
moment. Without another word, they left the barn and
crossed the yard to the pickup.

Gary stopped, hesitating. "You wanna come in, meet
my kids?"

Katie shook her head. She was physically attracted to this man, just as it was plain that he was attracted to her. But it was more than that, more than just the physical, and getting involved with someone wasn't on her agenda; it wasn't what she was here for. Meeting a guy's kids, that was heavy.

Again she shook her head no. "I gotta go."

Gary looked at her a moment, disappointed, then he nodded, holding his hand out to her. In it were the keys to the Scottsdale.

"I don't need it till mornin'," he said. "Go on, take it. Good ol' Dee-troit motor, runs good. You ain't that far. Straight up that road to the junction, take a left on County Route 203, you oughta be at the Lazy-Vu in less than twenty minutes." He dropped the keys into her hand and turned toward the house.

Katie stood looking after him until he disappeared through the front door. His walk was a casual amble, but his back was straight and his shoulders square; his body was lean and fit and more powerful than the casual eye revealed. Katie had the impression of coiled strength slumbering in his muscles. Something stirred inside her, something that was waking up hungry. Resolutely, she pushed it back down deep; let it starve. Katie Phillips was no Betty Jo Babcock to party with the first available man. The hunger could wait.

Sweat poured freely down Katie's cheeks as she wrestled the combine harvester down another furrow of wheat. Her lips were dry, the taste of salt was on her parched tongue, and she was so thirsty that all she could think about was beer, ice-cold, bitter-tasting, life-giving beer. The thought of it was torture, but she couldn't get it out of her mind. It was still hours to quitting time, but at that moment, Katie Phillips would kill for a cold bottle of beer.

Suddenly, as though her thoughts had taken on a life of their own and created substance, a frosty beer bottle materialized out of nowhere, held out to her by a little girl of about seven. A little girl in denim overalls, with her long hair braided into pigtails, who looked up at Katie with a pair of dark blue eyes exactly like Gary Simmons's eyes.

"Daddy said to bring it to you," she said, handing the beer up to Katie. "My name is Rachel."

"Thank you, Rachel," Katie said solemnly, accepting the beer with gratitude and pressing the icy bottle against her sweltering forehead and neck before she took a long swallow.

The little girl smiled, revealing missing baby teeth. "Daddy said to ask you to come to dinner with us tonight. Grandma's coming over and making a pot roast. Grandma makes the best pot roast in the whole world. She puts garlic in it."

"She does?" Katie smiled, enchanted. She loved children, and had warmed immediately to this one, possibly also because she was Gary Simmons's daughter.

Rachel nodded seriously. "She says garlic's good for you, but if I eat too much, I get diarrhea. Do you ever get diarrhea?"

"I sure try not to." Katie grinned.

"Is it fun riding up there?" The child looked wistful; her longing was apparent.

"You want a ride?" Katie threw the cab door open, and Rachel's little face lit up like a Christmas tree with freckles. Giggling with excitement, she clambered up into the cab beside Katie.

"Wait till I tell Joey! He's gonna have a shit fit!" she crowed.

Katie settled the child safely on her lap and put her small hands on the steering wheel. Together, they started up the harvester. As the long rotors began to turn and the combine went rumbling and roaring down the furrow, Rachel let out squeaks of excitement and joy. Katie, too, began laughing, infected by the little girl's delight.

Five hundred yards away, out of their line of sight, Gary Simmons stood watching the two of them, and a look of satisfaction crept over his face.

*   *   *

Supper time. Still damp and refreshed from her shower, Katie Phillips and her pickup truck arrived at the Simmons's house promptly at six. By day, she could see that the farmhouse was old, a tall, three-story affair with a deeply slanted roof, so that the heavy winter snows wouldn't pile up and loosen the shingles. Its exterior was covered in weathered clapboard painted white—not vinyl siding—and the windows bore old-fashioned shutters.

The house itself stood framed by a fence of pointed pickets painted white, behind which grew colorful zinnias and marigolds. A wide, screened-in porch wrapped around the house from the front door to the side, and a tall flagpole displaying the American flag stood proudly in the front yard. The house looked well cared for and inviting; although it wasn't dark out yet, lights shone cheerily from the windows, bidding Katie hello.

In the yard near the barn stood the usual clutter of vehicles that come with any working farm—cultivators, back hoes, a couple of junky cars, two John Deere tractors—one big, one little—a Jeep Cherokee, a flatbed Ford truck, and Gary's Chevy pickup, which he'd evidently reclaimed from the Lazy-Vu. There was also a heavy black Harley-Davidson motorcycle leaning on its kickstand, not new, but muscular and powerful.

Shorty and Wes were working on the caterpillar treads of the smaller tractor when Katie got out of the pickup. Dressed in oil-covered overalls, they were intent on what they were doing, but as they heard the cab door slam, they looked up.

"Evenin', Katie," called Shorty. He flashed her a good-natured grin and a wave.

Katie waved back. "Hi, Shorty." She waited for a greeting from Wes, but he said nothing, only ran his eyes coldly up and down her body in a way that was at once leering and contemptuous. Katie's cheeks burned, and she hurried to the door, wanting to get out of Wes Bond's line of sight as quickly as possible.

Suddenly, standing at Gary Simmons's, front door,

Katie felt shy. She was about to enter a situation unfamiliar to her. She was meeting a family, the family of a man she barely knew. Yet between the two of them there had already passed a current of hidden meaning, and she felt instinctively that this evening would be a test of some kind. She suspected that every minute she'd spent with Gary so far, every word she'd spoken to him, had somehow been checked and rated against a set of standards private to him and unknown to her. Even while it stimulated her, it made her uncomfortable. It was a challenge, and there was nothing that Katie Phillips responded to more than a challenge. Even so, she was still determined not to get involved with this man, tempting as he was. Involvement would serve no purpose, and only get in her way.

She raised her hand to knock at the door, but before Katie's knuckles touched the wood, the door was flung open wide, and little Rachel was standing there, smiling and licking her index finger.

"I stuck my finger in the roast," she announced. "Boy, is it good!" Turning, the child called into the house, "Grandma! Katie's here!" Then she grabbed Katie's hand and eagerly pulled her inside.

Whatever Katie may have expected to find, it wasn't this. The house was simple, comfortable, even beautiful. The living-room furnishings, like the house itself, were old and rather worn, but well cared for. The room was cozy and beckoning. To take the chill off the evening, a fire burned in the fireplace, its yellow-and-red flames casting a warm golden glow over the room.

A blue earthenware bowl filled with pink roses stood on a pine table behind a well-stuffed, pillow-covered sofa. At the windows hung simple cotton curtains, but they were clean and stiff with starch. Apart from the cooking smells, there was the scent of furniture polish and roses, an aura that put Katie immediately at ease, as did the feel of her hand still clutched tightly in Rachel's.

A color television set in a large wooden console cabinet took up one corner of the room. It was on, turned to the "CBS Evening News," although there was nobody to watch it. From the kitchen came a mingling of aromas so appetizing they made Katie's mouth water.

A tall, thin woman of about sixty, with a sweet face crowned by thick, curly, graying hair, came out of the kitchen, wiping her hands on a dishtowel. Like Rachel and Gary, she had dark blue eyes that looked straight at you. Katie could see immediately where the strength in Gary's face came from.

"Hi, I'm Gladys," she greeted Katie like an old friend. "I've got the roast ready. I don't know where those two are, probably out in the barn with that poor horse. Set yourself down. Would you like somethin' to drink?"

"I'll take a beer, please," said Katie, the last shreds of her nervousness disappearing under the older woman's friendliness. Gary's mother was nobody to be scared of.

"I'll have one with you. It's so darned hot—" Mopping at her face with the towel, Mrs. Simmons went back into the kitchen for the beer.

Katie sat down on the sofa and glanced at the news. Dan Rather was saying something, but before he could engage Katie's attention, Rachel piped up eagerly. "Do you want to see my dolls? I've got six dolls! They're real nice—"

At Katie's nod, the child scampered off.

"Hi," a voice said suddenly behind Katie. "This is Joey."

Katie turned. Gary was pulling off his denim jacket, and standing beside him was a boy of perhaps eleven, tall for his age, with a serious, solemn face and the familiar Simmons freckles and blue eyes. The boy turned to his father as if appealing for protection, but Gary put one hand on his shoulder and urged him forward.

"Nice to meet you, ma'am," Joey said shyly, offering his hand. He was very different from his outgoing little sister.

Katie suppressed a smile at the formal "ma'am." With the same polite solemnity, she accepted Joey's hand and shook it. "Nice to meet you, Joey."

Suddenly Gary spoke, and his voice held bitter sarcasm. "There he is, the next president of the United States," he announced. "Ain't *that* a kick in the ass."

Turning, surprised, Katie saw that Gary was scowling at the television set. On the screen, Jack Carpenter was making a critical speech. He had called a press conference, saying he had something to announce, and the media already had a good idea of what it must be.

For months now, Carpenter had been running hard for an independent nomination for the presidency. Even though he hadn't yet announced his candidacy for office, he had been making all the appropriate moves, turning up in the media at least twice a week, grabbing headlines, addressing himself to the public. Although not yet the front runner, he was gaining ground fast, covering the distance between himself and the leaders. Now it was obvious to the nation that if he declared, Jack Carpenter had more than a fighting chance at the nomination. Only in his late forties, he had looks, style, and charisma. He knew how to face a TV camera and look it right in the eye, and his speaking voice had a passionate timber that was convincing, no matter what his words.

As for those words, they were fighting words, superpatriotic words, arch-conservative words. Jack Carpenter was a staunch defender of the American ideal of small government and big business, of New Testament religion founded on strict biblical principles, of the sanctity of the American home, of the supremacy of the American flag. The idea of America as a possible second-rate power, an issuer of a declining currency, burdened by a national debt counted in the trillions, on the short end of the stick in the balance of trade, was loathsome to him and everything he stood for.

"I'm announcing my candidacy," Carpenter was saying now, "because it's time for someone to tell the truth. This country has been run by the Rockefellers, the Kissingers, and the Kennedys for too long. Your so-called East Coast liberals and their godless egghead friends have been sissifying America too long. All I'm really saying, I guess, is that we have to return America to real Americans."

Carpenter's hands clutched the podium with fervor. He had a handsome face, lean, almost ascetic, with firm lips and a determined jaw, large, piercing eyes set deeply under his broad forehead, thick, fair hair with no trace of gray. He looked . . . American.

"He's kinda cute," joked Katie.

Gary made a gesture of contempt. "He's a turkey. They're all turkeys."

Now the cameras switched back to the studio, and the newsman said, "With Carpenter at today's press conference was former National Security Council adviser Robert Flynn, who resigned under congressional fire last November."

Robert Flynn appeared onscreen. He was far different from Carpenter. Roughly the same age as the candidate, he appeared at least ten years older. Flynn's energy, unlike Carpenter's, wasn't the kind that blazed out openly; rather, it smoldered half hidden. Smaller, darker, burlier, with a hooded face that hinted of secrets, burning black eyes, and a thin-lipped mouth, Flynn habitually dressed in dark clothing, which gave him the appearance of a priest or a mourner.

"What this country desperately needs is leadership. Jack Carpenter is a leader who can put this country back on track."

"I'm glad you came," Gary said quietly to Katie.

"I'm glad, too." She smiled.

Gary switched off the television set and they went into the dining room to eat.

The family appeared relaxed and happy over the dinner table; even Joey lost some of his shyness around Katie. She looked around at all of them. Gary sat in the center of it all, at his customary place at the head of the table facing his mother, and he seemed to radiate pride and well-being. He was a very different man from the one Katie had met in the wheat field, much more like the man she'd seen in the stable, whispering his love to a dying mare. She was liking him better and better.

It was a family dinner right out of a Norman Rockwell painting, Katie thought. Kids with scrubbed faces, freckles, and bright eyes; a kindly grandmother whose careworn fingers had produced a magical meal for all to share; an old house filled with comfortable furniture of scrubbed pine. Almost too good to be true. Katie felt suddenly at home here, a natural part of it all. It was a good feeling, a happy feeling.

"This is *really good!*" she exclaimed, forking up another thick slice of pot roast and another portion of oven potatoes off the platter.

Gary grinned, watching her stuff her face. "She's still growin'." He laughed. "She eats like a mule."

"She looks just fine to me." Mrs. Simmons smiled.

"Me, too," admitted Gary.

Katie flashed him a quick, sharp look and went on chewing, but a small jab of satisfaction tickled her insides, and she couldn't help the tinge of red that stained her cheeks.

"When can you see my dolls?" pleaded Rachel.

Before Katie could answer, Gary intervened. "You guys wanna go watch TV?" It was a gentle but firm form of dismissal, and Rachel and Joey responded to it at once. They got up and left the dining room obediently, but Joey came running back, with Rachel behind him.

"Did you really give her a ride on your combine?" he demanded.

"I told you he was gonna get red-assed." Rachel grinned to Katie.

"Can you give me a ride sometime, too?"

"She's real busy, she gots work to do!" Jealous of her status, Rachel was reluctant to share it with her brother. She already considered Katie and the combine her personal property.

"Sure, I'd be happy to," Katie laughed.

The boy's face expressed his delight. "Thanks!" He turned eagerly to his father. "Can she ride on the merry-go-round with us tomorrow, too?" he pleaded.

"I don't see why not," Gary told him, looking over the

boy's head directly at Katie. Their eyes locked, and this
time Katie didn't look away.

"Neat-o! That's neat-o!" crowed Joey, and he and
Rachel raced back to the TV set.

"We got some white cake later if you want," Mrs.
Simmons called after her grandchildren.

"I love white cake," said Katie.

"It's real white cake, too. None of that factory-made
cellophane silliness. *I* still make it, even if nobody else
does." Gladys Simmons's voice had an edge to it.

Gary glanced sideways at Katie. "Mom goes on sometime," he told her apologetically.

But Mrs. Simmons didn't hear the apology. "Every-
thin' changin'," she continued in a rising voice. "Everybody leavin' or wantin' to. People leave here, diggin' into
God's earth all their lives, they take the kitchen sink with
'em, hopin' they can sell it. It ain't right."

"Don't get yourself all upset, Mom," said Gary sooth-
ingly, but a frown line appeared between his eyebrows,
cutting deep. Katie felt uncomfortable watching the two.

"You *know* it ain't right," his mother replied accusingly.

"You know I know it, Mom."

Cords stood out in the older woman's neck. A sour
twist to her mouth now robbed her face of its former
beauty. Her self-control had vanished, and in its place
was this deep well of bitter unhappiness that gushed forth
from her like a river in flood.

"It ain't the country I grew up in no more. Trash, filth
every place—"

"Mom," Gary said quietly, but so firmly that it cut his
mother's words off in midsentence. Mrs. Simmons looked
at her son's face and seemed to recollect herself.

"I'm sorry," she said in a low voice. "I'll go check on
the cake." She stood up uncertainly, as though a little
disoriented, and walked slowly into the kitchen, her shoulders bowed. All at once, she appeared to be at least ten
years older.

Watching Gary, Katie said nothing, but sat with her
hands clasped before her on the table. Gary's head

dropped forward as though he were very tired, and he sighed a little. Then he looked across at Katie and he, too, looked suddenly older.

"She's old," he said at last in a husky voice. "It's hard."

"I know," Katie answered him softly. "I grew up in a town like this."

There was nothing else to say, but the awkward moment they'd shared had drawn them somewhat closer together. Katie felt a deep sympathy for him, and his look told her that he recognized it and appreciated it. To a man and woman whose eyes are tightly linked, silence is natural.

Gary's mother appeared in the doorway with a large round plate on which sat a tall cake frosted with coconut icing. She was in control of herself again, and was smiling. Gary jumped from his chair and went to his mother's side, putting his arm around her waist and taking the heavy plate from her. Mrs. Simmons smiled feebly at her son, and her eyes begged his forgiveness.

"This is the best white cake in the world, that's what this is!" he announced proudly.

Gladys Simmons blushed like a maiden and giggled with pleasure. "Oh, you hush now," she told him, flapping at him with her dishtowel. Dodging the towel, Gary kissed her on the cheek and held her tightly.

Watching them, Katie felt a tugging under her ribs, a melting in the veins that lay beneath the surface of her skin. Gary Simmons was a man with a lot of love to give, and he gave of it freely—to his mother, his children, his friends, his dog, even to a dying old horse.

The tugging inside her told Katie Phillips that she, too, wanted to have some share in this love that Gary Simmons was giving away. The intensity of the emotion took her by surprise. It was an unwelcome feeling, but one that threatened to overwhelm her.

Chapter Four

The Fourth of July

If we could only see again with the eyes of a child on the Fourth of July! To be young and free of care and to taste again the excitement of fireworks, hot dogs, parades, carnival rides, flags flying, bands playing.

Coming at the very beginning of the summer, when school has only just let out, July Fourth brings with it all the exhilaration and promise of an endless holiday. In the big cities like New York and Chicago, July Fourth celebrations are enhanced by high-tech displays of computerized fireworks, sophisticated televised speeches by major public figures, free open-air concerts in the parks.

But if you want to know the true meaning of the holiday, you must go to heartland America. To the breadbasket, the dairy country, to cattle ranges and the little prairie towns like Denison. There, you'll find the whole town draped in red, white, and blue bunting; the American flag flies from every house. Houses that don't own flagpoles fly Old Glory out a second-story window, or drape the flag over the porch rail, but everybody, Democrat, Republican or what-have-you, shows the colors on the Fourth of July.

In little towns like Denison all over the U.S.A., the patriotic speeches are given by people whom the whole town calls by their first names—the mayor, Mike, who runs the real estate office; the barber Pete, chief of the volunteer fire brigade; Sam, wheat farmer and president of the local chapter of the Veterans of Foreign Wars; George, who heads up both the American Legion and the local savings and loan.

The parade marchers carry the colors with pride. Lodges and organizations are well represented—Masons, Kiwanis, Rotary, Elks, Odd Fellows, Moose, Jaycees, VFW, the Legion, the firefighter battalions, the National Guard. Their wives, still content to be "ladies' auxiliaries," march behind their men as though they'd never heard of women's liberation. The veterans' contingent spans three wars. The Second World War, the Korean "conflict," and Vietnam. Only a handful of World War I doughboys, now men in their nineties, are alive to be put on show as heroes, but these few go rolling grandly in their wheelchairs down Main Street. There are young men in wheelchairs, too, their bodies shredded and crippled in southeast Asia. The veterans wear their uniforms and their medals, their battle ribbons and hash marks as bitter souvenirs, and they're proud of them.

The bands playing in the parades are boys and girls from the local high schools. They may not be professional, or even good, but they are enthusiastic and loud. Sweating in their high-collared, brass-buttoned uniforms, the kids step high and dignified down the central streets of America, playing their hearts out.

If you want to see America, see it in the small towns of the nation on the Fourth of July.

Best of all, see it with the eyes of a child.

Rachel and Joey Simmons shrieked with joy at the sight of the carnival that had been set up in the town square. It was one of those traveling caravans that make their way from town to town to set up a canvas tent, a few mechanical rides, a tall ferris wheel, cotton candy and popcorn machines.

The whole town had turned out for the celebration; there would be fireworks later. Picnic tables and barbecue grills had hundreds of people milling around them. The smell of burning charcoal, sizzling hamburgers, hot dogs and mustard hung in the air. Fathers manned the grills while mothers bustled around with huge bowls of coleslaw and potato salad, and the children, a little sick from the ride, drank ice-cold Cokes to settle their stomachs. Younger couples with small babies sat on the grass with their picnic lunches spread out on old blankets, watching their infants learning to crawl and keeping a sharp eye on the toddlers.

Rachel tugged eagerly at Katie's hand, urging her toward the nearest ride, the Wonder Whip. Joey followed more slowly with Gary, who was holding a string of paper tickets. The four of them squeezed into a single car and hung on tight as the motor coughed and rattled and the ride got under way.

The Whip began slowly but within minutes was going very fast, "cracking" around the turns like a rawhide lash. The string of cars whirled one way, while each individual car spun in the opposite direction. Centrifugal force pressed them all against their seats and kept them pinned there. Rachel, her braids flying behind her, her eyes squinched tightly shut, was screaming and laughing at the same time. Getting into the spirit of the ride, Gary began to screech along with his little girl, and Katie caught the infection; she, too, yelled her head off.

But Joey didn't scream. Instead, he clung very tightly to the back of the seat, and his face was dead white, his eyes staring in fright. Seeing the boy so obviously afraid, Katie wrapped one comforting arm around him, hugging him to her. It was an instinctive act, not performed for Gary's approval.

The ride was soon over, the cars stopped their nauseating spinning and chugged to a stop, leaving them dizzy and laughing, even Joey. They staggered out of the little car and off the platform, their arms wrapped around one another, out of breath but happy.

"I wanna get a picture!" called Katie, taking a small Japanese camera out of her purse and sliding the lens cap off. She began snapping Gary and his kids, catching them in casual attitudes. A tall stilt walker in an Uncle Sam costume caught her eye, and she urged the children toward him, to get him into the picture.

"I'll take one of you guys," Gary smiled, taking the camera.

Katie pushed her dark bangs out of her eyes and put one arm around the shoulders of each of the children. Rachel smiled broadly at the camera, the gaps in her baby teeth showing, but Joey pressed quietly, trustingly, against Katie.

Gary took his time, enjoying the sight of the three of them in the viewfinder. Katie Phillips didn't look a whole lot older than Rachel and Joey. Dressed in a simple white shirt and jeans, standing straight and slim, dark hair loose on her shoulders, she looked more like a girl than a woman.

"Ribs!" yelled Rachel. "I smell ribs!" She scampered off, with Joey following. Gary handed Katie her camera.

"You hungry?"

"Starved!"

He gave a great shout of laughter. "What else is new?" Whacking her on her small, round butt, he ran after the kids, leaving Katie to follow.

Shorty was at one of the barbecue grills, cooking ribs, basting them with sauce in a long-handled spoon. The coals were very hot, and from the sizzling fat spattering up came an aroma that made Katie's mouth water. Mrs. Simmons had spread out a colorful cloth on a nearby picnic table, and was uncovering bowls of salad and platters of corn on the cob and taking the lids off the jars of chowchow and piccalilli. Home-baked pies and cakes winked temptingly from under Saran Wrap coverings. A portable radio was playing country and western loudly, but not as loudly as the Sousa marches blaring over the public address system. Running, laughing children and mothers with babies were everywhere; it was bedlam, but ecstatic bedlam.

Katie grabbed a folding aluminum chair near Gary's and gratefully accepted a plate heaped with barbecued ribs and corn and a frosty beer from a huge vat piled high with ice and bottles. She felt completely relaxed, her legs stretched out in front of her as she sat chewing on a rib and sucking at the beer. Hog heaven.

"How long you been on the combines?" asked Toby, a plump woman in a sleeveless blouse. She had arms as big as Smithfield hams and an equally fat baby on her lap. The baby was gumming blissfully on a rib, its chunky face awash in barbecue sauce.

"It's only just my first year," Katie replied.

"You like it?" Toby's husband asked. This was Dean Morgan, sheriff's deputy, and he was dressed in his full uniform, badge, gun, and all. He hated being parted from that uniform, even when he was off-duty.

Katie thought the question over. "I don't like the motels," she said finally. "They ain't no Howard Johnsons."

"Hey, Lyle," called Gary. "You know Katie?"

Katie turned. A tall man, his face wrinkled with age and hard work but his back straight as a rifle barrel, stood behind her chair.

"Pleased to meet you, ma'am," he said politely.

Instinctively, Katie extended her hand to shake his, but pulled it back quickly, turning red with embarrassment. Her hand was covered in greasy barbecue sauce.

Gary laughed. "Lyle went way back with my dad," he explained.

"Now *there* was a real man for you." Lyle's voice snapped the words off hard. "He could eat a bear for breakfast and shit bullets!"

His words met with laughter, but Katie was just a little taken aback. She glanced over at Gary's mother, to see how she was taking this remark, but Mrs. Simmons was busy helping Rachel and Joey to plates of food.

"How do you know he shit bullets, Lyle?" Gary grinned with lazy good nature.

"Your mouth fulla them *ob*scenities again, Gary Simmons?" demanded a silver-haired man in his fifties, approaching the table. He had a reddish, pleasant face and friendly eyes.

"Hiya, Reverend, how you doin'?" Gary waved, intro-

ducing Katie to the Reverend Russell Johnson, their
pastor. The minister, pressed hard by Gladys Simmons,
accepted a piece of her blueberry pie and carried it off
with him.

Even the voracious Katie was beginning to feel full.
There was still plenty of food left, and Mrs. Simmons
was still urging those who'd already eaten seconds to try
for thirds. Everybody was kicked back and feeling mellow; even Wes, who said very little, and nothing at all to
Katie, moved closer to the circle and almost smiled now
and then,

Buster Miller was heading in their direction, trailed by
his short, haggard wife and three small children. He was
carrying a bulging paper bag and grinning all over his fat
jowls.

"Hey, Gary," he called. "When the hell we gonna go
huntin'?"

There was a split second of silence, thick and almost
palpable, as the men exchanged glances among themselves, then Gary said easily, "I don't know, Buster, I'll
let you know." He turned to Katie. "You ever been
huntin'?"

"When I was little"—she nodded—"my daddy took
me."

Buster was dumping the contents of the large paper
bag onto the picnic table. Colorful wrappers and odd
shapes spilled out, fireworks of all descriptions.

"Cherry bombs! Snappin' crackers! Big Nukes!" crowed
Buster exuberantly, and the other men caught the fever,
pawing eagerly through the fireworks like little boys to
find their favorites. Katie took her little camera out of
her purse again and began snapping pictures.

"Hellfire, Buster!" Gary laughed. "You gonna blow
the town up on the Fourth of Jew-lie!" This struck the
other men as hilarious, and they roared with laughter.

"Hey, you hear old Ronnie Reagan's gonna put the
farmer back on his feet?" Shorty asked.

"How's he gonna do that, Shorty?" Gary wanted to
know.

"He's gonna take our pickups away."

This time the joke fell flat, too close to the bone to be comfortable. The laughter around the table rang hollow and bitter.

Suddenly Wes addressed Katie for the first time. "What you takin' all these pictures for?" he demanded in a hard voice.

Surprised and a little frightened by his aggressive tone, Katie took a step or two backward and froze, the camera dangling from her hand by its strap. "I . . . I take 'em wherever I go," she stammered. "I got a whole album."

But Wes's scowl didn't diminish, and the other men kept silent, looking uncomfortable. It was Gary who broke through the awkward moment.

"What the hell's the matter with you, Wes, you 'fraid your face is gonna bust the camera?"

Now the others were free to laugh, although Wes didn't join in. He went on staring at Katie with undisguised loathing in his pale eyes. If looks could kill, then Katie Phillips would be stone-cold dead, she was sure of it.

"Come on," Gary said, grabbing Katie by the hand and pulling her away. "Let's go and pitch us some horseshoes."

Katie followed him willingly, eager to be out of there. Whatever Wes Bond's problems with her was, she didn't want to have any part of it. Let him keep it all for himself. Katie had never met a man so hostile or so hard to read. Wes made her flesh crawl, with those light, hate-filled eyes of his, and that mean expression around his mouth. What was his problem? Why did he hate her so much?

When darkness fell, everyone gathered near the band shell. Those who could find seats took them, while the others spread out on the grass. Families grouped together; the kids, who'd been running around wild all day, came to join their parents, to stand with their heads against their mothers' shoulders or huddle in daddy's lap. This was the time they'd been waiting for, the time when the sun would go down and the sky above Denison would blaze with the light of a million billion stars. The time of the fireworks.

Katie sat huddled next to Gary; also close beside him were Rachel and Joey, between their father and grandmother. The fireworks started. With each dazzling burst of color, red, blue, yellow, green, then red, white, and blue, with each explosion of light and brilliance, a great collective "ah!" rose from every spectator's throat. As each rocket went out in a dying fall, leaving a sputtering trail of sparks in its wake, the "ah" died away to "awww." Cheers and applause followed the more spectacular bursts.

Someone started to sing "God Bless America," and more voices picked the melody up, then more and more, until finally, everybody was singing it together, sharing the moment and the feeling of communion as the spectacular fireworks display continued to turn the night heavens into a light show.

Gary watched Katie's face in the sporadic glow of the rockets. Her eyes shone exactly like a child's and her upturned profile, anticipating the next bright flare, was lovely in its purity. He was deeply moved, by the holiday and its meaning, by today's closeness with family and friends, and by the unsettling presence of this beautiful and independent girl so close to him. Almost without willing it, he bent over and kissed her softly on the mouth.

Katie looked at Gary in surprise, but she didn't pull back, nor did she turned her face away. When he leaned forward to kiss her again, more urgently this time, she closed her eyes and raised her lips to meet his.

Katie and Gary drove back to her motel in silence, but he took her left hand from the seat and tucked it under his leg, imprisoning it there as he drove. Katie felt the warmth of him and the muscularity of his thigh on her palm, and it dizzied her, making it difficult for her to think straight. She had kissed him, but now she was beginning to regret it a little. Everything was happening so fast, too fast; she'd been here only a couple of days. This wasn't what she wanted or intended to happen. Even though she knew Gary better now, had seen him with his family and his friends, knew what affection and tenderness he was capable of, felt the strong pull of physical attraction, she still clung to her defenses.

So, when they reached Katie's door at the Lazy-Vu and he pulled her tightly against him and kissed her deeply on the mouth, Katie broke off the kiss and pulled away from him.

Gary looked at her for a long moment. "You ain't gonna ask me in, are you?" he asked softly.

Katie found it difficult to meet his eyes; she could only shake her head.

"It ain't the time yet, is it?" He hooked one finger under her chin and turned her face up to his. Her expression showed him plainly that she was torn, unable to decide whether to go forward or back. It made him smile. Gary Simmons was a patient man; he knew that time was on his side.

Gary's smile tore at Katie. She stepped forward quickly and kissed him, much to her own surprise.

Gary's smile widened to a broad grin. "You better get in there, though. Unless you want me to make the bed for you."

Katie broke into an answering grin and socked Gary playfully on the chest. Then she turned and went inside, still smiling.

The smile remained on her lips as she watched Gary's Scottsdale drive off. It stayed there as she looked at her face in the mirror, studying the expression in her eyes to see if she could fathom her own mind and understand her own desires.

It stayed there until the telephone rang.

The shrill sound made Katie jump, and her smile faded. She looked at the phone for several rings, as though she were trying to decide whether to answer it or not. Then, crossing the room swiftly, she picked it up.

"Hello," she said.

She listened for a few seconds without speaking. Then, she said only "Yes," and hung the phone up.

It had started raining sometime during the night, and by the following morning the rain had settled in under swollen gray skies. It rained hard, soaking the land. Pools of oil-slick water collected in the ruts in the roads, and the narrow irrigation ditches began to overflow. There were puddles everywhere.

Katie slammed the pickup door shut and pushed her wet hair out of her eyes. She glanced at her wristwatch; she had very little time. A glance around the front yard of the Simmons farm told her that Gary was nowhere in sight; only Shorty was there, dressed in an old rain slicker and his customary cowboy hat, still working on the John Deere tractor.

"They're in the barn," he yelled, seeing Katie.

The barn was cold and smelled damply of wet hay. Rain clattered loudly on the roof. Rachel came running toward her, crying, throwing her arms around Katie and holding on for dear life. Over the little girl's head Katie could see Gary and Wes talking with a man she didn't know. Nearby, Joey was standing pressed against the barn wall. He, too, was crying, crying as though his world was coming to an end.

"It's . . . Beauty," Rachel sobbed. "She's too sick. Daddy says we're gonna have to put her to sleep."

"Ah, no!" breathed Katie, hugging Rachel to her. "No." She turned pleadingly to Gary's mother, who came to stand just inside the barn door as the veterinarian left with his black bag. But Mrs. Simmons only nodded sadly, confirming Rachel's words.

"She's gonna get well! I promise, Dad! I promise!" Joey ran to his father, sobbing.

Distracted momentarily, Gary turned to hug the weeping boy, then gently pushed him away. "Go with your grandma, son," he said in low voice that shook with emotion.

"Please, Dad, please!" Joey begged for Beauty's life.

"Daddy, please! Please don't, Daddy!" Now Rachel, too, ran to her father. Gladys Simmons hurried to pull the crying children away from Gary, hugging them tightly, trying to shush them and soothe them, all the while moving them out of the barn, away from what they all knew was about to happen.

Katie watched, heartsick, aching for all of them. But she wasn't a part of this; it was right for her to stay in the background. She could hear Ronnie whimpering as the dog began to sense the tension in the air.

Turning back to Beauty's stall, Gary reached into his pocket and drew out a Remington .45 pistol. As he clicked off the safety, he and Wes exchanged silent glances. Gary moved quietly up to the mare and aimed the gun at Beauty's head. He stood there for a very long minute, frozen in an eternal action, a man and his old horse and the gun that would end a relationship of more than twenty years. All he had to do was pull the trigger, and Beauty's suffering would be over for good. It was the right way, the merciful way, the only way.

But Gary couldn't do it. He didn't have the heart. Behind him, Ronnie whimpered again, insecure and afraid, his tail curved between his legs, tight under his belly. Gary's gun hand dropped, and he turned his face away from his old chestnut mare, tears burning in his eyes so that he could barely see. He shook his head and walked quickly out of the stall, handing the pistol to Wes.

Katie followed him out of the barn. Gary didn't see her, or if he did, he just kept walking anyway, not looking to the left or the right. Water ran in rivulets over his head and shoulders, dripping from the peak of his cap. But he didn't appear to care, or even to notice that it was raining.

Behind him, from the barn, a shot rang out. Ronnie started whimpering again, a high, whining sound, a strange sound to come from so large a dog.

Gary flinched and stopped walking. He stood very still, his eyes fixed upon the ground, while twenty years of his boyhood memories washed away into the puddles on the sodden earth.

Katie came up to stand beside him and Gary looked at her as though seeing her for the first time.

"I have to go," she said quietly, hating to hit him with this now, just when he needed everybody he cared for to stand with him in his pain. When he didn't say anything, she added. "My mama's gonna have an operation. I got a call. It's just her gallbladder. She'll be okay."

Gary took a long look at her while Katie's words sank in. Her face and hair were wet and glossy with the rain, but there were shadows under her hazel eyes and faint lines of tension around her mouth.

"When are you comin' back?" he asked her finally.

Katie shrugged unhappily. "Coupla days, maybe. Can't get any work done around here anyways. It's gonna take a while before all this dries out."

Gary nodded wordlessly. Wes came up to them and handed Gary back his Remington. He didn't look at Katie at all, and she kept her eyes turned away from him, so as not to see the naked hatred in his face.

Slowly, Katie and Gary walked to Katie's pickup, and she climbed in. Joey broke away from his grandmother and came running over, his cheeks wet with tears and raindrops. "Where you goin'?" he demanded.

"Her mom's sick," explained Gary.

"When are you comin' back?"

Katie couldn't find the words to make Joey feel better; his neediness, and Gary's, were so palpable that she felt pressured, unable to breathe.

"Aren't you gonna give me my ride?"

"Sure she is," Gary said hastily. But he looked at Katie in exactly the same way that Joey was looking at her, like a disappointed little boy who didn't quite understand why.

"You promise," demanded Joey.

"I promise." Katie nodded solemnly. She turned the key in the ignition, then hesitated, her foot suspended over the gas pedal. "I'm sorry about Beauty," she told Gary huskily.

Gary looked straight into her eyes. "I love you," he said.

It was a simple statement, simply delivered. Katie gasped, then she floored the pedal and pulled away, out past the picket fence and onto the road.

She didn't want to look, but she couldn't help herself. She knew damn well what she would see. Yet her eyes sought the rearview mirror, and there they were, the two of them, man and boy, their arms around each other, waving at the retreating pickup. Just standing there in the rain, waving at her like a pair of soaking wet damn fools.

"Aw, shit," Katie Phillips muttered out loud. "Shit. What the hell am I gonna do now?"

Chapter Five

Catherine Weaver

Catherine Weaver's high heels clicked on the hard marble as she crossed the wide plaza that surrounded the reflecting pool at the entrance to the office block. The July heat was scorching, and she felt uncomfortable in her tailored suit and panty hose. The combs that pulled her hair tightly back from her face and held it swept into a French knot were cutting into her scalp. At least the building would be air-conditioned, she thought gratefully.

A concrete and glass structure designed by a famous Chicago architect, the new multimillion-dollar office building had won several architectural awards and a place in the rank of notable twentieth-century constructions. To Catherine Weaver, it was nothing more than a place to work.

She came through the revolving doors into the coolness of the two-story, mosaic-walled lobby, and walked past the vast directories filled with renowned corporate names and the banks of elevators near the entrance, turning instead into an alcove where there were two elevators, the only two elevators that stopped at floors twenty-two through twenty-five. In front of these an armed security guard sat at a desk. Several people were waiting in line to be passed through, and Cathy joined the end of the line.

When her turn came, she opened her purse and took

out her laminated ID badge. The guard checked the photograph carefully, matched it against Cathy's face, and nodded.

"Don't forget to put your tag on, Miss Weaver."

As the elevator doors shut behind her, Cathy fastened the badge to the lapel of her suit.

She got out at the twenty-second floor and pushed through a door marked "Federal Bureau of Investigation, Chicago Division," into the reception area. This was a set of offices very different from the magnificence promised by the downstairs lobby. These were plain and pragmatic, designed not so much to impress as, perhaps, to intimidate.

Behind a long reception desk sat a tall young man in a dark suit and white shirt. His necktie was fastened to his shirt by a tie clip discreetly carrying a tiny version of the FBI emblem. Everything about his bearing would inform the wary visitor that he was armed and skilled enough to use a gun effectively. On the wall above his head was the Great Seal of the United States; on the wall across from him was the seal of the Justice Department. On a side wall, two photographs—the President and the director—flanked an American flag on a stanchion.

Efficiently, the receptionist checked Catherine Weaver's credentials and passed her through. No matter how many times she entered these offices, no matter how well the security officers knew her face, her identification was carefully checked on each and every occasion.

This time, as she entered the door marked "Authorized Personnel Only," Cathy almost wished they'd turn her away. She knew she was in for trouble, especially with Michael. It was Michael Carnes who'd assigned her to this case, and he wasn't going to like her report. Michael knew Cathy well enough, intimately enough, to know that behind her report there would be much more than the dispassionate observations of an undercover agent.

The Bureau was attempting to build a case against

Gary Simmons in the murder of Dan Kraus, and Cathy
Weaver, in her undercover identity of "Katie Phillips,"
had been sent to Denison to bring back evidence of his
guilt. Instead, she'd come back when they'd summoned
her, bringing nothing with her but two rolls of undevel-
oped snapshots and the conviction of Gary's innocence.
The Bureau wasn't going to like that, and most especially
Michael Carnes wasn't going to like that.

She'd have to be strong, convincing, sure of herself,
and Cathy thought nervously that she was none of these
things. This was her first undercover assignment, and she
was going to screw it up. An FBI agent isn't supposed to
get emotionally involved with a suspect, but Cathy had
been too vulnerable. Gary's last kiss still stung her lips,
Gary's "I love you" still rang in her ears, and when she
closed her eyes she could picture him as clearly as though
he were standing right there in front of her—strong,
serious, with those dark blue eyes and that beautiful
mouth. . . .

It was every bit as bad as Cathy had been afraid it was
going to be. She would have preferred to report to Michael directly, and alone. Instead, Michael's office held a
number of people beside himself, and there was barely
enough room in it for the extra chairs to accommodate
the larger number of personnel. Other agents were present; among them, Donald Duffin, as junior an operative
as Cathy. Also there was Marty Freed, the Chicago Police
detective lieutenant in charge of the investigation into
Dan Kraus's homicide. It was to this gathering that Cathy
was forced to recap the events of the past few days,
trying to sound as uninvolved and objective as possible,
knowing that she was muffing it. Even to her own ears,
she sounded partisan.

Worse, Michael came to the meeting prepared with a
fat dossier on Gary and his origins. Of course I knew
there was one, Cathy thought unhappily, why was I dumb
enough to forget he'd use it? This case is his baby.

All Cathy had to offer was her sincere belief in Gary

Simmons, and a couple of rolls of holiday snapshots; for the Bureau, it would hardly be sufficient evidence to prove a dossiered suspect innocent.

Worst of all, the Old Man, the Bureau chief, came in just as Michael was really getting warmed up. With him was a tall, handsome black man whom Cathy had never seen before, but who wore the unmistakable air of authority of an experienced agent. Everybody started to stand up when the chief entered, but the Old Man signaled them to go on as they were.

". . . his father—" Michael was saying. "Gary Simmons's father joined a group called the Sons of Liberty in 1978. He refused to pay his taxes. The IRS went after him. They put a lien on the farm. His father hanged himself."

"So what?" Cathy demanded hotly. "What does that have to do with anything?"

Michael's gray-green eyes shot her a reproachful look. His mouth took on that stubborn line she knew so well. "His wife divorced him and moved to San Jose—" he continued.

"That makes him a killer for sure, right?" Cathy felt that she was coming on too strongly in Gary's defense, but she couldn't help herself. She had a very clear memory of Gary's hand holding a gun, a gun he was unable to shoot. She saw again the gun pressed against the mare's head, then the hand dropping helplessly. If he couldn't put a dying horse out of its misery, how in God's name would Gary Simmons be able to shoot a man down in cold blood?

But Michael Carnes was not to be so easily put off. He was young, smart, and ambitious, a man on the way up. The Bureau had its eye on him, and this case assignment, the assassination of a celebrity, a hate killing that was still making national headlines, was the most important plum handed to him so far. He wasn't about to let it be plucked from his fingers.

"A year later she was killed by a hit-and-run driver,"

he continued to read from the file he was holding. "The driver was never apprehended." He looked up at the Old man. "Her body was so badly bruised that we think whoever hit her put it in reverse and drove over her again."

"Was he out in California when she was killed?" Cathy asked levelly.

Michael frowned, annoyed. He hated not having every *i* dotted and *t* crossed. "We're still checking."

"That shouldn't be too hard to check," retorted Cathy with a sarcastic edge to her voice.

The two of them locked eyes angrily, then Michael looked away. He directed the rest of his presentation at the chief. "He almost won the Medal of Honor in Vietnam. He threw himself into a VC bunker and killed five Viet Cong—after they had shot him in the shoulder."

"Great!" Cathy burst out. "We ought to hang him for that!" She stopped, checking herself, in the knowledge that she had just gone too far, had stepped over an invisible line.

"What did *you* find?" the Old Man asked in his dry voice. "Weaver?"

Cathy's jaw set stubbornly. "Nothing."

"For the moment," Michael put in hastily. "She's still—"

"I don't think there's anything *to* find." Cathy looked earnestly at the chief, trying to convince him by directness and sincerity. "I think it's a wild-goose chase, sir."

"A car like his was seen speeding away from the garage," Michael insisted.

Cathy whirled to confront him. "Yeah, a half-drunk witness identified *two digits* of a license plate on a car *similar* to his."

"Whose side are you on, anyway?" demanded Michael. It was the question Cathy had been dreading, the question to which there were no easy answers. Her only defense was attack.

"Don't you even start that shit with me, okay, Michael?" she rasped, furious. "You're gonna tell me I'm getting in too deep, right? Then you're gonna accuse me of getting my loyalties all screwed up. Don't even start it! Just don't!"

"I didn't say anything about your loyalties getting screwed up—*you* did," Michael pointed out, equally angry. The two of them glared at each other, breathing hard. Then Cathy shook her head in frustration.

"What the hell are we doing? Targeting him now? On what basis?"

"My *gut's* basis," yelled Michael. "I have a very sensitive gut. It comes from long proximity to certain erogenous zones." It was a low blow, personally meant and personally taken. Cathy recoiled from the intimate shot, and looked around to see how the others were taking it. But they were operatives trained to reveal nothing, and sat as expressionless spectators at the battle. Whatever they were thinking, they chose to keep it to themselves.

The Old Man's next question was addressed to Michael. "What about the Chicago PD? What are they coming up with?"

Michael turned to Marty Freed. "Marty?"

"We've got more than a hundred guys on this case, sir," the police lieutenant told the Bureau chief. "We've got nothing, zip." He shrugged. "As far as we're concerned, Gary Simmons is a real long shot."

Cathy shot Michael a look of triumph. Vindicated.

"Did you see any guns?" asked Duffin.

Cathy smiled. "There are more guns in that part of the country than people. I didn't see any Mac-tens if that's what you mean." She felt calmer now, surer of herself and more certain of her ground. "Kraus was a lightning rod. Anybody who's got a radio could've killed him."

"So?" Michael Carnes wasn't letting go so easily. "Gary's got a radio, hasn't he? I bet he's got two or three."

But Catherine Weaver was on a roll now, counting suspects off on her fingers. "Dog lovers, Republicans, Democrats, left-wingers, right-wingers—maybe they all got together. Maybe this is the kind of conspiracy that would have got Mr. Hoover's rocks off."

If she expected a laugh or a gasp at the desecration of the late, great director's name, she was disappointed. Only the Old Man cracked a smile.

"You skipped the fat ladies," Michael pointed out with some sarcasm. "You wanna know my real gut instinct? The fat ladies got him."

"They certainly had cause!" retorted Cathy.

The Bureau chief stood. "Let me know what you decide," he said to Michael, and left the room. The black man remained behind.

Michael handed over Cathy's rolls of film to Duffin and made the introductions. "Al Sanders. He's in from D.C. Catherine Weaver."

Sanders and Cathy shook hands, while Cathy wondered what the Washington agent was doing here in Chicago. D.C. was heavy, and rarely interfered with local operations. This case was even bigger than they'd suspected if the Bureau was widening its involvement.

"I admire your balls," Sanders told her, grinning.

Michael Carnes uttered a short, barking laugh. "She doesn't have any balls, Al," he scoffed. "Look at her. Let's not carry this sacrosanct equality bullshit too far. It's the first time she's been undercover. I bet she's like a sixteen-year-old on her first date."

"I love sixteen-year-olds," Duffin put in with a leer.

"You're sick, Duffin. All you fucking yuppies are sick."

But Cathy wasn't paying attention to any of this byplay. She was leafing through Gary Simmons's dossier, paying special attention to the photographs of Gary. He was so young in some of the pictures that her heart melted to see them, especially the ones in his army uniform; in those, he was little more than a boy. But he still had that same sweet, serious expression in his eyes.

Duffin went off to develop Cathy's film, and Al Sanders went along with him.

Michael and Cathy were alone. At once, his face relaxed, became more boyish. Not conventionally handsome, Michael Carnes had a head-on kind of charm that

had more to do with the strength in his face and his
direct gaze than with his features. Only thirty-four, he
possessed all the fire and optimism of a young man. To
Michael, there weren't any questions in life that didn't
have answers. If you just looked for them long enough
and in the right places, you'd find the answers to everything. Life had not yet taught him otherwise.

"It's nice to see you again, anyway. You look great,
Cathy."

She gave him a weak smile, hoping it would put him
off. A new photograph caught her eye and she picked it
up and stared at it. It was the picture of an extremely
attractive young woman, with light brown hair and level
brows. Cathy thought she could trace something of Rachel and Joey in her features, although both children had
Gary's eyes.

"His ex-wife," said Michael, coming over to stand
beside her and look over her shoulder. "I missed you."
He leaned over, and before Cathy could pull away, he
kissed her on the lips.

Cathy made an impatient gesture and slammed the
folder down, stalking out of the office with Michael following behind her.

"I always did like this view." Michael grinned, appre-
ciating the fine contours of Cathy's rear end.

"Cathy spun around, scowling. She hated it when he
put their working relationship on a physical basis. "You
really piss me off, Michael!"

"Good. That means we still feel the same way about
each other."

She hesitated, not wanting to hurt him but still wanting
to make her meaning very clear. "No, we don't," she
told him gently and a little sadly.

But Michael didn't hear the sadness in her voice, only
the gentleness. Grasping her by the shoulder, he pulled
Cathy back into his office and pushed her up against the
wall, pressing himself against her, breathing into her
hair, searching for her lips with his own.

A couple of months ago, the feel of his strong, hard body would have excited her, caused her to respond. Now, all she felt was weary and turned off. Had she ever really cared for him? The naked longing in Michael's face disgusted her. Over his bland features her mind's eye superimposed another face—older, more rugged, the eyes darker, the mouth softer, the same look of longing in the eyes.

"Don't," she told him, trying to push Michael away.

But he was aroused and not easily discouraged. "I really did miss you," he murmured into her throat. "Very much." His hands searched over her body, and it took all her strength to pry him loose. But she managed to slip past him, shaking her head, moving quickly out of his office as proof that she wasn't merely teasing him. She really *didn't* want to be alone with him.

Angry, frustrated, hurt, Michael watched her go.

A couple of hours later, they gathered in the company cafeteria—Cathy, Michael, Al Sanders, and Donald Duffin—to look over eight-by-ten-inch glossy blowups of Cathy's pictures from the Fourth of July picnic. There, over Styrofoam cups of bitter coffee and tuna sandwiches as tasteless as cardboard, Michael and Cathy resumed their dispute over Gary Simmons.

"Come *on*," Cathy argued, "his dad, his ex-wife—what the hell does that mean? Circumstantial bullshit! He's a war hero! Are we going to hold that against him, too?"

"Not in the eighties, we ain't," said Sanders. "Heroism is back in style."

"Honest to God, Michael, you want J. Edgar to come flouncing back from his grave?" Cathy demanded.

This made everybody smile. "No, thank you," conceded Michael.

"Gary's no more violent or racist than anybody up there," she continued.

"What does *that* mean?" Michael's suspicions flared up again.

Cathy shrugged. "It means they tell black jokes."

"You mean nigger jokes?" asked Al Sanders.

Cathy nodded. "I'll bet they tell black jokes in this building."

"The hell they do!" flared Michael.

"They tell 'em just loud enough so this nigger's gonna overheard them," Sanders said without rancor.

"You didn't see *anything* suspicious?" Duffin asked again. "That *must* mean he's our man. There's always something suspicious about really innocent people."

"All I saw was two scarecrows he and his little boy used for target practice. Is that suspicious enough for you?" snapped Cathy.

"What kind of scarecrows?" persisted Duffin.

"*I* don't know." Cathy shrugged. "Scarecrow-scare-crows."

"What's a scarecrow-scarecrow?" Duffin looked genu-inely puzzled, but with Duffin it was sometimes impossi-ble to tell when he was playing it straight or when he was goofing on you. He lacked the reverent demeanor that marked the typical young FBI agent.

"A scarecrow-scarecrow's a scarecrow, right, Weaver?" Al Sanders smiled at Cathy with his eyes, and she felt a rush of genuine liking for this tall, quiet man.

"Right." She smiled back.

"Jesus Christ!" Michael Carnes burst out impatiently. "Enough about the fucking scarecrows! What about Zog?"

She turned to him earnestly, leaning her elbows on the cluttered table. "Michael, what did you think I'd find? 'Zog' painted on the barns right next to 'Duane loves Mary'?"

"Who's Duane?" Duffin asked with deceptive innocence.

Michael pointed to a picture that included Gary's Jeep. "How come he's got all this mud on his plates?" he demanded.

"Because, Michael, when it rains, farm fields get muddy," Cathy said, as though explaining to a small and not very bright boy.

But Michael didn't buy it; he kept shaking his head no. "This guy smells too good," he said slowly. "I've been around the track too long. I can smell it. This is the kind of guy who needs an Alamo to defend. He's perfect for the part."

"You *want* him to be perfect for the part." Cathy pointed an accusing finger at him.

Michael's hands were busy with the sheaf of photographs. Now, something occurred to him as though for the first time. Pulling out one picture, he laid it on the table faceup. It was a picture of Gary, Gary grinning at the camera, his cap pushed back on his dark hair, Gary looking like an American boy, a farmer, and pretty damn good.

"He's a good-looking guy, isn't he, Cathy?" Michael asked softly. He didn't take his eyes off her face, watching for her reaction to his loaded words.

With an effort, Cathy kept her face a blank. It took all her training. She knew that Michael was fishing for; she could see where his detective's mind was going. "You want something, I'll give you something," she said finally. "He's got a dog named after Ronald Reagan."

"Well, he ain't *all* bad." Sanders laughed.

"What's wrong with Ronald Reagan?" demanded Duffin. "I voted for Ronald Reagan."

Michael took Cathy home in a cab, but a few blocks before they reached her apartment building, they got out and dismissed the taxi. They needed privacy while he briefed her on her cover story. Side by side they walked slowly down the overheated streets. Catherine Weaver lived in a high rise near Lake Michigan; ironically, not far from where Dan Kraus had lived and died. From time to time a cool breeze off the water made the street bearable for a few seconds, then July rushed back at them more aggressively and more brutal than ever.

"Your mother had her operation at Saint Joseph's Hospital in Dallas," he informed her. "She's in Room 302. Her name is Emma. She'll be home in a week in Wells. We'll have an agent there. Your home phone number is 312-555-1701. Memorize that."

Cathy nodded.

"If you need me," Michael said, suddenly anxious, "there's an airfield. I can be there in an hour and a half."

"You're getting paranoid, Michael." Cathy smiled. "Nothing's gonna happen to me."

He stopped walking and grabbed her by the arm, turning her around to look at him. His face, with its wide brow, clear eyes, and strong chin, looked troubled. "I didn't recruit you off that campus to lose you five years later," he told her in a low, serious voice.

Cathy shook her head. "You already lost me, Michael. It's a wild-goose chase, I told you that."

"You like the guy, don't you?" Michael accused. "It won't kill you to spend another week with him, will it?" He watched Cathy's face change, grow angry and stubborn, and he put his hand out to her in apology. "I didn't mean to put it like that," he pleaded. "You do like him, though, don't you?"

Cathy hesitated for the length of a slow heartbeat. But she went way back with Michael. She owed him some honesty, if nothing else. "Yes."

He might have been expecting that answer, but he wasn't expecting the rush of pain that came with it. Even the sight of her face, so lovely and so dear to him, hurt like hell, and he had to look away. He didn't want to say anymore, but some self-destructive instinct in him forced him to probe further.

"You like him a lot, don't you?"

For the first time, Cathy faced the question squarely in her own mind. As the song says, you gotta know when to hold 'em, know when to fold 'em. Katie folded all those defensive cards that she'd been keeping so tightly to her chest and laid them out on the table.

"Yeah, I like him a lot," she admitted to Michael and to herself, and a surge of unexpected joy swept over her. She felt suddenly free.

Michael only nodded, not trusting himself to speak. Enough words had already passed between them. For a long time they just looked at each other, a man and a woman who'd shared a piece of important time together, and whose time together was over now. Then Cathy kissed him softly on the cheek and turned to go.

"Hey!" Michael called after her, and she turned. "What's your mother's telephone number?"

"312-555-1701," recited Cathy.

He nodded, satisfied, and they went their separate ways.

Chapter Six

A Shadow

Katie Phillips came back to Denison eagerly, with an open heart, prepared to let down all her defenses and open herself to Gary Simmons. All she really wanted was to see Gary again, to find out if he really did love her, and to love him back, to give him as much as he had offered her. She wanted to share his life, his family, his dreams, to become a part of all of them. That she was still on the case, still undercover, and still surveilling Gary's movements, was almost secondary. Maybe Michael was right; maybe her loyalties *were* confused. But she couldn't help her feelings, and she knew now that she didn't want to.

Before she left Chicago, Cathy changed from her business clothes into Katie's combine-driving outfit—jeans, pullover sweater, and boots. She pulled her hair loose from its citified chignon and braided it into one pigtail down her back; on her forehead, her bangs were loose, fluffing up in the July humidity. While she was braiding her hair, Catherine Weaver took a good look at herself in the mirror; a stranger looked back, a stranger named Katie Phillips.

Driving to Denison, Katie felt happy yet impatient, both anxious and at ease, everything crowding in at the same time. What she felt for Gary was right; she could believe in that. She trusted her emotions. As to what the future held—well that's what futures are for. To be hidden from the present. Someday, all of this would be behind them, and she could be honest with Gary. The case would be solved, the killer caught, and Katie Phillips could become Catherine Weaver again. Katie and Gary would have something to talk about in the long evenings she planned for both of them, something to laugh over. When that day came, Katie hoped he wouldn't be angry, or feel that she had betrayed him. After all, hadn't she championed him to the Bureau, believing in his innocence, and hadn't she returned undercover mostly to bring back further proof of it?

Pulling up in front of the Simmons farmhouse, she jumped out of the pickup and almost ran to the front door, so eager was she to see them all. Before she reached it, the door opened and the Simmons family came out, all of them together, Gary and his children and his mom.

They were dressed up as Katie had never seen them. Rachel was wearing a starched and ruffled dress instead of her overalls, and Joey was dressed in a jacket, tie, and slacks, not his usual jeans and T-shirt. Even Gary was wearing a suit, Katie was astonished to see. Not exactly a business suit, not your three-button gray flannel, but a matching jacket and pants with western styling—top stitching and a yoke across the back. Gladys Simmons was sporting a flowered print dress and a neat little hat with a veil. In her gloved hands Mrs. Simmons carried a large black Bible.

"You came back!" yelled Rachel, launching herself at Katie and hugging her tightly. Joey beamed at her shyly.

"I told you I would," Katie answered, hugging her back, but never taking her eyes off Gary.

His gaze was fixed on her face, and in his eyes was the expression that Katie was hoping to see there. He had missed her; he wanted her; he loved her.

"We're goin' to church," he told her. That explained the Bible and hat and the Sunday-go-to-meeting clothing. "You wanna come?"

"I've gotta go check the field." Katie shook her head. "What for? It's still too wet," Gary pointed out. "Ain't gonna do no wheat-whackin' today." Mrs. Simmons nodded agreement, urging Katie to come along with them, and Rachel and Joey joined in with their entreaties.

Katie bit her lip, embarrassed. She had totally forgotten that this was Sunday in Christian America. Back in Chicago, Sunday was a day for sleeping late and pigging out in the living room, sitting on the floor reading the *Sun-Times* and the *Trib*. Sunday meant three cups of coffee in a big blue mug, croissants and strawberry jam, not church. A feeling of shame and even guilt stole over her, as though up to now she'd been living wrong.

"I'm not dressed," she told them awkwardly, holding out her denim jacket to prove her point.

"Sure you are," Gary grinned. "You can come in what you're wearing. Hey, you gotta hear old Russell. He preaches like the devil's after him with a red-hot pitchfork."

"The devil doesn't *have* a pitchfork!" Rachel piped up.

"How do *you* know?" scoffed Joey. "You seen him?"

What could Katie do? She didn't have a leg to stand on. Besides, now that she saw him again, it would take more than a devil—pitchfork or not—to pull her away from Gary. She smiled and gave in, and they all piled into Gary's Jeep Cherokee for the drive to church.

The Christian Reality Church was a plain building with only a steeple to show that it was a house dedicated to worship. No stained glass, no large crosses, no church choir in purple robes. Inside, a small pipe organ and unadorned wooden pews, a spartan altar surmounted by a modest cross. The biggest thing in the church was a huge American flag stretched across the wall behind the pulpit, where every eye could be fixed on it.

When they moved into the Simmons pew and sat themselves down, Katie looked around curiously. She recognized so many faces here—there was the sheriff's deputy Dean sitting with his fat wife Toby. Over there, Shorty Richards was scrubbed within an inch of his life, his plump body busting out of his dark suit. Buster was in a pew at the back, surrounded by his scrawny wife Ellie and their three homely children. Lyle, the older man who "went way back" with Gary's father, was two rows in front of them. It was like Old Home Week, or maybe an alumni reunion, Katie thought.

The Reverend Russell Johnson—"Old Russell," as Gary had called him—certainly lived up to his advance billing. He preached a hellfire-and-brimstone sermon on the declining, decaying state of modern life that had his congregation yelling out their enthusiastic agreement.

"What are we turning into?" he yelled at them, his friendly face turning a dark indignant red. "The most cowardly, sheepish bunch of degenerates that have ever littered the face of the planet!"

Scattered cries of "amen!" came from all over the church. Katie sat astonished, saying nothing. This wasn't what she had expected. This was more a diatribe than a Sunday sermon.

"We're mugged on our streets and our neighbors are afraid to help us! Our children's minds are poisoned by filth and our judges are afraid to cast that filth into the fires of righteousness! Our cities are dying of sexual disease; the Lord's wrath comes down on them who live by promiscuity and perversion!"

"Amen!" "That's the truth, Reverend!" "Tell it, Reverend!"

Reverend Johnson's face grew darker yet, and a vein pulsed in his forehead, so swollen and evident that Katie was afraid he was going to have a seizure right there in the pulpit. Yet all around her, people were leaning forward in their seats, eyes shining, mouths agape, eagerly drinking in the preacher's every enraged syllable.

"Listen to me, Americans! *We* are the descendants of the Lost Tribes of Israel, the beneficiaries of God's blessings!"

"Amen, brother!"

Katie sneaked a look at Gary to see his reaction. He sat quietly, his eyes fixed on the reverend, a slight smile on his face. His expression was impossible to read. Was he really believing any of this? she wondered.

"We're all the dragons of God!" bellowed Johnson. His arms waved about in the air as though he were wielding a flaming sword against the demons of unrighteousness. "We aren't the sons of Cain, come from that illicit coupling between Eve and Satan! We're the sons of Abel! We must awaken! The time is coming! A long forgotten wind is starting to blow!"

"We hear ya, Reverend!" "Amen to that!" More and more voices in the congregation now were raised to join in the responses. There was a rustling in the pews as men and women half rose from their seats, stretching out their arms, reaching out to their minister as though touching him would solve their problems, would grant them holy grace.

"Amen!" Gladys Simmons yelled loudly, and Katie jumped a little, startled. Mrs. Simmons's face was ecstatic; it glowed with fervor. The sermon had evidently gotten right down to her core and stirred something powerful inside her.

"Amen!" Rachel yelled suddenly, and Katie's eyes widened in surprise. Was the child serious or only parroting her grandmother? Surely she was too young to be caught up in all this religious fury. How much can a baby like Rachel understand of all this talk?

Katie had never witnessed so dramatic and deliberate a rousing of human emotions. Doubtful and filled with reservations, she looked over at Gary. Was he swallowing this performance whole? But he turned just then and winked at her, and she felt a rush of relief. Shakily, she returned his smile. He seemed quite normal, an island of sanity in an ocean of pseudo-biblical frenzy.

"I told you he was somethin' else." Gary grinned as the family left the church after the sermon. Katie could only nod; she didn't trust herself to speak. But "somethin' else" was as good a description as any.

"You gonna come to Grandma's for dinner?" wheedled Rachel. "We're gonna watch a cowboy movie. Daddy loves cowboy movies."

"Sure she is." Gary smiled, giving his daughter a hug.

"Pick some beer up on the way for Katie," Mrs. Simmons told her son.

"That's okay," Katie started to protest, but Gary cut her off.

"I'll get it from home. You guys go with Grandma." Grabbing Katie's hand, he led her toward the Cherokee. Katie turned back to watch Mrs. Simmons shepherding Rachel and Joey home with her. She felt a tiny pang of envy; she'd never had a grandma of her own like Gladys Simmons, and the little girl inside her longed for one. Just as the woman inside her longed for children of her own like Rachel and Joey.

"I love your family," she said wistfully.

"Know what?" Gary's handsome face broke into a grin. "I do, too."

As soon as they were inside the Simmons homeplace, Gary pulled her roughly into his arms and kissed her for a very long time. This was the first occasion that Katie and Gary had ever been alone under a house roof. It occurred to her, as soon as she was able to think, that Gary had brought her here for that very reason, so that they could be alone together, and that he was about to make love to her. It was the right time at last. A little butterfly of fear trembled in Katie's belly and fluttered up through her chest to her throat. But the fear was mingled with the delicious thrill of anticipation.

"What are we doing?" she whispered.

"We're lookin' for the beer," Gary whispered back, reaching for her again.

Katie closed her eyes, uttered a little moan, and surrendered herself utterly to sensations. She lost herself, becoming a mouth, a pair of hands, breasts, a body. The hungry beast that she'd kept imprisoned and starved burst out with a roar. She smelled Gary, drank him, felt him near her, around her, over her, inside her. The strength in him that she admired before she now revered, as he used it to bring her to ecstasy, while she writhed and shuddered beneath him.

They made love, and it was like no lovemaking that Katie had ever known before. In the past, she had been more passive with her lovers, sometimes simply allowing the act to take place in the physical present while her mind went roaming elsewhere and her emotions remained detached. Even during the times she was energetic and reciprocating, it was for the act of love and not for the lover.

But now, with Gary, she threw herself and her emotions fully into his possession, her defenses willingly destroyed. In the past, apart from passion she wanted nothing from her lovers. Now, with Gary, there was nothing Katie *didn't* want—his body, his mind, his spirit, and, above all else, his strength. It was his strength that drew her like iron filings to a powerful magnet, drew her and held her fast.

Katie's eyes closed, and she let pure pleasure wash over her as Gary Simmons made love to her, devouring her with a hunger to match her own, then gently, as though her body was the most precious, fragile thing in the world. When at last her eyes opened, she saw his face above hers, sweating, handsome, tender, savage, and she felt the heart in her turn over at the sight of it.

I love him, she thought. Oh, I think I love him. Out loud, she cried "Yes!" and again "Yes!"

Later, after a long, long time, they lay still at last. The rays of the late-afternoon sun, slanting through the lace curtains at the windows, made filigree shadows on the ceiling, traced the faded roses on the wallpaper, and built a road of dust motes toward the bed and over the patchwork quilt that covered their still-quivering bodies. Then the ray settled on the monitor of Gary's computer, reflecting off the silent screen and creating a glare that hurt Katie's eyes. So she closed them again, and settled down beside her lover, cradling her body against the strength of his.

It was very quiet in the bedroom. Outside, birds sang

in the trees and there was a heavy drone of bees as they went about collecting pollen from the flowers. Gary sighed. "It's the first time . . . since my wife died," he said in a low tone.

Katie raised her head from its resting place on his shoulder to look into Gary's face. "How did she die?" she asked softly. She held her breath, waiting for the answer. His file, the dossier Michael Carnes kept on Gary Simmons, had already supplied her with the answer. But she needed to hear it from Gary himself.

He turned his face away for a long moment, as though staring beyond Katie into the past. Then he pulled away from her, sitting on the pillows and reaching for a cigarette.

"She left me," he said flatly. "She went out to California . . . she got hit by a car." His face contorted with emotion; Katie's heart ached for the pain evident behind Gary's blunt, bitter words. He had told her the truth, and she was glad of it.

"Maybe I worked too hard on the farm. Maybe I . . . didn't pay enough attention . . . to her . . . I don't know. Maybe she read too many magazines . . . I guess it was my fault." His lips quivered, making Katie ache to kiss them. Then he turned back to her, looking straight into her eyes so that she could read his meaning.

"I learned from it," he told her simply, and leaned down to kiss her. Katie wound her arms tightly about his neck and pulled him against her, hard and demanding.

And then they were making love again, and this time it was less hungry, but much, much more tender, as each vied to give the other the most pleasure.

It was barely dark when Gary fell asleep, his arms wrapped tightly around Katie. But rest didn't come quickly to her. For a long time, Katie lay staring into the darkness of the room, feeling the weight of her lover against her back. Her thoughts would not allow her to fall asleep. Second thoughts.

What had she done? Surrendered herself to a man she was investigating, compromised herself, the investigation, and possibly even the Bureau. Of course he *was* innocent; nevertheless, she had broken the cardinal rule of the underground investigator—she had become personally involved in the case. You couldn't get more personally involved than lying naked in the arms of a suspect, could you? It's a good thing Michael couldn't see her now.

Then, too, think of Gary. Katie knew what she owed to the Bureau. What did she owe Gary Simmons? It was pretty obvious that he was head over heels in love with her. Just as she had made herself vulnerable to him, so he had opened himself and his loneliness and pain to her. He had come to Katie raw and aching, like an exposed nerve. But who was the woman he loved? A spunky, independent, blue-collar farm worker named Katie Phillips, a girl who spoke the same language he did and held many of the same beliefs, a cussin' Texas gal who drank beer, drove a pickup, and was comfortable only in blue jeans.

Gary Simmons wasn't in love with Catherine Weaver, college-educated, trained in deception, a highly paid investigator for the FBI, a woman who represented governmental surveillance, anathema to a man like Gary Simmons, a woman who wore tailored suits and high heels and told her lover a false name, wore a false identity, gave him a false sense of security. Gary Simmons, who loved Katie Phillips, would probably loathe Catherine Weaver. The sure knowledge of that fact made Katie squirm with guilt.

What was she going to do now? Reveal herself to Gary? Tell him the truth? Impossible. That was out of the question—at least, for the present. Later, when the case was over and Gary Simmons was completely exonerated, she could come back to him and tell him what had gone down. Would he still want her when he knew the truth? When he knew how she'd lied to him and spied upon him? Or would he turn her away, feeling betrayed? If he did, how could she blame him?

And what did Katie want? To leave the Bureau, her career, the excitement of her work, and go live on a farm

in Middle America? On the one hand, there were her
ambitions, the satisfactions she gained from feeling that
she was working on the side of the angels. On the other,
there were the frequent isolation and loneliness, especially now that she was going undercover, living lives that
weren't hers by right. Living, in short, a lie. What Gary
offered was not only his own strength and love, but the
affection of his two darling children, the protection of his
mother, a place in his warm, established home. These
were no small considerations; they had always been missing from Catherine Weaver's life, something she hadn't
realized until she'd become so familiar with the Simmons
family. What they had together had touched her immea-
surably.

So Katie lay awake, her mind tormented by unanswer-
able questions, her emotions caught in the turmoil of
conflicting priorities. It wasn't until very late that she
finally fell into a deep sleep. And even then her sleep
was troubled and made anxious by dreams.

In her dreams an angry Gary, who accused her of
deceit and treachery, kept turning into an angry Michael,
who accused her of being unprofessional and becoming
too involved. She dreamed that she had almost solved
the case and was happy that it would soon be over, only
to see the solution fly out from between her fingers and
vanish forever. She dreamed that innocent little children
were yelling out, over and over, "Zog! Zog!"

Zog. Zog.

"I don't wanna be Zog!" cried Rachel unhappily.

"It's your turn!" Joey insisted.

Katie opened her eyes. The sun was up; it was morning. Behind her in the bed Gary lay sleeping soundly,
one arm still flung across her back. Outside the window,
her dream continued, as Rachel and Joey played noisily.

"I don't wanna play Zog! I wanna play Dolly!"

"You always wanna play Dolly!" accused Joey angrily.

Stunned, Katie sat up in bed. Was she hearing right?
How could it be possible? Their childish voices were loud
but still indistinct. Was it Zog or another word she was

hearing? Slipping silently out of the bed, Katie went to
the window, hopping as she pulled on her jeans and
slipped her T-shirt over her head.

She forced a smile onto her face as she came around
the house to the backyard. Rachel and Joey were still
arguing.

"Hi!" said Katie brightly. "What are you playing?"

"Dolly," answered Rachel, holding up two dolls for
Katie to see. "He never wants to play Dolly."

Katie turned to the little boy. "What do you want to
play, Joey?" she asked him carefully.

"I don't like dolls!" Joey scowled.

Katie took a deep breath. "What's Zog?" she asked,
as casually as she could.

"I don't know," said Joey sullenly.

"We don't know," Rachel echoed.

"Dog," said Gary behind her. "One of 'em's the dog.
The other's the cat." He slipped his arms around Katie
from behind. "Good morning," he whispered into her
ear.

Still yelling at each other, the kids ran around the side
of the house, leaving Katie and Gary alone together.
Katie looked after them, chewing on her lip, deeply
troubled. She still wasn't certain if she'd dreamed "Zog"
or not. Rachel and Joey said they didn't know what the
word meant; were they telling the truth? What could
innocent children that young know about Zog? Was it
merely a coincidence, a nonsense syllable, part of a childish game?

"What's the matter?" Gary asked, seeing the distress
on Katie's face. "Didn't you sleep good?"

Katie turned to him slowly, looking into his eyes,
trying to read any mystery in those dark blue depths. "I
slept okay," she said finally. But her voice was distant,
and Gary picked up on it at once.

"Love 'em and leave 'em, Katie, huh?" Behind the
joke was an anxious question.

Katie smiled and shook her head. "No." She wasn't
about to leave Gary, not now. She'd dreamed it, must

have. Didn't the kids say they didn't know what Zog was? Why should they lie about a thing like that?

Joey came running back around the house to the yard. "Can you take me on the ride now?" His voice was pleading. Katie exchanged glances with Gary, who nodded his permission. "Sure," she told the little boy, and Joey's little face became the picture of excitement.

"Hot shit, Dad! We're gonna go on a ride!" As Gary laughed, Joey grabbed Katie's hand and began dragging her toward the waiting combine.

Just as she had with Rachel, Katie set Joey up behind the wheel, allowing him to drive the big rig while she guided his hands. The ground was still damp from the heavy rains of a few days earlier, and it was hard going through the fields, yet the heavy vehicle lumbered forward, the long rotors spun around, slicing and gathering in the grain for the thresher.

"You wanna come huntin' with us tonight?" Gary's face appeared suddenly at the cab window. Working shirtless in the heat, his body gleaming with sweat, he'd hopped up on the moving combine and was clinging to the side.

"I'm tired." Katie shook her head.

"You are?" Gary grinned knowingly. "How come?"

"Can I go hunting, Dad? Please?" begged Joey.

"When you get bigger," Gary promised his son.

"I'm big, Dad!" the boy protested.

But Gary's attention was all for Katie. "Come on. I really want you to come," he coaxed.

Katie didn't say no, but she wouldn't say yes. She knew that hunting was a common occupation in this part of the world, but she couldn't get over her loathing of violence. The thought of spilling an innocent animal's blood for the sport of it turned her stomach. All during her weapons training for the FBI, she'd silently prayed that she'd never be compelled to pull a trigger on another living creature. Push come to desperate shove, she wasn't sure she'd be able to do it. It was a fear she'd never revealed to anybody, not even to Michael when she was sleeping with him. It was just one more secret she was forced to keep.

"Goddamn, it's hot!" Gary took off his cap and mopped at his face. "You wanna go look for some more beer later?" He threw Katie an insinuating grin. On his face was the possessive expression of a man who knows every inch of a woman's body, who considers that body his.

Without a word, Katie gave a hard spin to the steering wheel. Caught off balance, because his cap was in his right hand and he was clinging to the combine with his left, Gary was knocked loose and tumbled to the ground.

He came up laughing, prouder than ever of his girl's feistiness, and Katie laughed, too.

But Gary Simmons wasn't laughing later in the day when they sat in his pickup waiting in line for their turn to unload their wheat at the grain elevator. The sun beat down with merciless fury, baking Katie and Gary as though they were in a roasting pan in a hot oven. The inside of the cab was airless. Dusty motes of chaff rose off the heavy sacks of grain in the truckbed and clung to their eyelids, irritated their nostrils, and parched their throats dry.

The grain elevator had met with some mechanical accident, and a long line of trucks snaked along the road leading up to it. The line was unmoving, and Gary's truck was stuck right in the middle of it. Uncomfortable and impatient, Gary was furious, and he didn't care who knew it.

"Goddamn elevator, it always breaks down!" he fumed to Katie. "Get the parts for it in Abba Dabba or some damn Ay-rab place. Get the parts in Abba Dabba, send the wheat to Russia, feed the goddamn commies so they can sell the goddamn equipment to the goddamn Abba Dabs so they can sell it to us so we can set out here and goddamn boil ourselves to death—I sure as goddamn shit don't get it—"

Gary broke off and leaned his head out the window to look up the line. Up ahead, he spotted a farmer with a better vantage point, and yelled out, "Goddamn it, Elmer! What in the goddamn shit is goin' on?"

But Elmer merely shrugged. Nothing was happening. Nothing was *going* to happen. All a feller could do was to sit and wait; what was the point of getting mad? Wasn't the first time this had happened; wouldn't be the last.

Cursing under his breath, Gary switched off the motor and climbed down from the truck's cab. "Coke machine works, least they don't make it in that goddamn Abba Dabba . . . I don't think."

Katie followed Gary to the big old dented red Coca-Cola machine standing under a shed roof near the grain elevator. There was a small group of farmers crowded around it, mostly men in their forties and fifties, drinking soda, sharing the little piece of shade, and waiting patiently for the elevator to open again.

Gary plunked some change into the Coke machine, and two icy soda cans came tumbling out. Handing one to Katie, he took a long, deep drink from the other, wiped his mouth on his sleeve, and asked her again, "So, we goin' huntin'?"

She couldn't stall him forever. "I hate huntin'," Katie began to explain, but Gary interrupted her eagerly.

"Hey, you're gonna *like* this hunt. This here hunt's a—" Gary broke off as he took notice of a farmer approaching the soda vending machine with a couple of his friends. "How ya doin', Del?" he called.

The man called Del ignored Gary, dropping his coins into the Coke dispenser without a look in Gary's direction. A muscle tensed in Gary Simmons's jaw, but he kept his voice level and even friendly.

"Good crop this year, Del? I got a pretty good crop myself, how about you?"

Del collected his soda and turned to leave. He still hadn't said a word in reply, or even looked in Gary's direction.

"I'm talkin' to you, Del." Suddenly Gary's voice was thin-edged and hard. He put one hand on the older

man's arm to detain him. For the first time, Del looked
at Gary, and the two men locked gazes.

Now Gary broke into a friendly smile, but there was
steel beneath it, ice cold and dangerous. "I'm talkin',
Del, one neighbor to another, chewin' the shit, that's all.
I ain't heard you give me no answer, *Del*." His voice bit
the name off, underscoring it, giving it a menacing
emphasis.

Del shook Gary's hand off his arm. "You ain't no
neighbor of mine," he said, and there was contempt in
his tone. Around the pair of them, the other farmers
stood watching, wary, but nobody said anything or stepped
forward to take one side or the other, or to get Gary off
Del's back.

What the hell's going on? Katie thought, watching.
This was almost an exact replay of that scene in the bar
the other night, between Gary and the man called Hank,
the man who wouldn't say a simple "howdy" to Gary
Simmons.

Now another man did come forward to intervene, anxiety written across his face. In a mild, placating voice he
said, "Come on, Gary, we don't want no trouble. We're
just mindin' our business, same's you—"

"What's that you got on your face, Jud?" Gary asked
suddenly, turning his attention to the other man.

Jud took a step backward and put one hand up to his
face. "It's just a sun rash, Gary."

"Yeah? You sure about that, Jud?" Gary's grin, close
to a knowing leer, pulled his lips back like a wolf's, but
his eyes weren't smiling. "It ain't one of them spots you
get from that there AIDS, is it, Jud? You ain't been airin'
your back door, like one of them dying spotted faggots,
have you, Jud?"

The unwarranted viciousness of this attack made Katie
gasp. This was a side of Gary she hadn't imagined ex-
isted. She couldn't reconcile this sudden cruelty and bru-
tality with the familiar gentleness and sensitivity he showed
to his family and to her.

What's going on between Gary and his neighbors? she

wondered. Why don't they want to talk to him? Where's all this hostility coming from? What happened? How long ago? What started it?

Jud just looked at Gary, and the hatred was as plain in his face as the pain. "You son-of-a-bitch," he said quietly.

But Gary met his eyes coolly, and it was Jud who hung his head and turned away.

"Don't fuck with me, Jud. You hear me, Del?" Gary held Del's eyes in turn, until the other man, too, dropped his gaze and turned to go. The other farmers moved toward their trucks, and they were suddenly all old men, shambling and shuffling, with their heads bent. Del's defeat was their defeat; by keeping their mouths shut in the face of Gary's attack, they shared it equally with him.

"So, how's your crop this year, Del?" Gary called after him.

Del turned back, shamefaced. "Pretty good," he mumbled. Humiliation was written all over his features, along with something else. Fear. And it wasn't only Del who was afraid. They were all afraid of Gary Simmons; not one of them had the courage to stand up to his bullying.

What power does he have over these men? Why do they hate him so much? Why does he treat them like this? Why do they all seem to be afraid of him? Katie asked herself. And a shadow fell across her soul, a shadow it would be up to Catherine Weaver to identify and, if she could, dispel.

"Glad to hear it, Del. Glad to hear it." The old familiar friendliness returned to Gary's voice, and he turned to Katie, smiling. He seemed to be his old self once more, but he was now a man whom Katie didn't know as well as she thought she did. Who was he?

Katie didn't return Gary's smile. Instead, she confronted him face-on. "Why'd you do that?" she demanded.

Gary's eyebrows shot up to the peak of his John Deere cap. He appeared surprised at the question. "I'm not the one who started all of it," he told her, and Katie knew it was the only answer she was going to get.

Easy now, she told herself. Don't make an issue of

this, not here and not now. But for the first time there
was a shadow present between them, vague, amorphous,
indefinable, yet real and definitely there. Katie blamed
herself as much as Gary. She hadn't been watchful enough;
she'd been blinded by partiality, by the physical attraction—Katie hesitated to say "love," even to herself—that
they felt for each other.

Yet what did her suspicions amount to, after all? Kids
playing, calling out a syllable that sounded like "Zog."
And what if it *had* been "Zog"? Was that enough evidence to tie Gary to a murder case, that his children said
the word "Zog"? And the other farmers didn't like him,
were afraid of him. So what? Since when is not being
"Mr. Popularity" a crime? Maybe they were just jealous
of Gary, because of his youth and strength and integrity.
None of this was exactly hard evidence, certainly nothing
you could take before a grand jury.

What *was* hard evidence was the way the two of them
had joined together like a volcano erupting. Could she
be so wrong about anybody whose hands and mouth
could be so gentle? About somebody who had told her "I
love you" and seemed to mean it? And it wasn't as if
Gary Simmons didn't have friends. He had *lots* of friends,
including a sheriff's deputy. And what about Shorty? Her
mind jumped to Wes Bond and skittered away again. She
didn't like to think about Wes.

Even so, the shadow was there, and Catherine Weaver
was too good an operative to ignore it totally. But here
and now were not the time or place. From now on, she'd
keep her eyes open a little wider, her ears a little keener.
After all, she wasn't here to reap wheat. She was working on a murder case so large in scope that the feds had
involved themselves in it.

"I'm gonna get down on my hands and knees, right
here, with alla them lookin'," Gary told her, and he
meant it, "unless you come huntin' with me. You know
that, don't you? Yes I am, right here, right in this dirt
here." He started to go down on his knees, and Katie

reached down to pull him up, embarrassed. Everybody was watching them.

"All right! I'll go!" she yelled. "Now get the hell up and stop makin' a damn-fool ass o' yourself!"

Gary stood up, grinning from ear to ear, and Katie sighed inwardly. "You'll love it," he assured her again.

I'll hate it, she thought. But I gotta go. Maybe I can just hold the rifle and not fire it. Why not? I can always say I didn't get a clear shot at the target. Or I can shoot wide, and miss. Either way, I'm not gonna kill any helpless animal. Not if I can help it.

But could she help it? That this was yet one more of Gary's tests Katie had no doubt. He'd made too big a deal of it, had pressed her too hard to give in, for the hunting to have no hidden significance to him. Otherwise, why would he keep pushing at Katie, poking and prodding and testing to see if she really had guts?

Why was a public display of Katie's courage so important to him? Why had this hunt tonight become such an issue between them? She knew she had to go or he would become suspicious. But why suspicious? The only suspicious people are those who themselves have something to hide.

Again, that vague shadow made its presence felt, and despite the intense heat pouring down from the afternoon sun, Katie Phillips was suddenly cold.

Chapter Seven

Mudhunt

Thunder was rumbling in the western sky when Gary opened the passenger door of his Jeep Cherokee. Before Katie could get in, Ronnie the German shepherd bounded past her, almost knocking her over in his eagerness, and jumped into the front seat. Still filled with misgivings, Katie followed slowly. She climbed in with reluctance, but the fact that it was after midnight eased her mind a little. In the dark it would be relatively easy to miss a shot, or maybe, with some luck, she wouldn't have to fire at all.

Gary was in a fine mood, cheerful and exhilarated. It was obvious that he loved hunting, the masculinity of it, a shotgun, a big dog, a 4×4—these were things he understood and appreciated, things that gave him pleasure. Katie felt a little selfish about not being able, or even willing, to share these pleasures with him. The gap between them was widening, and she was starting to feel a sense of loss.

She wondered squeamishly what prey they would be stalking. Obviously something nocturnal—raccoons? But raccoons seemed a little Mickey Mouse for a man like Gary. She imagined a larger game, deer maybe. It had been a good year for deer; they'd had plenty to eat and their numbers had increased dramatically. There might even be some justification in killing to thin out the herd, so that the smaller number would have a better chance to survive next winter. Even so, to Katie it was like killing Bambi. Grizzlies? Were there grizzly bears in this part of the world?

Gary glanced happily over at Katie. She was looking real cute in his old army fatigue jacket, a set of camos that matched his own. They looked good together; they fit together just right, Katie and Gary. He was pleased with his woman. She was turning out just like he'd hoped, someone he could count on to stand by him, go where he went, do what he did, see things his way.

"Those fit you pretty good," he said.

She nodded, peering out into the darkness, wondering just where they were going. "I never been huntin' at night."

The rumbles of thunder had been growing louder and, suddenly, lightning split the sky wide open, like a knife through a ripe peach. The smell of ozone lingered in the air. It began to rain, a few scattered drops, then it pelted down hard and fast. Gary switched on the wipers, and Ronnie moved closer to Katie for comfort; the heavy, sour smell of dog breath was somehow comforting to her, too.

Gary looked out at the earth turning to muck under the wheels of his Jeep. "It's gonna be a real mudhunt tonight," he observed.

"What are we huntin', deer?" asked Katie.

"It ain't deer season." But he didn't name the quarry.

They drove through the rain for another twenty minutes. The fields of wheat and the farms became farther and farther apart, and the terrain grew more rugged. Uncultivated acreage replaced the rows of grain, and tall stands of timber began to appear, demarcating the upward slope of the ground toward the foothills. At last they reached a large field, beyond which was a deep wood, almost a forest. Gary swung the Cherokee off the road. They jounced over the rutted ground, tires squishing in the mud.

The field was already occupied by a circle of vehicles,

cars, pickups, four-wheel drives. Their headlights, left
on, illuminated the figures of the men and women waiting there in the circle of light. As they got out of the
Jeep, Katie recognized Shorty, Lyle, Dean the deputy
and his fat wife Toby, Buster and his skinny wife Ellie. It
was Gary's usual group of friends; only Wes was missing.
They were all dressed in boots and hunting clothes, fatigues and camouflage suits. No one was carrying a rifle
or a gauge, which was a surprise to Katie. Where were
their guns? In this part of the world every second pickup
carried a gun.

"Y'all know Katie," said Gary.

Katie smiled nervously, but, oddly, nobody smiled back.
They all gave her hard, cold looks, as though they'd
never seen her before, as though they didn't trust her for
shit. There was no acceptance on their faces, only suspicion and dislike. Gary's friends had not expected to see
her here, and it was plain that none of them was happy
about it.

But it was Gary Simmons they'd been waiting for.
Gary was their leader and this was his woman, so, like it
or not, they had to accept her. Shorty was the first to
break into a smile.

"Hiya, Katie," he said, and the others echoed him.
The tense moment had passed.

Wide streaks of lightning crackled overhead, followed
by thunder booms. It started raining harder.

We're getting soaked here. Why the hell don't they
call this stupid thing off and everybody go home and get
dry? wondered Katie.

But Gary had no intention of calling anything off.
"Let's do it," he said to Shorty.

Shorty nodded and went to the trunk of his car. He
pried open a carton and hauled out powerful high-beam
flashlights, handing one to each of them. Then he went
for the guns.

Katie was expecting to see the shotguns and rifles
coming down from the gun racks. But it was neither
gauges nor rifles that Shorty Richards was passing around.

She looked at the two weapons he was putting in Gary's hands and froze. Each of them weighed close to nine pounds, with a stocky grip and a two-inch barrel extended by a silencer. Black and menacing, an automatic, efficient, rapid dealer of death. They were Mac-10 machine pistols.

Mac-10s! Jesus Christ! What the hell was going on here! And then an even more chilling thought: Just what the hell were they hunting?

Gary handed one of the guns to Katie. "It's a Mac-10 submachine gun," he told her calmly. "Just pull on the little trigger and say hallelujah."

Numbly, Katie accepted the gun and stood staring at it as though she'd never seen a weapon before. Her thoughts were racing, and she could feel her heart pounding under Gary's old army jacket. Mac-10s. A mercenary's gun, a killer's gun, the gun that had ripped Dan Kraus's body to ribbons. The gun Katie had been so sarcastic about back in Chicago.

There are more guns in that part of the country than people. I didn't see any Mac-10s if that's what you mean. Cocky and confident, she'd shot off her mouth to the Bureau.

Well, here they were. Mac-10s with all the deadly solidity of reality. Now she *was* seeing them, and her self-confidence was crumbling fast. Katie was suddenly, horribly aware that her error in judgment could have fatal consequences. She had already compromised herself and the investigation. Think! She had to have time to think!

Lyle had been watching her closely, seeing the numb, sick look on Katie's face, and the trembling hands that held the deadly weapon so awkwardly. He took it for cowardice, and his grizzled mouth twisted in contempt.

"She ain't got no place here!" he spat.

"Shut up!" Gary barked, and Katie saw again that he was the undisputed leader of these people.

The sound of a car motor made everybody turn. Gary's pickup was bumping toward them, over the marshy ground.

It stopped about two hundred yards from them, and Wes Bond climbed out. Now they were all here. Now the hunt could begin.

Walking around the front of the truck, Wes opened the passenger door and dumped something out on the ground. Something large. Then a smaller something landed on the ground inside the first thing. Wes climbed back into the truck and drove toward the circle of assembled hunters. Ronnie started barking furiously, and so did Buster's dog Duke.

"Git up!" Shorty's voice, amplified many times by the bullhorn, made Katie start in surprise. She looked around her. Man and woman alike, they were all holding Mac-10s as if they knew how to use them, and their eyes were grimly fixed on the large bundle on the ground.

For a long moment, nothing happened. Then the bundle began to move; it came to its knees on the muddy ground and stood up shakily. It was human. Katie suppressed a gasp. This wasn't happening. Not in this country, in this decade!

A flash of lightning, only a few miles off, lit up the sky. For one split second, the figure was illuminated as though by daylight. A black man, young, handsome, perhaps no more than twenty-four or twenty-five. He was bare-chested, wearing only blue jeans. A gash above his right eye was still bleeding, and the eye itself was almost closed. On the man's face was a look of terror and disbelief that Catherine Weaver would never forget for the rest of her life.

Shorty's words came roaring through the bullhorn. "Run, nigger! Pick up the gun and run! You got six bullets!"

The young man stood frozen, fixed to the spot by his fear. No one said anything; they just waited. Their grim silence was a terrible thing.

Now Dean, impatient, grabbed the bullhorn from Shorty. "You're gonna die, nigger!" he yelled, and fired. The bullets sped silently from the gun hitting the ground near the black man's feet, making a sickly *thock, thock.*

They were not intended to kill, only to frighten. It was much too early to kill. Dean's shots were intended to show the nigger they meant business. Move it or lose it.

Hurling himself to the ground, the young man grabbed the pistol, a cheap .38-caliber copy of the police Smith & Wesson, a gun they call the Saturday Night Special. He scrambled desperately to his feet and began running as hard as he could, heading for the tree line and a chance at life. The hunt was on.

Sickened, Katie could only close her eyes while her world came crashing down around her, and she saw clearly how she had been betrayed by her emotions.

Behind her, Shorty uttered a harsh, excited laugh, more like a growl. Every vestige of good nature had disappeared from his affable face, leaving only a mask of hatred. "Go, Ronnie! Go, Duke!" he yelled, egging the dogs on.

Barking in excitement, the dogs began the chase, running swiftly on their powerful legs. When they were only ten yards from their quarry, the young black man turned and fired. With a yelp, Buster's dog Duke pawed at the sky for a moment, then toppled over on his side, screaming in pain.

"He shot Duke!" Buster shrieked, hysterical with rage. "Goddamn him to fuckin' hell! He shot Duke!"

Now the others began to move, running across the open field with the high beams of their powerful flashlights cutting through the blackness like searchlights. Buster rushed to his dog's side, and knelt close to him, cradling the wounded dog in his arms. There were tears in his eyes.

Katie stood rooted to the spot, her eyes tightly shut, her mind saying no no no nonononono . . . over and over again. No no no. Please, God, no.

"Come on," Gary said, tugging at her arm.

"No." Unable to look at him, unable to stop shaking her head from side to side.

"I love you," he said harshly, like a man in pain. "I gotta be honest with you."

Katie opened her eyes to look at him, and the tears spilled over and coursed down her cheeks. "No. No. No." As though the negation would make it go away.

Gary pulled her close to him, stroking her shoulders and back, rubbing his jaw over her hair. "It's your first hunt," he told her tenderly. "You'll get used to it. You gotta learn to defend yourself just like they are."

"They" were out there, stalking human prey. "They" included a man who could weep for a wounded animal, but gave no thought to the taking of a human life when that life was encased in a black skin. Who were "they"? Gary couldn't be "they." Not this man whose body she had held in her arms, whose mouth had burned with her kisses. "How can you . . ." she wept. "You're not like them . . ."

"Trust me," he whispered. "It's nothin'."

It was true, then. He was "they." Packaged more attractively, perhaps not quite as obvious, which made Gary all the more evil. Katie turned away from him, choking her tears back. Inside her breast, her heart's destruction was complete. She had loved him, and he was evil. He was a killer who could hunt down another human being, for sport. What was she going to do?

Katie looked over at the field. The black man had disappeared into the trees, with the mob behind him. Only she and Gary were left behind. Katie and Gary and Buster, still weeping over Duke. And Wes.

Wes Bond was standing at the pickup truck, staring at her. In his hands he was cradling a Mac-10, as though it was a natural part of him, an extension of his body. His face was cold, and his eyes, even at this distance, were filled with hatred. And, she knew now, with suspicion. Wes had waited for this moment, knowing it would come, knowing Katie would fail and would have to face the consequences of that failure.

The sight of Wes's face put the pieces together with a click inside Catherine Weaver. She knew with certainty what Gary wanted her to do, what the rest of them expected of her. Could she do it? Could she convince him that she was the same Katie Phillips he'd come to love? She had to, or she'd lose Gary.

Without Gary Simmons, Katie had no power base, no space in which to operate. As an undercover, she was finished. If she cut and ran now, say, tomorrow morning before first light, she'd make it back. Chicago was a haven; nobody would ever have to know how she'd screwed up. The Bureau would send other operatives; Katie would give them names and descriptions, but for her the game would be over and she'd be safe.

If she stayed with Gary, under his protection, she could watch and witness, gather evidence, keep the investigation going. She'd have to convince him that she was his woman, that whatever he wanted was okay with her. She'd have to lie, turn her back on every decent thing she believed in. For the first time, she realized what peril she was putting herself in. It would be the same as walking barefoot into a mine field. The world could explode at any moment. If she slipped, if her cover was blown, "they" wouldn't hesitate to kill her.

In a split second, Katie made her decision. She owed everything to the Bureau, to this investigation, to bringing murderers to justice.

She gave Gary her right hand, keeping the Mac-10 in her left. Side by side they ran across the field toward the hunt. Up ahead, beams of light from the flashes lit the trees eerily; the shrill sound of Ronnie's barking cut through the noise of running feet, the shouting of many voices, and the muffled staccato bursts of fire from the Mac-10s.

A single shot cut through the air.

"Four left," called Shorty derisively. "Don't miss, nigger!"

Another shot. "You're down to three!" followed by the sound of men's raucous laughter, and a high-pitched giggling from Toby.

Gary had reached the trees now, and went dodging through them, running swiftly and keeping low, Nam training. Katie followed him as quickly as she could, panting a little with the exertion. It was raining steadily now, a hard, driving downpour, and the ground was slippery underfoot. Thunder cracked again and again, its volume deafening, and eerie green lightning played around the tops of the trees, casting a torchlike glow over the scene being played out below. Each fresh flash of lightning that lit up the sky showed the man running desperately, zigzagging from tree to tree in search of safety. But there was no safety, there would be no escape.

Gary was near his quarry now; hearing him coming up behind, the black man turned and fired, his bullet ricocheting off a tree near Gary's head. Little splinters of wood hit Gary's face, and leaves showered down over his fatigue cap.

Elated, Gary grinned as the bullet missed him. This was what hunting was all about. The hell with shooting anything that couldn't shoot back; where was the fun in it?

The running man turned and fired again, hitting the tree where Gary had been only a moment ago. But he wasn't there now.

"One more, Satchmo!" taunted Gary.

"You better make it count, Satchmo," echoed Dean.

The man had disappeared into a thick copse, and Gary ran after him, keeping low. The others followed with shouts, all except Katie, who trailed slowly at a distance, silent.

She couldn't see Gary now, and neither could the others. The black man, too, had vanished from sight. Both of them were out there, somewhere, and both were armed. But one man had an automatic weapon, its clip filled with bullets, and the other had only one bullet left in a cheap handgun.

A gun fired from inside the stand of trees. One single shot. The last bullet from the quarry's shoddy gun.

"You missed." Gary's voice, triumphant.

They were all around him now, with their flashlights and their submachine guns, closing in on the cornered black man. For the hunters, this was the climax of the chase, the moment they'd been waiting for. This was what made worthwhile the rain and the mud and the scratches and cuts they'd gotten dodging the tree branches. This is what they were here for.

The black man was nowhere in sight, but Gary, grinning, held his finger up for silence. When the hunters quieted down, they could hear the muffled sound of sobbing. Gary shone his flashlight on a tree. Behind it, the cornered man was shaking uncontrollably, crying, knowing that his death would be now.

"Looks like we got ourselves a coon in a trap," snarled Lyle, and the others laughed, then fell silent. The hunt was over. All that was left was the kill. But whose would be the finger to pull the trigger?

"It's her first time." Wes's voice was cold and hard, and they turned to look at him. He was staring at Katie. There was no mistaking his meaning. He meant Katie.

Shorty nodded. "First blood, Katie," he told her cordially, as though he was granting her a favor. "It's your kill. Go git him."

For a long moment, Katie's mind refused to function. Kill him? Kill an unarmed, defenseless man for no reason on earth? Is that what these . . . people . . . expected of her? She looked around. They were all staring at her, waiting to see what she would do. Katie could sense their doubts and hostility. And, above all, their suspicions. Wes was watching her with a thin, sarcastic smile on his face, as though he could read her mind. As though he knew what torture he was putting her through. Only Gary was regarding her with any kindness. He was sure of her, sure that she would do whatever he told her to, just like a good woman who obeyed her man.

"Walk over, point the gun, and pull the trigger," he said gently, as though giving a teenager her first driving lesson.

Catherine Weaver's mind raced. The man was doomed to die, if not by her hand then by some other's. This was the ultimate test of her allegiance, the test that all the others were leading up to. If she pulled the trigger, Gary

Simmons would accept her and trust her. She would have
passed this hideous test for which he'd set her up. As for
the others, they would have to follow his lead. Their
suspicions would be lessened, because, in a single split
second, Katie Phillips would have become one of them.
Only then could she be the effective undercover agent
she was sent here to be.

Shakily, she raised the Mac-10, forcing her mind away
from the enormities of the situation, forcing herself to
believe that this was a dead man already.

"Don't, please don't. Please."

The weeping man begged passionately for his life, and
his eyes met Katie's. She saw not a dead man but a living
person, one who walked and talked and loved and laughed
and cried, a man who'd been stalked and shot at, forced
to run for his life, forced to beg and plead to save
himself. A man hunted down like an animal, who was not
an animal, but a human being.

Her hand wavered, and the barrel of the Mac-10 pointed
down.

"You can do it, Katie," Gary urged.

The pleading in Gary's eyes matched the entreaty in
his voice. Both told her how crucial this act would be to
him. She lifted the gun, telling herself that this murderous act would be committed for a righteous reason, that
good would come out of this evil, that she had to remain
effective, that these people must be convicted in a court of
law so that they might never commit acts like this again.
That he was dead anyway, whether she shot him or not.

Her finger curled around the trigger, but before she
could squeeze off a burst, her hand dropped. She couldn't
pull that trigger, not to save her life, not even to save
America. Catherine Weaver was simply unable to kill,
and she couldn't compel Katie Phillips to kill for her.

"Shit!" Wes barked behind her, exultant. His vindica-
tion was total, his loathing of Katie now fully justified.
Gary looked at her with sorrow in his eyes; he was
deeply disappointed in her; his woman had let him down.

Now Wes Bond, Mac-10 in hand, was stalking toward

the tree behind which the black man wept. His purpose was plain; he would show Gary's pussy just how things were done in a real man's world. But before he could take aim, the black man burst forth from the trees, his empty gun in his hand, and he ran screaming, headlong, straight at Wes. It was the desperate act of someone who had finally been pushed over the edge, pushed into primal rage.

But Wes didn't flinch. He took aim calmly and fired a burst of bullets at his prey. The gun chattered softly in his hand, muffled by the silencer, but the bullets found their target, even without making a sound. The man shuddered under their impact, then crumpled to the ground and lay still.

With terrible calmness, Wes walked over to his victim and fired again, the coup de grace shot blowing the back of his head away. Then he wheeled around and lifted the Mac-10, taking aim straight at Katie Phillips.

Katie just stared at him mutely, her mind deadened by the night's hideous experience. Rain poured down over her head and face; her thin body under the fatigues trembled with exhaustion. He'd kill her in a minute; she had no doubts about it. Yet, oddly enough, she didn't feel afraid. She felt . . . anesthetized. She wanted to think, but she couldn't. The finality of the man's death had numbed her.

"Don't even think about it, Wes," said Gary coldly. His own gun was aimed at Wes Bond. The two men stood looking at each other for what seemed an eternity, while Catherine Weaver's life hung by a thread.

"She knows," said Wes.

Gary looked hard at Katie. He saw the numbness in her eyes, the shock, the horror on her frozen features. Wes was right. She knew. She knew and she could talk. She wasn't really one of them after all. She'd failed the test. Maybe she'd never be one of them. Maybe she wasn't made of the right stuff. Maybe he ought to let Wes kill her, right here and now. They could bury the body so deep in the soft, wet ground of these woods that nobody would ever find her. Just as they would with the dead nigger.

But the thought of Katie's young body riddled with machine-gun bullets, torn and bleeding, the body he'd made love to, hungered to make love to again, was more than Gary Simmons could stand. His feelings for her were so strong they overpowered his natural sense of caution. No woman had moved him since the death of his wife, no woman until now. She'd come around. She loved him; he was sure of it. She'd come around to his way of thinking. She was smart and tough and she had courage; he could train her. She'd learn. She could even be valuable to them.

"She knows," Wes said again, more insistently.

"It doesn't matter," said Gary.

Wes expelled his breath in a hiss of hatred and walked away. Gary Simmons was leader, and leader's word, however hard to swallow, was law. Watching him go, knowing that the moment of her death had passed, Katie felt her legs buckling, going out from under her. If Gary hadn't caught her in his arms she would have fallen.

Half dragging, half carrying her, Gary moved Katie out of the woods toward his Jeep. The others followed, all except Shorty and Lyle, who stayed behind to dispose of the corpse. Behind them, on the sodden ground in the pelting rain, the hunters left the still-bleeding quarry. The mudhunt was over.

Chapter Eight

Cut and Run

By the time they reached Gary's Cherokee Katie Phillips was able to walk without help, but she was a long way from regaining control of herself. For one thing, she couldn't stop shivering. She was soaked to the skin, her hair plastered over her forehead, the fatigue jacket rumpled and soggy against her chest.

But it wasn't the wet clothing or the night chill that was making her tremble so. The hollow, numb feeling was starting to wear off, and terrible memories began flooding in to sear her brain. Imprinted on her mind was the imploring face of the young man when he realized this wasn't simply a sadistic game, that he was going to die for no reason at all. That moment when his eyes had begged her for his life as Katie held the murderous machine gun trained on him, when he had wept, "Please, don't," that agonizing moment would never leave her. It would haunt her forever.

And she'd done nothing! Just stood there and watched as he'd been shot down coldly by someone who cared no more for a black man's life than an insect's! The fact that Katie herself had almost been caught in the same trap, had been close to a brush with death only minutes before, only added to the horror she was feeling now. She pushed herself as far away from Gary as she could get, pressing her body tightly against the passenger door of

the Jeep, unable to control the shivering that shook her
like a leaf in a windstorm. Guilt and humiliation and
helplessness tore at her, threatening to overwhelm her.
And rage. Rage deep and terrible.

Gary himself was as calm as though nothing gruesome
had taken place back there in the woods, as contented as
Ronnie the shepherd dog, who snoozed peacefully,
sprawled out at full length on the back seat. He looked
over at Katie, whose thin frame was shaking badly, whose
teeth were chattering.

Poor kid's wet to the bone, he thought, most likely shit
scared. I reckon it's been kinda heavy for her, maybe too
heavy all at once. But she'll get used to it in time. She
has to, if she loves me like she says she does.

"I'll give you somethin' to warm you up when we get
home," he promised, thinking of them in bed together,
remembering the pliant, passionate heat of her body
under his.

"Take me back to the hotel," Katie said in an empty
voice.

Gary's eyebrows shot up in surprise. "It was just a
nigger, don't make too much outta it," he told her cheerfully. "There's plenty more where he came from. Their
birth rate's seven times the size of ours." He treated
Katie to a wide, boyish smile. "You'll feel better in the
mornin'," he promised, and reached over to squeeze her
thigh.

Katie turned on him almost savagely, pushing his hand
away. For the first time, he saw how upset she really
was; she *was* taking this hunting thing seriously.

"I didn't want there to be nothin' between us," he told
her intensely. "I love you that much, I wanted you to
come."

But Katie said nothing, staring ahead of her, her face
as expressionless as a stone. His "I love you," once so
precious, was now totally repugnant.

Gary put both hands back on the wheel and gripped it
hard. His voice was very quiet, almost resigned. "If you

love me, I got nothin' to worry about. If you don't, I don't care about goin' to jail."

He waited for Katie's reaction, but there was no sign from her. Not a word. She just sat there, looking out through the windshield at absolutely nothing, her face an unreadable blank.

"We're gonna raise the kids," he went on. "We're gonna have babies. We're gonna kick the shit outta fuckin' Zog."

There was a long silence, then Katie asked softly, "Who's Zog?"

"Zionist Occupation Government," Gary answered eagerly, glad to get her talking again. "It means the fuckin' goddamn Jews are runnin' our country."

Zog. There it was, and Catherine Weaver saw now that it was so simple. Economics was the key. Like so many blind hatreds, it came down to dollars and cents. A twisted anti-Semitism, a warped belief held by a man who might never have seen a Jew in his life . . . unless it was Dan Kraus in the last moments before he died.

A belief shared by others, men and women disappointed in the American dream that had been promised to them in the schoolroom, by their parents, by the media, by the propaganda machines of government and industry. The dream had been killed, so they went looking to pin its death on a recognizable enemy. Hard work and honesty were supposed to count for something, supposed to bring prosperity, but they hadn't.

Instead of prospering, these people were floundering helplessly in debt, mortgaged to the teeth, seeing the value of their labor going for next to nothing. The banks owned their bodies and their souls were owed to the company store. Raised to be totally independent, they found themselves dependent on the federal government for up to forty percent of their annual income.

Others did prosper, though. Bankers were rich, and Jews were rich, everybody knew that. It was a well-known, well-documented international conspiracy. In their paranoia, these bitter men and women reached out ea-

gerly for a traditional scapegoat. Dirty Jews were the
sworn enemy of hardworking, God-fearing people.

Kill the enemy. Kill Zog.

Oh, my God, Katie thought, it's worse than I thought.
Much, much worse.

The Cherokee drew up at the Lazy-Vu. Gary switched
off the ignition and sat watching Katie anxiously. She
was still in pretty bad shape, still trembling like a deer
when the dogs have it cornered. He moved closer to give
her a comforting hug, but before he could reach her,
Katie came to life, pushing the passenger door open and
jumping out. Without a backward look she ran to her
motel room and slammed the door shut behind her,
turning the lock and putting up the chain.

Gary just sat behind the wheel for a few minutes,
smoking, gnawing at his lip and wondering what he should
do. What he burned to do was to follow Katie inside and
take her into his arms, holding her and kissing her until
she was herself again, and all his. Instinctively, though,
he knew that the best thing was to leave her alone, at
least for now. She was tough, she'd get over it. The worst
part was over. She'd seen the hunt and, horrified though
she was, she hadn't opened her mouth. From now on,
things would get better. Tomorrow was another day, and
they'd start up from square one again.

He threw the still-lit cigarette out the window, switched
on the motor, and drove away.

Katie stood pressed against her door, shaking and crying,
waiting for Gary to leave. When she heard the Cherokee
drive off, she had a feeling of relief, but it was short-
lived. The bile rose in her throat, burning her, and her
stomach churned in revolt. Gagging, she ran to the bathroom, barely making it in time. She threw up again and
again, until there was nothing left except the scorching,
bitter bile.

Her throat raw, she drank two large glasses of water,
washed her face, and brushed her teeth twice. Then and
only then, Katie Phillips went to the telephone. She was

still shaking as she placed the call; try as she might, she couldn't control the goddamn shivers.

There's an airfield. If you need me, I can be there in an hour and a half, Michael had told her. Well, she needed him. Now she knew what Zog was, and who was behind the killing. The case was solved, the evidence gathered. Her job was finished, and she was glad. Time now for the Bureau to take over, let Katie Phillips go back to being Catherine Weaver.

It was almost two in the morning, but Katie knew exactly where to reach Michael, knew also that the lateness of the hour was of no consequence compared with the enormity of what she had to report.

"Michael? Katie, I mean Cathy. I have to see you."

"Now?"

"Yes, now. I'm sorry to wake you—"

"No, forget it. I'll be there. Give me about two hours, maybe less. You know where the airfield is?"

"Yes—" Before Katie could say another word, there was a click in her ear and then the dull buzz of the dial tone. Michael was on his way.

The contact made, Katie left her motel room hurriedly. All she wanted was to escape from this murderous madness, to get to that little airfield and wait for Michael. She headed for her pickup truck at a dead run, her boots crunching on the gravel of the motel parking lot.

She was still so shaky that she put the truck in reverse instead of forward gear, and backed up fifteen feet before she realized it. Katie stepped on the gas, and was heading out of the parking lot when, suddenly, another pickup truck, a Dodge Ram, pulled out ahead of her, about forty feet away, blocking her exit.

The door opened and Wes Bond got out. He left his motor on, and the high beams of his headlights shone directly into Katie's eyes. Slowly and deliberately, he sauntered toward her.

"Where you goin', sugar?" he asked insolently

How long had Wes been spying on her? And what was he going to do now that he'd caught her attempting to leave? He would cheerfully have killed her back there in the forest, gunned her down and stuffed her into the same shallow grave as the black man, left them to rot together, until the melting flesh of one corpse had joined with the flesh of the other in unholy marriage. And that was only on suspicion!

The danger was real, almost palpable. Wes was a proven killer who enjoyed killing. She had to do something. Katie didn't think twice. Her booted foot hit the gas pedal hard, and her pickup jackrabbited forward, toward Wes. He had only a split second to jump out of the way, because sure as God she would have rolled right over him. Motor gunned to top speed, Katie's pickup crashed into Wes's, smashing in the whole left side and knocking it out of her way. The crunch of glass and metal was deafening, but Katie didn't stop to hear it. Pedal to the metal, she kept on going.

She was three miles from the motel before she collected herself sufficiently to look into her rearview mirror. There was nobody following her. The damage she'd done to Wes Bond's pickup had saved her for now, but she'd better not meet up with him alone again. She wouldn't, of course. By tomorrow, she would be safe in Chicago, her written report on the Old Man's desk. They'd already have issued FBI arrest warrants. Wes and Gary and the whole damn gang of hunters would be behind bars, awaiting indictment for murder. If she couldn't pin Kraus on them, at least she had the murder of the black man. She'd been there; she'd witnessed it.

All Katie could think of as she drove to the airport was that she wanted to be home, back in Chicago. She wanted to put all this behind her, to take off the persona of Katie Phillips like a torn dress to be thrown away. She wanted to wear her own clothing, her own personality, become Catherine Weaver again. For her the danger would soon be over; Michael would take her back with him. Cut and run. Katie would cut and run.

If Michael was correct and *would* be here in Denison less than two hours from her phone call, Katie still had a

good hour to wait. She reached the tiny airfield outside
the town, a little rural airstrip stuck in the middle of
nowhere—no tarmac, only a few landing lights, and,
instead of a control tower, a ramshackle office in a hangar with a tin roof.

She spent the time pulling herself together so that she
could deliver a cogent, coherent report to her superior
officer. But it didn't work. For more than an hour she
had kept her mind shut off deliberately, refusing to allow
it to focus on the hunt, on the murder of that poor young
man and the danger that she herself had been in.

Now, as she went over the gruesome details of tonight's awful events, to fix the time and the place and the
names and the happenings in their proper order, the
horror of it all, combined with the guilt and the fear,
returned to wash over Katie in full force. Once more the
hot bile flooded her throat as her gorge rose, and she
gagged and retched miserably, her stomach already emptied. Tears rolled down her cheeks unheeded. A man
was dead. He'd been killed without mercy and without
human reason, and she, a federal officer of the law, had
done nothing to stop his murder. Instead, she'd cut and
run. Katie moaned out loud, but she was so distraught
she couldn't hear the sound of her own voice.

By the time the tiny six-passenger Cessna landed and
Michael Carnes climbed out, followed by Al Sanders and
Donald Duffin, Katie was a wretched mess, her eyes
swollen with weeping, her body curling in upon itself and
shaking uncontrollably, her face a zombie mask of horror.

"Christ!" Michael exclaimed when he saw Cathy clinging to the cyclone fence like a shipwrecked sailor to a
spar of floating wood. "What the hell happened?" He
looked around, always the FBI man. "Are you sure you
weren't followed?"

Cathy could only nod speechlessly. She was shaking so
badly she couldn't talk.

"Hold me," Michael said gently, taking a step toward
her. "Just hold me."

Cathy let go of the fence at last and allowed Michael to

take her into his arms and hug her tightly. Part of her responded to the touch of another human being, but another part of her shrank away from it. She felt as though she never wanted to be touched again.

After the three men had led her into the office in the hangar, Cathy smoked a couple of cigarettes, which helped to calm her nerves. Then she told her story, her voice shaky but clear, leaving out nothing. Once or twice she had to stop and get herself together, choke back the tears, and hug herself tightly to stop the trembling. Michael, Duffin, and Sanders listened in silence, never once interrupting, their faces a study in grave attention.

At last, the gruesome narrative came to an end. Cathy had detailed everything that Katie had experienced—Zog, the mudhunt, Wes Bond's killing of the young black man—everything. She sighed deeply, lit another cigarette, and sank back in her chair, completely drained. There was a hollowed-out feeling in the pit of her belly, and she was so tired she couldn't think anymore.

Michael leaned forward in his wooden chair, his eyes probing deeply into hers. "We'll never find the body, Cathy," he reminded her gently.

"I can testify. I was right there. I didn't . . . do . . . anything."

"You couldn't do anything. They would have killed you. They're guilty. You're not."

She looked around at the others. Duffin was standing against the wall, silent for once. Even he couldn't find anything funny in this. The black agent, Sanders, his face impassive, sat perched on a corner of the desk. Their eyes met, and Cathy turned away.

She stood up and began to pace nervously. She was beginning to perceive what Michael was getting at, and the silence of the other two confirmed it. Her story by itself wasn't enough for them to go on. "It wasn't the first . . . hunt . . . they were on," she stammered.

"No shit," remarked Sanders dryly.

"We'll never find the bodies, Cathy," said Michael softly, his tone forcing her to look at him, to see in his face what she didn't want to see, was afraid to see. It was there. "I want them for Kraus. We can put 'em in jail forever for Kraus," he told her intensely. Michael waited for Cathy's answer, but she didn't speak. She wrenched her eyes away from Michael's and looked at Sanders, but the black man's impassive expression delivered the same message, telling her what she already knew.

"You've gotta go back in, Cathy," said Michael.

"No!" The cry was wrenched out of her deepest being. It wasn't fair! She'd brought them their goddamn evidence, hadn't she? Nearly getting herself killed in the process? She'd made a murder case for them, hadn't she? She'd even brought them the connection—Zog. Zionist Occupation Government. She was willing to testify. What more did they want? Cathy looked at Michael. She knew what he wanted, and it terrified her. She *couldn't* go back undercover! She'd already cut and run, and Wes Bond was more suspicious than ever. Her life would be in danger every moment. But there was more to it than Katie's fear. There was Gary.

"No," she said, more quietly, but choking with emotion. "I couldn't stand . . ." She was about to say, "him touching me," but she caught herself and finished the sentence, ". . . looking at him."

It wasn't enough. Even to her own ears, her excuse sounded lame and insufficient. Cathy took a deep breath. "I couldn't stand him . . . touching me again . . . I feel dirty . . . just having been . . ." She broke off, unable to bring herself to say the actual words.

Michael flinched. He looked as though something had hit him hard on the forehead, right between the eyes. Sanders said nothing. Duffin made a small, suppressed sound.

The hurt on Michael's face made Cathy suddenly furious. She turned on him. "*You* sent me in, Michael!" she cried accusingly.

"I didn't tell you to go to bed with him, did I?" Michael flared back. "*Did* I?" How could you have . . . I thought we . . ." He broke off, agonized and angry. *"Why?"*

"I didn't just go to bed with him," said Cathy coldly. "I made love to him."

Michael's face whitened and he took a step backward as though she'd hit him. Then his hands balled into fists, and he raised them instinctively as if to lash out with them. A muscle in his jaw twitched and jumped as his teeth clenched hard.

"Cool it, man," Sanders cut in with quiet authority. His words had an immediate effect on Michael, reminding him of who they were, what they were doing here, and what they still had to do. He nodded and turned to Cathy quietly.

"You've gotta go back in," he said again.

"Is that why you want me to go back in?" demanded Cathy hotly. "To punish me for—"

"No!" Michael's face was tortured. "You feel dirty? What's more important? Putting them in jail or . . ."

Cathy's eyes widened angrily and she opened her mouth to speak, but Michael cut her off. "How many others are they going to kill? How dirty would it make you feel if you didn't do anything about it?"

Cathy gasped. It was a low blow, but a telling one. It hit her where she lived. Turning away from him, Cathy bowed her head against the hangar wall, pressing her forehead against its coolness, huddling her body close to it as though the wall could give her comfort where the world could not.

"How could I have been so . . . wrong?" she moaned, more to herself than to the others. "How could I have allowed myself to be so blind . . . so stupid . . . My God! I . . he . . . he can be so gentle . . . his family is so . . ." Cathy broke off, the words strangling in her throat.

"Maybe your instincts just aren't very good," Michael said without a trace of pity.

It was like cold water dashed in an unconscious person's face. Cathy winced, but she regained her awareness. She straightened up and gave Michael a long, assessing look. Then she looked at Sanders and Duffin. Their expressions confirmed it. They were Bureau, FBI officers with an important job to do. Personal considerations, private feelings, even fear for one's life had no place in this. First and foremost, they were team players, law enforcement agents, professionals.

And so was she.

"Yes or no, Cathy? What's it going to be?" asked Michael.

But, even before she spoke, they already knew the answer. Catherine Weaver was going back in.

Chapter Nine

Back Inside

The three agents walked Cathy back to her pickup while Michael gave her a last-minute pep talk and briefing. Cathy moved stiffly, like an automaton, her eyes empty. She said nothing. What the hell was the point? They wouldn't listen to her anyway.

"Don't go along too easily," he advised her. "Their garbage is new to you. Play it normal. Don't convert too easily. You don't want him to think you're an easy lay, do you?" He couldn't resist that cheap parting shot, his ego was still too badly bruised and his feelings had been genuinely wounded. Cathy could see that, but his anger didn't make her unhappiness any less. She felt cheap and dirty enough as it was, without his making it worse.

Now Duffin took a stack of photographs out of an envelope. Among them was the snapshot of Wes that Katie had taken at the July Fourth barbecue, the one that had enraged him so and excited his suspicions.

"Wesley John Bond," said Duffin soberly, "paroled from San Quentin three years ago. He headed up a white racist group called the Aryan Brotherhood in the joint. He's got a sheet going back fifteen years, all of it in California. Forcible rape, sodomy, aggravated assault. Nice guy."

"I wish I knew how the hell he wound up here," Michael said thoughtfully.

"Shit floats, that's how he wound up here," Sanders replied in his dry, rather sour way.

"Stay clear of this guy, Cathy. This guy's not just a freak, he's a freak's freak." Michael looked closely at her to see if she was listening to his warning, but it was impossible to tell. She looked stoned, dazed, as though she were walking in a fog.

"We've got nothing on the others," admitted Duffin, stuffing the pictures back into the envelope. "They seem like a bunch of losers."

"I'll bet Gary likes losers," Michael retorted bitterly. "If I were Gary, I'd like losers, too. You treat losers right, they make great soldiers." He smiled coldly. "I learned that in the marines."

"I learned that in the FBI," said Sanders, his eye on clumsy Duffin, who scratched his neck uncomfortably and dropped one of his photographs. Michael bent quickly to retrieve it before Cathy could see it, but not quickly enough. She put her hand out for it, and after a moment of thought, Michael gave in and placed the photo in it.

Cathy stared at it for a long moment. It was a study in affection, the picture Gary Simmons had taken of Katie with Rachel and Joey the day they all went to the fair and went on the rides. She remembered how Joey had been so scared, and how she'd had to put her arm around him to give him confidence. Looking at the picture, Cathy recalled her happiness that day, her brand-new, clean, sweet feelings for Gary, her sense of belonging to the Simmons family. That picture was taken less than a week before she and Gary had . . . made love . . . for the first time. Woodenly, she handed the photo back and climbed into her pickup truck.

"You're doin' a job, girl," Al Sanders said with gentle sympathy. "That's all there is."

Now Michael was pulling a gun out of his pocket, a .22-caliber pistol small enough to be hidden in a woman's handbag. He gave it to Cathy. She accepted it automatically, but made no move to stow it away. Instead, she let it dangle from her fingers.

"Take it," Michael urged.

"If he finds it, I'm dead," Cathy said, shaking her head.

"Make sure he doesn't find it," Sanders said with the quiet authority of the senior agent present.

Cathy looked from one face to another, trying to read her chances in their expressions. It was impossible, and she realized that this was the way it was supposed to be. Her chances were her chances, neither more or less. The Bureau had little to do with it. It was up to her to better the odds. Without a further word, she switched the motor on, floored the pedal, and drove back to Denison.

By the time she reached the Lazy-Vu Katie was dog-tired. Her watch said 5:46 in the morning. The first light of a July day had dawned nearly half an hour ago, and the sun had already cleared the horizon and was climbing its upward road across the eastern sky. All she wanted was to sleep, to sleep for hours and hours, to put off dealing with anything for as long as she could. She knew she'd have to face up to Gary Simmons sooner or later, but later was better than sooner. She needed some time to herself, to think, to plan, to work out contingencies. And she needed some privacy to restore the integrity of her body, which no longer felt like her own.

But when Katie let herself into her motel room, she saw that her options, few as they were, had been taken out of her hands. Gary was already there waiting for her, lying on her bed. She'd have to deal with the situation here and now, even in her exhausted state.

"Mornin'," he said to her pleasantly. "Where you been?"

Katie forced herself to look him in the eye. She'd lost ground with him, she knew that, and she had to regain it. "I drove," she said simply. "I got past the Interstate." Then, in a lower tone, "I came back."

"Come here," said Gary, tapping the bed next to him.

He hadn't taken his eyes off Katie's face, as if he were probing behind her eyes, to see into her very brain, to learn what she was thinking.

Slowly Katie walked over to the bed and sat down next to Gary. He put one hand lightly on her arm. "How come you came back?" he whispered.

She knew what he wanted to hear. "I don't know," she whispered back, turning her face away so that he couldn't see her eyes.

Gary's hand tightened on her arm. "Yes, you do. Say it."

Katie couldn't bear to look at him. She understood what was required of her, by Gary, by the Bureau, even by herself. But, oh God, if she could only have a few short hours to herself, to shower and rest and get up the nerve and the heart to go through with the rest of this awful business . . . but even that little bit of time had been stolen from her.

"Say it!" Gary insisted, his fingers digging in hard, bruising Katie's arm. "Say, 'I love you, that's why I came back.' "

She turned to look into his face. Gary Simmons was still handsome, still boyish, but to Katie Phillips he had become hideous. If he had so much as an inkling of what she was thinking, of who she was and what she was here for, he'd kill her without mercy, and it would all be for nothing. He mustn't be allowed that inkling. Michael's words burned in her memory: *You don't want him to think you're an easy lay, do you?*

Wrapping his powerful arms around her, Gary pulled Katie onto the bed and bent his face down to hers, kissing her with a passionate fury that bruised her lips. Instinctively, she fought him off, pummeling him with her fists and trying desperately to pull herself away. But Gary was stronger than she. Rolling over with her in his arms, he pinned Katie underneath him on the bed. Katie could tell by his coarse breathing that he was enjoying this.

"Say it!" he whispered hoarsely.

The words rose to Katie's lips, but stuck in her throat; she wanted to say them and get it over with, but she couldn't.

His hands were on her body, the heat of them burning her through her thin summer top, and his fingers began to unbutton her blouse. It was now or never. She was starting to lose her nerve.

"I love you," said Katie. Gary uttered a triumphant shout of laughter.

She sobbed when he entered her, and Gary took it for a sob of joy. The tears that rolled down her cheeks through closed eyelids as he made love to her he saw with pleasure, as the visible sign of Katie's capitulation. Now she was completely his; now she understood who was the master. Katie's silent weeping stimulated Gary, it increased his pleasure and his passion, and his love-making became more furious and more protracted.

Underneath his hard, surging body, Katie lay crying in humiliation, shame, anger, yet with a kind of ferocious joy. She almost welcomed this invasion of her body; Gary's domination of her flesh gave her a new strength, a new courage even while it abased her. Had he been gentle and tender, it would have been even harder to bear; this way, it was so much easier to hate him. At the moment of his climax, she feigned one of her own, and her fingernails bit deeply into his back, drawing blood. He had his satisfaction; this was hers.

Later in the morning, the combine crews left. The harvest in this part of the state was over, and it was time to be moving on to the next county, where the ears of grain still stood tall in the fields, waiting for the rotors to arrive and slice them down and feed them to the threshers. That meant that the combine girls would have to be moving on, too.

The parking lot at the Lazy-Vu was a hive of noisy activity as the operators packed their vehicles—cars, four-wheels, pickups—with their belongings. They called out to one another, saying goodbye to the boyfriends they'd picked up in this town and were leaving behind. There'd be new boyfriends waiting in the next county.

Gary Simmons stood at the window of Katie's room, staring out at the scene. Katie came up to stand behind him, wrapped only in a sheet. She took a look over his shoulder.

"Combine's gonna be leavin'," she said.

Gary didn't turn from the window. "I want you to stay with me," he answered.

It was the offer Katie had expected, and it was what Cathy needed if she were to keep her cover going. Even so, there was a jolt of revulsion in her belly, and her gorge threatened to rise again and make her sick. But she fought hard against showing it. Walking away from Gary, Katie got hold of herself. Michael had told her not to convert too easily. Gary knew what kind of girl Katie Phillips was. Any deviation made too soon from her independent, feisty character could trigger his suspicions.

"What did you kill him for? Just for fun?" she demanded, as though this were the bone of contention between them.

Gary turned to look at Katie. "It ain't never fun killin' anything," he said quietly. He saw the challenging look of skepticism in her eyes, saw her chin lift stubbornly, and he turned his face away.

"It was self-defense. He had a gun. We was just protectin' ourselves," he went on. "That's all we're tryin' to do, protect ourselves. It's self-defense."

Katie's eyes grew wider. Self-defense? Nine against one? A six-shot revolver against high-tech automatic weapons? Was he serious? Did Gary Simmons actually believe this line of horseshit?

"I don't like killin'," she told him flatly. "I don't like people hurt."

"They ain't people. They're mud people," said Gary,

and Katie could see that he was being perfectly sincere. He *did* take seriously what he was saying. He believed in his white supremacy as fervently as she believed in the sanctity of human life, obedience to the law of the land, and respect for the individual, any and every individual.

There was obviously no reasoning with the man. Katie grabbed up her jeans from the floor and began to pull them over her naked hips.

"You could move in with me," Gary said from the window. "Help me with the farm and the kids. We could be a real family again."

A real family! Just two days ago, the idea of it would have made Katie feel warm and happy. Now the thought brought only revulsion. But she had a job to do and she needed the cover of a relationship with Gary Simmons to do it. She needed to infiltrate his organization through acceptance within his family unit. She finished buttoning her blouse and went over to Gary, who was still standing at the window looking out.

Betty Jo Babcock was out there, kissing her young lover goodbye. Her eyes opened and met Katie's, and she waved a little sadly. She understood that Katie and Gary had something permanent going, and Katie wouldn't be coming along to the next town. Betty Jo would have to make a new friend, but that would be no problem for her. She formed her friendships with nonchalant ease, and broke them just as easily.

Betty Jo's life was so beautifully uncomplicated. She worked, she ate, she drank, she made love, she danced, she fussed with her makeup, hair, and clothes. And that was enough for Betty Jo. The future, whenever it came, would take care of itself. Katie felt a stab of envy.

The marks of Katie's nails on Gary's back had not yet healed. There were ribbons of fresh blood all along the scratches, and Katie put one wondering finger up to touch them. Then she curled her fingers into claws and dug them in again.

Gary winced and turned to her. "You're a real wildcat,

aren't you?" he asked with a grin. "Well, I'm gonna tame you. I'm sure gonna tame you."

So began the most difficult period of Catherine Weaver's life. Not that she had taken her job or the Bureau lightly before; Cathy was a person who took everything just a little too seriously. She rarely lightened up or cut anybody slack. Not that she hadn't realized that it could be dangerous, but so far the danger had been only theoretical. *There,* but not *real.* But somehow she had never expected her first undercover assignment to be so hateful as well as so dangerous.

When Cathy Weaver pictured her first assignment back when she was in training, it was always some kind of sting operation, stylish and cunning, that would net the FBI a bagful of greedy fellows, politicians perhaps, or maybe influence peddlers. She'd imagined herself playing the role of the "baiter" or even the "hook," but it was always a role played in clean clothing, enacted without a gun in her leather shoulderbag. And she'd always thought she could go home at night, to sleep in her own bed.

Cathy hadn't pictured the grim ugliness of this racist murder case. She had never imagined that she'd be playing a role twenty-four hours a day, seven days a week, or that to relax the disguise for even one instant would be to invite death. And she'd never, ever pictured an enforced sexual relationship with a man she'd once loved but had come to loathe. Or that she'd be compelled to pretend she still loved him, still wanted to share his life.

Now she followed that man up the stairs to his bedroom, to take up the semblance of a life with him.

Gary put her case down and looked around his room a little uncertainly. The situation was obviously awkward for him. He hadn't made a commitment of this kind since the death of his wife. He didn't want to start off on the wrong foot with Katie. Bad enough she was so damn independent. He admired it, but it also made him nervous.

"There's a lot of room," he said at last, opening a

closet door to show her how empty it was. "Ain't nothin' in here, see?"

"I only got the one suitcase, Gary."

Ill at ease, they faced each other, not sure of what to say or do next. This was a new situation for Gary, and a perilous one for Katie. Two people with totally opposite agendas.

The sound of running footsteps broke the uncomfortable silence. The next moment, the children burst into the room. When they saw Katie with their father, they came to a halt, staring with wide childish eyes.

"Katie's gonna be stayin' with us," said Gary.

"Are you gonna be our mommy?" Rachel's voice squeaked with excitement.

"Mom's dead," said Joey sternly. He scowled unhappily at Katie.

"I don't care!" Rachel's braids swung from side to side as she shook her head stubbornly. "I don't hardly even remember her."

"*I* do. *You* do, too."

"Rachel? Joey?" Mrs. Simmons called from the kitchen below, and the kids went racing down to tell their grandmother the news. Katie and Gary followed.

"Katie's gonna move in!" yelled Rachel, getting down the stairs a step ahead of Joey.

Gladys Simmons's back stiffened. "Is she?" she asked. It was less a question than an expression of disfavor. She looked hard at Katie, a glare even more disapproving than Joey's scowl. It took Katie somewhat by surprise. She thought that Mrs. Simmons liked her. It seemed that her only friend in the family, besides Gary, was Rachel.

This was going to be harder than she thought. She needed the mother's trust and approval if she were to secure the son's. Following the older woman into the kitchen, Katie stood in the doorway, her face a question mark.

Mrs. Simmons busied herself with the dinner preparation, refusing even to look at Katie. But after a long minute in which neither woman spoke, she said at last, in a distant voice, "He's been hurt once. I don't want him hurt again."

Katie drew a deep breath, feeling like a class-A shit. "I'm not gonna . . . hurt him," she lied.

But Gary's mother didn't relent, and dinner was a silent, uncomfortable affair. After dinner, Mrs. Simmons drove home almost immediately, leaving the dishes to Katie.

Katie worked in the kitchen, her arms deep in soapy water and her mind deep in thought. Somewhere in the house Rachel and Joey were talking together. She could hear Joey's voice, sullen and unhappy, but she couldn't make the words out. It seemed that, instead of making Gary's life easier, she was about to make it more difficult. This wasn't good for the investigation; it was vital that Gary Simmons be lulled into complete trust in Katie Phillips.

Washing the milk glasses, she glanced out the kitchen window. The yard light was on, and she could see Gary out by the barn. Wes Bond was with him, and although she couldn't hear what the two men were saying, they appeared to be quarreling bitterly. Suddenly Gary lashed out with his right hand and shoved Wes back against the barn door, then stormed toward the house. Katie bent her head over the sink, and when Gary came into the kitchen, he found her scrubbing out a roasting pan as though she'd seen nothing.

He stood looking at her for what seemed a long time, then he began rolling up his sleeves. "I'll help you," he told her.

"I'm almost done." Katie shrugged. Gary came over to stand next to her at the sink, picked up a dishtowel, and started to dry the dinner plates.

" 'Wash and dry together, laugh and cry together,' my mama used to say that." Katie smiled.

But Gary wasn't amused. His face was stony, and his expression distant.

"What was that all about?" she asked.

"What?"

"You and Wes."

For a moment Gary said nothing. Katie was just beginning to believe she wasn't going to get an answer when he finally shrugged. "He thinks you're a grasshopper."

Katie's eyebrows shot up. "A grasshopper? He is *weird*. I don't *look* like a grasshopper, do I?"

Gary didn't crack a smile. In a deadly serious voice, he went on, "The kinda grasshopper gettin' in people's hair all the time. FBI, CIA, KGB, JDL, NAACP—that kinda grasshopper."

Suddenly fear caught Katie by the throat and squeezed tight. For a couple of heartbeats she couldn't breathe. Then, very casually, she said, "Oh," as though the parade of acronyms held no significance for her. She picked a pot lid out of the sink and rubbed the steel wool over it, hard.

"You a grasshopper?" Gary asked seriously.

Katie looked up from the sink, straight into his eyes. "Shit, yes."

She grabbed the end of his dishtowel and dried her hands, then kissed him quickly on the lips. "I'm gonna go kiss the kids good night," she said, and left the kitchen while there was still strength in her legs. Gary stood looking after her, smiling. She was too damn much! She wasn't afraid of anything. A wave of love for her washed over him.

Rachel and Joey slept in the same room, a large room with a sloping ceiling and three dormer windows. There were twin beds and a definite line of demarcation between the boy's half of the room and the girl's. On Joey's side were robot cars, realistic-looking plastic guns, GI Joe and his toy military gear, and a poster of Stallone as Rambo, with his bare chest crossed by bandoliers filled with bullets. On Rachel's side, numerous dolls and stuffed animals—Strawberry Shortcake, Cabbage Patch, Barbie, complete with clothes and accessories.

The room was dark, and both children were already tucked up in bed. Katie stood in the doorway, looking at them, feeling guilty and loving at the same time.

"Good night, sleep tight, don't let the bedbugs bite," she told them, coming over to the beds. She kissed Rachel first, and the little girl threw her arms eagerly around Katie's neck and hugged her hard.

"Good night, Katie. Daddy said we don't have to have no secrets anymore."

Katie straightened up. "What kind of secrets?"

"About the niggers and the rabbis."

"And the race traitors," added Joey, piping up from the other bed.

"And Zog! They're the sons of Cain!" Rachel was as excited as if she were describing a birthday party with presents. Zog again! Katie thought. So she hadn't been mistaken about Rachel and Joey. They knew about Zog.

For a long moment, Katie stared at them disbelievingly, then she asked, very softly, "What's a rabbi, Rachel?"

"*You* know."

"He's got a big dirty beard," Joey offered.

"With lice in it," Rachel confirmed brightly.

"And he does it to little kids!" Joey warmed to the subject.

"Niggers do it, too! They do it in the back, in the butt!" Rachel was determined to top her big brother.

"That's gross!" Joey sputtered, making a yeccchhh face.

"We're the good guys," Rachel confided to Katie. "One day we're gonna kill all the dirty niggers and Jews and everything's gonna be neat!"

With a sick heart and a disbelieving mind, Katie heard this filth spewing forth from the innocent lips of children too young to understand the horror of their words. What kind of monsters did this to children? What kind of monsters twisted and warped little kids' minds and taught them to hate people they'd never even seen? What kind of monsters had children using the word "kill"?

God, this was getting worse and worse.

*   *   *

"What's this?" Katie asked casually, standing in front of the computer in Gary's bedroom. She was wearing only a towel around her body and another wrapped turban-style around her head, having just emerged from the shower.

Gary grinned appreciatively at her half-exposed body and went over to his pride and joy, eager to show it off. He switched it on, sat down at the keyboard, and punched in a code number. Katie came and stood by his shoulder, her eyes riveted to the tiny screen.

The screen lit up. "PASSWORD," it demanded.

Gary typed out "SUMMER LIGHTNING."

A moment passed while the data banks scanned the password, found it acceptable, and allowed Gary's hookup access.

"WELCOME TO THE AMERICAN LIBERTY NET—DEVOTED TO FREE EXCHANGE OF IDEAS." The screen scrolled down, and more words began to appear. "PREPARE YOURSELVES. THE DAY IS COMING. WE WILL EXECUTE ALL FEDERAL AGENTS, CONGRESSMEN, JUDGES, AND JEW COLLABORATORS."

Kate watched, fascinated and horrified, taking mental notes, but saying nothing.

"THE WIND IS STARTING TO BLOW." There was more to come, but Gary wasn't ready to let a stranger see it, not even Katie Phillips.

Shutting the computer down, Gary turned to Katie with a big smile. "I can talk to anybody I want," he told her proudly. "We got systems operators all over the country." He stood up, unbuttoning his shirt. "My dad, when I was a little kid, he'd say to me, 'No amount of carryin' on is gonna make the wheat grow faster. Don't rock the boat.' He changed his mind later on."

He slipped out of his jeans and stood naked. "We're gonna rock the damn boat." He went over to the bed and stripped the patchwork quilt off with a flourish. It was obvious that he had sex on his mind.

Inside, Katie shrank away, knowing what would come

next. On the outside, she remained calm, even smiling at him in a kind of welcome. And, when Gary asked her mischievously, "Can I borrow your towel?" and put his arms tightly around her, she forced herself to smile.

But as they sank onto the bed together and Gary's lips began trailing across her naked breasts, his hands searching between her thighs, Catherine Weaver made a promise to herself: to bring this case to a rapid conclusion so that no man she didn't love could ever touch her like this again.

Chapter Ten

Camping

For days now, Gary had been talking about going Camping. Every time he said the word, Katie heard the capital C in his voice. Rachel and Joey, too, were excited, looking forward to Camping as the high spot of their summer vacation. They talked endlessly about campfires and sleeping bags. It appeared that all of them were going, Gary and the kids, and, of course, Katie.

Gary could hardly stand to be away from her long enough to get the day's work done. He had taken to coming home at lunchtime, eating the hot lunch Katie would prepare for him, then grabbing Katie's hand and pulling her up the stairs to the bedroom.

Each time Gary made love to her, Katie found it harder to handle than the time before. She used every discipline in her mental arsenal to distract herself and keep herself from thinking about it. But try as she might, she couldn't turn her mind off and simply let it happen. Each new time was always a new violation, a new rape. The hardest thing she had ever done in her life—equal to watching that black man die—was to go on pretending that she was enjoying it, that she was loyal to Gary Simmons and loved him more than ever. How long could this possibly continue?

Maybe camping, with Gary's family all around them, would give her some respite from his ardor.

C-Day, as Katie had begun to think of it, arrived at last. Rachel and Joey were so excited they could barely choke down their breakfast. Gary spent the morning packing bags and boxes with his tent, some sleeping bags, camping equipment, and other gear that Katie didn't get a look at, because Gladys Simmons arrived with sandwiches, potato salad, and other food for them to take along on the trip, and was needing Katie's help in the kitchen.

Gary's mother hadn't softened much toward Katie in the short time that Katie and Gary had been together. Plainly Mrs. Simmons still didn't trust her. Whether it was Katie's youth, or her beauty, or some other, more threatening aspect of the girl that made her suspicious and hostile, Katie couldn't tell, but she hadn't won her over, so it would be good to get away from her influence for a while. Much as he loved Katie, Gary set great store by his mother's opinion.

The Jeep Cherokee, large as it was, was just about packed full. The back seat held Rachel and Joey and the dog Ronnie. The camping gear took up the rest of the room. Katie and Gary carried the last of the parcels out to the car and stowed them. All Katie was taking along was one small bag; in it she'd packed the camos, the army-issue green camouflage suit Gary had bought for her, and she wore her little Japanese camera slung over one shoulder. Gary stowed the last bundle and started to get in behind the wheel.

"Ain't you gonna lock the door?" Katie asked, surprised.

"What for? We never lock the door."

Katie couldn't help a thin smile. "What about all those people you gotta protect yourself against?"

Gary turned toward her, grinning. "Hell, this ain't one of them nut places like Hellifornia or Jew York. You yankin' my chain?"

"Have you ever known any Jews?" Katie asked.

"Hell, no!" Gary exploded. "Y'are yanking my chain, ain'tcha?"

Katie shook her head.

"Yeah, y'are. You're ain't gonna need that camera where we're going." Gary took Katie's little camera off her shoulder. "You don't wanna get it broke. I'll take it back in." And he hurried back inside the house with it. Stunned, Katie watched her camera disappear, and an uneasiness crept over her. Why, if he trusted her, did he want to take the camera away? Unless he *didn't* trust her as completely as he pretended. And why couldn't she take the camera on a simple camping trip? Unless it wasn't as simple a trip as she had imagined.

"This is gonna be so fun!" Rachel cried, eager to be going.

"Yeah," Joey echoed. "Lots of fun."

"Yeah." Katie nodded somberly. "Fun."

Katie had asked Gary exactly where they were going, but all he would tell her was "Campin'," with a grin. He loved his little mysteries, Katie decided, and he loved to keep her guessing. It was part of his power trip, part of his sexual domination of her. But maybe, just maybe, there was something beyond that.

The children seemed happy enough, singing old camp songs with their father as they drove, songs like "Red River Valley" and "She'll Be Comin' Around the Mountain," songs in which Katie joined only halfheartedly. Rachel and Joey were surprisingly not cranky, very different from other kids taken on long trips. In the long hours of the drive, they didn't fight, or whine for food or the bathroom. Being with their father put them on their best behavior. They loved Gary, but they were scared of him, too.

Katie was antsy. There was something a little wrong about this trip, something she couldn't quite put her finger on. The kids were *too* good, for one thing. The distance was too great. And Gary himself was almost hectically cheerful, a little larger and louder than life. The whole thing put Katie off balance and made her anxious.

Just before they reached Wyoming, they stopped for

lunch, picnicking on the grass near the highway on the food Gladys Simmons had sent along. The children appeared unusually subdued, and Gary was impatient to get going again, reminding them that they had a very long drive ahead of them. He was obviously itching to get there, wherever "there" was.

The rural highway stretched for miles, past farms and small communities. Every now and then they'd pass an ugly stretch of road, built up with automobile body shops, fast food restaurants, and mini-malls. It was near one such place that Katie saw the billboard, an advertisement for Dan Kraus and his radio show out of Chicago. The sign showed Kraus's picture, with the legend: "WLD, the Voice of the Midwest." Katie stole a look at Gary. If he noticed the billboard, or felt any sense of irony at seeing it, he gave no outward sign.

But to Katie, the billboard was a symbol as clear as the one that God showed the emperor Constantine. It was the visible reminder of why she was here, of the job she had to do. The Jew Dan Kraus had been murdered. If Gary Simmons was the man whose finger had pulled the trigger, then he was a man who by his own admission had never known a Jew. He had killed, then, out of ignorance and paranoia, out of a fear ungrounded in reality. It struck a fresh chill into Katie, and it reminded her that she was in a dangerous position that grew more perilous with every moment. She mustn't let up for one second. The charade had to be perfect, her cover intact and seamless. She snuggled up to Gary and put her head on his shoulder.

They drove for hours—west, then north, picking up Highway 85 at the South Dakota/Wyoming border and following it into Bowman, where the highway made a junction with 12. On 12, they were already in Montana, driving through Miles City, Roundup, and Twodot, where they turned onto a county road.

Ahead of the Jeep could be seen the treetops of tall pine forests; the terrain became more rugged and rose toward the foothills of the Rocky Mountains. If they kept driving due west, they would soon be into natural forest land, preserved by the government in its original magnificent state. But they were still on private land. Not much later, the peaks of the Rockies loomed up even above the tops of the giant pines and redwoods.

The Cherokee turned onto an unmarked road, little more than a trail into the woods. Night had fallen, and it was pitch black. The 4×4 bumped and jounced its way across the narrow road, which rose upward in a steep gradient. Even the power of Gary's strong headlights did little good in the tree-choked darkness. On both sides of the road, giant pines spread long branches to form a thick canopy, keeping out any illumination that the moonlight might give.

Yet Gary Simmons drove confidently, as though he'd been on this road many times before. On the back seat, Ronnie and the children were sound asleep, Rachel and Joey cuddled up to the dog. Katie dozed fitfully, her head on Gary's shoulder. Suddenly, almost out of nowhere, a chain-link fence with a closed gate appeared in the Cherokee's high beams. Gary pulled to a stop.

Out of the darkness, four men, dressed in full paramilitary gear complete down to their boot knives, surrounded the car, one of them shining a powerful halogen flashlight on the Jeep. They were armed with Mac-10s, and they looked like they knew how to use them. In an instant, Katie came wide-awake. Where the hell were they? Who were these guys? Why were they pointing guns at them?

"Hey, Gary, you can go on through." One of the men waved. It was clear that the face of Gary Simmons was recognized and respected here.

Gary scowled. "Aren't you supposed to check your list?" he demanded sternly.

"Yes, sir, Gary, I just thought—"

"Then check it!" Gary's bark had the ring of military authority. Wide-awake, Katie sat silent, watching every move. The man in the camouflage outfit had a clipboard, and on it was fastened a list of names that seemed to be many pages thick. While he went down the list, looking for Gary Simmons's name, the other three ran their flashlight beams inside the car, checking everything out. Miraculously, Ronnie and the children managed to sleep through it all.

Gary's name checked out. "Go on." They waved him through, hurrying to open the locked gate.

"Thank you," Gary said with some contempt, and drove through. On the other side of the fence, the road wound into the tall pines.

"I thought we were going camping," said the mystified Katie.

"We are," Gary replied shortly, and Katie decided it was best to keep her eyes and ears open, but her mouth shut.

There came the sound of singing from the distance, growing louder as the Jeep headed toward it. In the back, Rachel and Joey woke up and rubbed their eyes, and Ronnie kept barking until Gary hushed him.

Strong light came flickering through the trees. There was evidently a bonfire somewhere, a big one, big enough to light up the night sky. Now the singing was very loud, the sound of many voices, women's as well as men's, but mostly the deep voices of men. The song was a hymn, "Amazing Grace."

And then they were driving into the clearing, a vast meadow carved out of the forest. Katie's eyes snapped open in astonishment. Even she, a trained agent whose suspicions had been put on red alert by four men armed with Mac-10s, was not expecting this!

There was no bonfire. Instead, the flames that leaped up into the night sky came from a gigantic burning cross. The clearing was lit up by the fiery cross, and Katie could see hundreds of men and women around the circumference of the meadow, singing and watching the cross burn. In the center of the clearing stood uniformed members of the Ku Klux Klan, costumed in their white robes and hoods, the badges on their breasts echoing the cross they were burning. Their leaders were dressed like them, only in black satin instead of white cotton. Some of the watchers wore battle dress or para-military outfits, camo suits or army fatigues. Most of them were armed.

Holy Jesus! thought Katie. This is like some enormous scout jamboree, only with white supremacists, Nazis, and militant fascists instead of Boy Scouts! If it weren't so goddamn terrifying, it might even be funny!

There were flags everywhere—American flags, rebel flags of Dixie. But also, there were Nazi flags of red and white, with black swastikas. A squad of fully uniformed neo-Nazis, garbed in World War II Nazi uniforms complete with high polished boots and swastika armbands, goosestepped around the circle's perimeter, their arms extended stiffly in the Hitler salute. Others, spectators, wore Nazi or KKK armbands, or T-shirts with White Power slogans printed on them. Dozens of little children were present, watching everything, their eyes round with wonder.

And all to the background of "Amazing Grace"! Behind her, Katie could hear Rachel join softly in the singing, and she could barely suppress a shiver. Exposing children to a scene like this was unforgivable.

But they didn't stop, and the hymn receded in the distance as the Cherokee drove past them and farther into the woods. Katie twisted her head backward for a last look at the KKK and the burning cross.

"Did you bring us some sheets to wear, too?"

Gary Simmons shot her a look. Was she being serious or what? Nah, she must be kidding around. "I don't believe in no clown outfits," he joked back.

All along the road, on both sides, a procession of parked vehicles—cars, Jeeps, ATVs, trucks. Almost every one of them bore a pugnacious bumper sticker:

THIS CAR PROTECTED BY A PIT BULL WITH AIDS
GUN CONTROL IS HITTING YOU WHERE YOU AIM AT

RED, WHITE AND BLUE: THESE COLORS DON'T RUN
FIRE-POWER IS THE BEST POWER FOR WHITE POWER

And inevitably, AMERICA: LOVE IT OR LEAVE IT.

People were milling about everywhere, dressed in down vests, jeans or overalls, and plaid shirts. Some wore more elaborate military or survival gear. Katie's eyes went from one group to the next, taking mental note of their weapons. She saw crossbows, assault rifles, ballistic knives, powerful handguns in hip or armpit holsters, but mostly she saw automatic weapons, almost all of them American-made.

"I'm real hungry," Gary said. "You guys hungry?"

"Yeah!" yelled Rachel and Joey enthusiastically.

But it would be a while before they got any dinner. First, they had to find a campsite, then set up their tent and unroll their sleeping bags, one each for Rachel and Joey, a double-sized one for Katie and Gary. Next they had to unpack everything from the Cherokee. While they were doing the unloading, Shorty came by in search of Gary.

"They been down here every ten minutes lookin' for you," he told Gary.

"Well, I'm here."

"Hi, Shorty." Katie smiled.

"How you doin', darling?" The fat man grabbed her up into a big bear hug.

"Fine." Katie smiled back.

They walked to the campfire together, Katie leading Rachel and Joey by the hand. The kids, half asleep, kept bumping into her legs, slowing Katie down. Sitting around the campfire were some old familiar faces—Buster, Dean, Ellie, and Lyle. Did they go everywhere that Gary went, like Mary's lamb? Evidently so. Dean's wife Toby was standing near the fire, stirring a large pot of something that made hungry Katie's mouth water, it smelled that good.

"Hey, people," Gary called.

They greeted both of them, but their eyes were on Katie. She knew she mustn't put a foot wrong here, she had to be on her guard every moment.

"We gotta feed these kids somethin' and get 'em to bed, they're tired," she said to Gary.

"Toby made a whole big pot o' stew," volunteered Ellie, handing Gary a big spoon. He dipped it into the pot and took a mouthful.

"Goddamn, this is good stew, Toby." He put the spoon back into the pot again and offered a taste to Katie, feeding it to her because her hands were still locked in Rachel and Joey's.

Katie closed her eyes and swallowed. "Mmmmm, I'm gonna pig out!" she declared, and everybody laughed, relaxing a little.

"They want you down to the trailer," Wes's voice cut icily through the night. As usual, he had been standing in the shadows, watching without being seen.

Gary continued eating his stew calmly. "I'll be along, Wes."

Katie felt rather than saw the look of naked hatred Wes flashed in her direction as he left to deliver Gary's message. But she didn't look in Wes's direction; it was too dangerous. All her attention was on Gary's children, as she played the role of the perfect mama.

"Come on, you two. Hurry up and eat, and then you're goin' straight to bed."

"Can't we stay up a little, Katie?" Rachel pleaded.

"No, you can not," Katie answered with mock sternness, but she bent down and gave the girl a kiss and a hug to take the edge off her denial. "We got the whole day tomorrow." Then, to be fair, she kissed and hugged Joey, too, while Gary's friends around the campfire watched her with his children. Katie knew they were forming judgments.

The kids were asleep almost before their heads hit the air pillows of their sleeping bags. Katie watched them for a minute or so, her heart aching for them, that such young children were being force-fed ignorance, hatred, and prejudice. Then she sighed and stepped out into the cold night air.

The campfire was almost deserted. Only Shorty still sat there, staring into the flames. He was singing softly to himself, a lovely old Scottish air, "My Bonnie Lies over the Ocean," a lament for Prince Charlie and the abortive Jacobite Rebellion. Katie went over and stood next to him, singing along with him until the song was finished. As the last notes died away, they smiled companionably at each other.

"Where's Gary?" she asked.

"He'll be back in a while. Set on down here and warm your toes, it gets nippy up here."

Katie pulled up an aluminum folding chair and sat next to Shorty. For a little while they sat in comfortable silence, sharing the firelight and their own private thoughts. Katie's private thoughts were involved with going over and memorizing the details of everything she'd seen tonight, for her report to the bureau. Then Shorty said, "You're real good with them kids, girl."

"They're real nice kids," answered Katie, meaning it.

Another long pause followed. "How do you feel about all this?" Shorty asked at last.

A thrill of fear shoot through Katie's veins. Easy now, she told herself. This could be a trap. You've got to stay in character. You've got to sound believable, sincere. Don't go too fast. Don't make mistakes.

"I . . . I don't know," she said slowly. "It's all . . . new to me. I've never really known any . . . Jews . . . or any . . . niggers. I never . . . hurt . . . nobody. I don't like hurtin' nobody."

For a long time Shorty's eyes stayed on her, probing her, while he said nothing. Then he looked away from the fire, off into the distant darkness. "I don't, either," he said with a small sigh. "I don't even like seein' a fight."

He waited for Katie to make a comment, but when she didn't he continued. "But if we don't fight back, they gonna take it all away from us, the whole country. Jewboy judges, bankers, politicians with their nigger police."

Where on earth do they get these ideas? Even a seemingly good-natured guy like Shorty?

Out loud, Katie said, "I never even liked guns that much."

Shorty Richards laughed. "Hell, I don't, either. I gotta close my eyes every time I pull the trigger."

Katie forced herself to chuckle over his horrible little joke.

"You got a good heart, girl. Ain't nothin' wrong with that. You'll learn you gotta do what's gotta be done," he told her in a kindly voice. "I learned it, too." Shorty's eyes took on a faraway look and his voice dropped to almost a whisper. "All I ever wanted to do was raise the crop and raise my boy. Bank took my farm, Vietnam took my boy. I ain't got nothin' left to take. I ain't in it for myself no more. I got a good heart, too, girl, just like you."

He smiled at her with some affection, and put his hand over Katie's, giving it a squeeze. She squeezed back.

"I can't sleep! I hear noises!" Katie turned when she heard the child cry. Rachel was standing there sobbing, rubbing her eyes with her knuckles. She was clearly frightened by the new situation and the strange sleeping bag, just a little girl who wanted to be home in her own bed.

"Ah, whatsmatter, honey?" Katie ran over to Rachel and gathered her up in her arms. "It's gonna be all right. Everything's fine. Daddy will be back in a few minutes and Katie's here. Don't cry, honey." She hugged and kissed the child affectionately, carrying her back to the tent and tucking her in, sitting with her and stroking her hair until the little girl fell asleep.

For a long, long time, she lay in the sleeping bag, smoking cigarettes and waiting for Gary to come back. There was no way that she could fall asleep, no way she even wanted to. Her mind went racing into the darkness, trying to see ahead to tomorrow. Why were they here? Why were any of them here, let alone an army of thousands of rabid haters from the lunatic fringe, armed to the teeth with grenades and automatic weapons? Why were they all playing soldier? And what was going to happen tomorrow, in daylight?

Chapter Eleven

School

It was after four in the morning when Katie finally fell asleep. Gary had not yet returned. She slept until well past seven, emerging from the tent only half awake to find the others already gathered around the campfire eating breakfast. It was a glorious day; the air was mountain-clear, the sky a deep, rich blue. Beyond the treetops the peaks of the majestic Rockies were visible in all their snow-topped splendor. The smell of strong boiling coffee and fresh, sweet pine needles tickled Katie's senses; she yawned and stretched like a cat.

"It's beautiful up here!"

"Mornin', lazy," Gary called.

Joey came up to hang over his father's shoulder. "Can we play ball now, Dad?"

Gary shook his head no. "You gotta go to school first," he reminded his son.

"Aw, Dad!" protested Joey, disappointed.

"Go on, now. Lyle's gonna take you."

The older man stood up and set his coffee cup on the ground. He gave one hand to Rachel and the other to Joey. "Come on, kids, let's get going."

"Hey, Lyle," Gary called after him with a wink at Katie. "Have a nice day!"

The old man turned sharply, his face purpling with

anger. "I done told you not to say that to me! I done told you!" he yelled. He was spitting mad.

Everybody at the campfire broke out in roars of laughter. Gary turned to Katie to explain the private joke. "Lyle thinks 'Have a Nice Day' is a Jew plot to put us all to sleep."

"He does?" Katie was flabbergasted. How could a grown man be so naïve?

"He sure does. How about you, are you ready to go to school?"

School?

"School" turned out to be a firing range. The "teacher" was Gary, the "pupil" was Katie. The "subject" was a target. The "textbook" was a Mac-10.

Gary put the gun into her hands, arranging Katie's stance in front of the target. But here was no ordinary target. This was a scarecrow figure dressed in black. Katie drew in her breath when she saw it—the same scarecrow that she had found in the wheat field that first day on the combine. That figure had been shot to pieces, and most of its black shirt had been blown away by ammo. This one was new, completely intact. Over its shirt, where the heart would be on a live human being, was fastened a large Star of David. This target was a symbolic Jew. Everything fell into place now. Even a field of wheat under a Midwestern sky could hold sinister secrets. Katie remembered how embarrassed she'd been to be frightened of a scarecrow. But her first instincts had been correct after all. It was a scarecrow with a terrifying message.

Katie felt a kind of paralysis; she could only stare at the target, her thoughts in turmoil. She held the light, boxy automatic weapon awkwardly, loose in her hands. Her heart was pounding and her palms were covered in cold sweat.

"Hold it nice and gentle," Gary advised. He came up close to Katie and steadied her arm. "It ain't gonna bite you." He moved her shoulder a little, as a golf instructor might when trying to perfect a student's swing. Only this wasn't golf school, it was kill school. "Lookit the Jewboy right in the eye and squeeze."

Katie drew in her breath and aimed the Mac-10. But the scarecrow was too disturbingly human. The Star of David was staring back at her, and there was no way she could fire.

"Go on, now," Gary urged, and Katie realized that she had no choice but to obey. She closed her eyes and pulled the trigger. There was a suppressor fitted to the gun's barrel, and the burst of fire came almost silently from the weapon, but the target remained intact. She'd missed.

"Don't close your eyes," Gary instructed her patiently. "Try again."

Katie pulled herself together, silently counting to ten. Here was one more of Gary Simmons's tests, a major one. She could not afford to let her personal feelings get the better of her; she had to go on playing Gary's game or she might jeopardize the entire investigation. Gary was watching her closely, waiting for Katie to act.

She lifted the Mac-10 and held it in the perfect firing position, braced against her shoulder as she sighted. Whirling toward the target, she fired off a long, sustained burst. Every shot that came out of the barrel ripped through the Star of David, blowing it away in tatters.

"Holy shit!" Gary exclaimed, almost speechless with astonishment. He'd never seen a woman shoot like that, and damn few men, either. What was her story?

"My dad taught me to shoot," lied Katie, who'd made the sharpshooter roster during her agent training, and had the medals to prove it. She fired again, this time blowing the scarecrow's head to smithereens.

"You connin' me all the time, huh?" Gary Simmons gave her a sharp look.

Katie looked boldly back into his face, the adrenaline still pumping through her veins. "No," was all she said.

But Gary was grinning with pride. This woman was dynamite, and she was all his.

When they left the firing range, Katie and Gary took a

walk through the camp, while he pointed out the more
interesting activities. Katie kept her eyes open and her
brain ticking, checking everything out. She wasn't the
greatest weapons expert in the world, but she did recognize some serious hardware here, a fortune in state-of-
the-art weaponry and equipment.

This was no survival camp or imitation jungle, where
weekend shooters gathered with their CO_2-powered rifles
to blast away at one another with harmless paint bullets.
These weren't soldier-of-fortune games they were playing.
All the people here were dead serious. Hidden behind
locked gates, a secret from the outside world, an army of
fanatics appeared to be drilling for some dire purpose.
What the hell was going on? Every militant right-wing
group was represented in this "camp," and all were heavily armed. Whatever was going down, this was much,
much bigger than anybody at the Bureau had imagined.
Katie had never heard of a secret camp like this one, and
she doubted that the FBI had a dossier on it. It was
possible that her report would be the first—if she lived to
make it.

Now that she'd shot expert on the range right under
Gary's nose, Katie knew that the .22 buried at the bottom of her handbag was more incriminating than ever. If
by some mischance it should come to light, she'd have no
excuse of feminine timidity for carrying a concealed
weapon around him. She could never say that she didn't
know how to fire it anyway, therefore the gun was harmless. It was now a deadly concealed weapon in the hands
of an ace, a genuine threat to Gary's life and security.
Katie wished now she'd never let Michael Carnes force it
on her.

Walking with Gary through the camp, Katie saw men
in full camo dress, their faces painted in green and black
camouflage stripes with army-issue greasepaint that smelled
like Juicy Fruit chewing gum. She took note of others, in
sniper training gear, men whose faces were hooded in
burlap netting, burlap wrapped around their rifles to
mask any glint the sun's rays might strike off the metal

barrels. She even saw ghillie suits, those ragged Velcro camos that make a sniper in the wild look exactly like a harmless bush.

Those men who weren't in military or para-military uniforms wore plaid flannel shirts and denim overalls, like hunters. She saw T-shirts with jingo slogans like "America's Dove is Russia's Pigeon," and many military badges and Special Forces green berets, the kind of stuff anybody can buy from the ads in the back of *Soldier of Fortune.* But if the T-shirts were tacky, the armament was far from Mickey Mouse. It was professional and staggering in its diversity.

No Uzis or Galils and no Kalashnikovs or AK-47s, of course. This crowd wasn't into buying Israeli, Chinese, or Soviet-bloc weapons, no matter how cheap or efficient. Katie took mental note of American and Canadian assault rifles, powerful crossbows, fully automatic AR-15s, M-16s with ballistic knives attached, and everywhere, the Ingram Mac-10. The Mac seemed to be the automatic weapon of choice. Many of the men she passed as she walked with Gary were carrying stun guns or grenades, and she could almost swear that she caught a glimpse of rocket-powered grenade launchers over in the next field. The hardware here was more than impressive—several million dollars' worth, at least, possibly more, if the heavier armaments were being kept under wraps. There was enough firepower here to start World War III. Was that what they were up to? World War III?

Firing ranges were set up in a number of places, for shooters of varying skills. Katie observed women in military outfits practicing with handguns—mostly combat pistols and Smith & Wesson Magnums, heavy to manage but with a deadly effectiveness.

This wasn't a camp, it was a training ground in which lethal skills were being taught and perfected.

But the most mind-boggling practice range of all was the "school" where the children were being taught to use real weapons. Dozens of boys and girls, none of them more than ten or eleven years old and the youngest no older than six, were being schooled in the deadly craft of the Mac-10. The children were dressed head to toe like miniature soldiers, in full sets of camos. Each child was assigned an individual instructor, to show him or her how to hold the gun, how to aim it, and how long to keep their chubby little fingers on the trigger to fire an effective burst. This was real weapons training.

Targets had been set up for the kids to shoot at. One was a gross caricature of a Hasidic Jew sitting on a toilet. The other showed a black man running with a terrified expression on his exaggeratedly Negroid features. The children were firing away at both of them, shooting and laughing.

When Katie saw Rachel among the other children, a Mac-10 in her hand, she barely suppressed a horrified gasp. Rachel! How could they! But Rachel appeared happy enough, she was even enjoying herself. On seeing Katie and Gary, the child came running up, excited and glowing.

"I got two niggers and a Jew!" she yelled proudly.

Gary beamed. "That's great, honey."

"Isn't that great, Katie?" Rachel asked insistently.

Katie couldn't bring herself to say the words, although she knew that Gary's eyes were fixed on her, watching her reaction closely. She smiled and nodded at the little one, but tears of sadness sprang to her eyes and she had to turn her face away so that Gary wouldn't see them. What a waste of a precious child's innocence, to teach her hatred, anti-Semitism, racism, and to promise her that all her problems could be dealt with by choosing scapegoats and filling them full of lead.

Gary *did* see Katie's tears, but his interpretation of them was different. He thought that Katie's emotion stemmed from pride in Rachel and tenderness for her, and that Katie was too independent to show it. Putting his arm around her shoulder, he pulled her close, giving her shoulders a hard squeeze. "You know what?"

"What?"

"Now we're a real family."

Inside, Katie shuddered. God help me, she thought. What kind of man is this who finds sentiment in the lethal potential of a woman and a seven-year-old girl?

They headed back to their own campsite, Gary's arm still tightly around Katie, hers wrapped around his waist. Near their campfire, three neo-Nazis sat talking to Lyle and Shorty. They were dressed in their full regalia, swastika armbands, high boots, jodhpurs, Sam Brown belts, black shirts. In their holsters were large Luger pistols.

Lyle was laughing loudly and slapping his thigh as Gary and Katie approached. "Look at that," he said to Gary, holding up a greeting card with Adolf Hitler's picture on it. "They're for Jews' birthdays. Listen to this: 'May his memory refresh your soul and give you inspiration.' Ain't that a pisser?"

Gary scowled. His handsome face darkened and his brow drew together. "Get outta here!" he barked at the Nazis, his fists clenching in anger.

"What did you say, brother?" The uniformed men looked justifiably startled.

"Listen, shithead! My dad got a Purple Heart fightin' uniforms like that. I don't wanna hear nothin' about Ay-dolf Hitler. Go on! Git! Go jack off your goddamn Lugers!"

Without a word, the three neo-Nazis stood up and walked away.

"What'd you do that for?" demanded the aggrieved Lyle.

"They're assholes," spat Gary. "They're losers. You're an asshole, too, Lyle. Sometimes I think we got more assholes here than they got in California." With a snort of disgust he grabbed Katie's hand and marched her off.

"What the hell did he mean by that?" Lyle watched Gary stalking off and turned to Shorty.

"Beats the shit outta me, Lyle." Shorty had to muffle his smile into a phony cough.

It had been a very long day and Katie was exhausted. Her fatigue was not only physical, but mental. She'd seen and heard some heavy things today. And she was certain there was more to come tomorrow. What she'd observed might be only the tip of the iceberg. She wanted to stay awake for a while so she could put her day's observations in order in her memory. Writing them down was of course out of the question. But she couldn't keep her eyes open. Her brain felt fried; so much had happened that she hadn't yet sorted through. When she climbed into the sleeping bag, Katie fell asleep almost at once.

Gary curled up behind her, wrapping his arms around her body, content just to feel her next to him. He was very pleased with Katie. She'd done him proud today, not only with the way she looked after the children, but the expert way she shot on the firing range. With her spirit and guts, she could prove very useful in the organization. Even his intimate circle of friends was coming to accept her as Gary's lover, beginning even to trust her.

Not Wes Bond, of course. Wes despised Katie and was suspicious of her. But then Wes hated damn near everybody and there wasn't anybody he *wasn't* suspicious of. Suspicion was born into Wes's nature and bred in his bones. He especially hated women, and a girl like Katie— tough, lippy, and independent—was guaranteed to make his hackles rise. Sometimes Gary thought that Wes was even suspicious of *him*. Well, maybe not. Not with the secrets the two of them held in common.

As if he'd materialized out of Gary's head, thought made flesh, Wes Bond slipped into the tent, silent as a cat, and signaled to Gary. He was armed, carrying his Mac-10 with silencer.

Evidently, Gary had been waiting for this signal. He eased himself out of the sleeping bag, taking care not to wake Katie up, slipped into his jeans and a shirt, zipped up his down jacket, thrust his feet into boots, and followed Wes out into the night, leaving Katie sleeping.

But Katie Phillips was not sleeping. As soon as Gary had begun moving around the tent her eyes had opened. Something was going on. Something big was about to happen, or else why would Gary be getting up in the middle of the night? Why would Wes be carrying an automatic submachine gun? Every sense alerted, she continued to lie still, breathing in slow, measured rhythm like a sound sleeper. But fifteen seconds after Wes and Gary left the tent, Katie scrambled naked out of the sleeping bag and ran lightly to the front flap, peering out, watching the direction the two men took. They had already moved past the campfire and were headed for the edge of the campsite clearing, in the direction of the line of trees that demarcated the beginning of the woods.

In less than ninety seconds she was dressed, her shirt stuffed into her jeans, boots on her feet. Cautiously, Katie put her head outside the tent and took a quick look around. The campfire was deserted except for Shorty Richards, who was sitting in an aluminum chair, nursing a beer and staring moodily into the flames. If she left the tent by the front flap, she'd be directly in his line of vision, because he was between her and Wes and Gary, who had nearly reached the tree line.

Katie moved silently to the other end of the tent, past the sleeping Rachel and Joey, and lifted the back flap. Making her cautious way outside, she stood still for a long moment, her back pressed against the tent, checking to see that she wasn't being observed. The other tents nearby were silent; nobody was stirring at this late hour. There wasn't anybody in sight. With her heart in her mouth, she took off quickly for the tree line, following the path the two men had taken.

It was rough going. Up ahead, she could see the moving beams of two high-beam flashlights as Gary Simmons and Wes Bond lit their way through the woods. But Katie didn't have a flashlight, and even if she had one, she wouldn't dare to use it. A city girl born and bred, she was no Indian scout in silent moccasins. Every now and then a branch would pull at her hair or snag her clothing, or she would stumble over a tree root or a stone in her path. The first few times she made a sound, it was cloaked by the crunching of the pine needles under the men's feet, but at last, as luck would have it, she tripped over something in her path, and the sound of her stumbling feet carried.

"What was that?" Wes turned sharply, alert to danger. He flashed his beam around, down the path toward Katie. She dodged behind a tree and held her breath.

"Nothin'. Come on!" Gary barked impatiently.

But Wes was far from satisfied. His innate alarm system had been triggered. Pointing his light through the trees, Wes gave the path a good raking with the beam. Katie stood very still, willing herself not to move a muscle. Finally Wes gave up and moved grudgingly forward with Gary. After a few seconds, Katie emerged from behind the tree and followed, taking great care where she set her feet.

Midway through the tall stands of pine there was another clearing, and it was to this that the men were heading. Parked in the center of the clearing was a closed-bed army truck with military plates. Around it stood several young soldiers in uniform.

"You stay here," Gary ordered Wes.

This didn't set well with Wes. His eyes narrowed and the muscles in his jaw tightened, but Gary was the leader, so Wes was forced to obey. He remained on guard at the edge of the clearing while Gary approached the truck.

Katie crept closer. Wes Bond stood as a barrier between her and the clearing, but she had to take her chances. She must see what was going on. This was federal business; this involved the U.S. Army. She could see Gary talking to the soldiers and watched as they took several large wooden crates out of the back of the truck. They opened the crates and took out a weapon of some kind, handing it over to Gary, who handled it carefully, with obvious pleasure.

Was was it? Katie craned to see better. From where she was standing the weapon looked like a mortar or even possibly a rocket launcher. And there were several large wooden crates, all filled with them. A major weapons buy was going down here. Some soldiers had evidently decided to go into business for themselves, dealing arms. But were they merely entrepreneurs or part of a larger conspiracy? Was money involved or, even worse, was it doctrine?

I've got to get a closer look! Katie thought, took a step or two forward, and stepped on a branch. It broke under her feet with a snapping noise. Instantly, Wes Bond wheeled around, his eyes and ears searching for the source of the noise. Katie moved again; her foot hit the same branch, which crumbled under her heavy boot with a loud crack like thunder.

The sound reverberated horribly. It broke the silence of the woods into a million noisy pieces. The Mac-10 rising in his hand, Wes Bond began to run rapidly and silently toward the tree line. Katie froze. He was headed straight for her. She turned and ran for her life.

She was no match for Wes; Katie knew that. She knew that her only chance of survival was escape. Small and light and wiry, Katie was fast, but she wasn't as sure-footed as Wes. The woods were treacherous going even at a crawl. At a run they were an obstacle course. Katie had a head start, but Wes had two major things in his favor. He had a flashlight, and he had a Mac-10. Bullets travel faster than feet.

Wes aimed his flashlight ahead of him. A figure was disappearing through the trees, but for a split second, he caught part of it in the beam. He couldn't see the face, just a piece of the shirt and the jeans. The figure's back was to him, but he saw that it was small-built and very slim. He fired, raking the trees in front of him with a burst of silent nine-millimeter bullets.

Katie raced desperately onward, keeping low, bullets whizzing past her, striking the trees near her head. Her only chance was to outrun Wes, get back to the campsite before him. Death was behind her, in front of her, all around her, staring her in the face. The night was very black, and trees loomed up ahead of her, offering a kind of shelter, but also a series of hazards, with treacherous branches to snag her, roots to trip up her unwary feet. Behind her, running fast, came Wes, firing again and again, each burst of bullets coming nearer to Katie. Any one of them might have her name on it.

Wes reached the edge of the woods. Beyond him, the campsite. He stopped to look around. Everything was quiet—no sound, no movement anywhere. The tents stood in a row like soldiers on guard. Shorty Richards was still sitting by the campfire, dozing a little with an empty Coors can clutched in his hand. Other than that, no sign of human life. Wes turned back to the woods, his flash-light sweeping through the darkness. Nothing. Nobody.

He turned reluctantly and headed back down the rug-ged path to the clearing. Gary was waiting for him, having concluded a deal for the weapons. Wes Bond felt cheated. Somebody had been out there; he'd seen it, he knew it. Somebody he'd have to catch up to and kill, and the sooner the better. Katie Phillips was dangerous. She was too goddamn nosy, and she already knew far too much. Under his breath, Wes cursed Gary for being a pussy-whipped asshole.

His footsteps died away down the path. Still trembling, covered in icy sweat and breathing with difficulty, Katie climbed out of the ditch where she'd been hiding under a pile of fallen leaves. Moving as silently as she could, she circled around behind Shorty and ran lightly past the backs of the tents until she reached the one she was sharing with Gary Simmons. She raised the back flap and slipped inside.

It took Katie a long minute to actually comprehend that she was safe, at least for now. The memory of those silenced bullets speeding past her, aimed at her back, was still too fresh and too terrifying. She drew in a long, deep breath and tried to stop her body from trembling.

Gary might return at any moment. He mustn't find her like this. Katie stripped her clothing off quickly and climbed back into the sleeping bag, curling up as though she had never left its warmth and shelter to run through the awful night. She closed her eyes. Sleep would be the best thing for her now. If Gary Simmons were to find her really asleep, it would never occur to him that she'd left the tent.

But sleep was unattainable. *I may never sleep again,* thought Katie. Certain pieces were beginning to fit into the puzzle; other, more important pieces still eluded her. And the puzzle itself was much larger and of a more ambitious design than anybody had suspected.

Gary Simmons himself was a bigger cog in the wheel than the Bureau had supposed. It was now evident to Katie that Gary was no simple wheat farmer, no mere rural right-winger with a grudge against Big Government. He was the undisputed leader of his little cadre, but he might possess an even greater and more sinister authority. Why else would a small band of farmers be buying up an entire truckload of high-tech combat weapons? Where was the money coming from? "Conspiracy" was the word that came into Katie's mind, hammering at her brain.

But a conspiracy on what scale? And involving how many? Funded by whom? For what purpose? These were the vital questions she must find the answers to, the questions that refused to let her sleep.

Wes Bond, still carrying the deadly Mac-10, came into the tent. He stared at Katie. She was sprawled on her belly in the sleeping bag, one naked arm exposed, her eyes tightly shut, her breathing regular, to all outward appearances soundly asleep.

But Wes wasn't fooled. "I saw you, bitch," he hissed at her, his deep voice thick with hatred.

Katie felt the thin edge of his rage as a dagger aimed at her, felt rather than saw the silenced barrel of the machine gun so perilously close to her naked body. She knew that Wes Bond's pale eyes, the eyes of a remorseless killer, were staring at her, silently willing her to move so that he would have the excuse to shoot her in the back. Her nerves were raw with terror and exhaustion, and they cried out for her to bolt, to run, to get away. But Katie forced herself to remain still, forced her

eyes to stay closed in feigned sleep, even though she
knew she wasn't really fooling Wes.

"What the fuck—" whispered Gary angrily, coming
into the tent and finding Wes standing over the sleeping
Katie with his Mac-10 poised. He grabbed Wes hard,
twisting the other man's shoulder savagely, and shoved
him out of the tent.

"She was out in the woods!" Wes snarled. Gary took a
step backward, startled, but he didn't let go of Wes.

Shorty Richards shook his head. "Nobody was nowhere," he volunteered. "I been settin' here the whole
time."

Wes's lips set in a thin stubborn line. Didn't matter a
damn what that fool Shorty said. He knew who it was
he'd fired at, and it weren't no possum or raccoon. It was
Katie's shirt and Katie's jeans and Katie's butt.

Gary's breath came raggedly and his face was a mask
of fury. "You touch her and I'll kill you," he said, meaning it. The two men glared at each other ferociously,
until Wes's eyes dropped and he was forced to look
away. Gary Simmons was the leader, and his word was
law. But there would come a time, Wes Bond vowed
silently to himself, when he'd catch that cunt in the act.
Then neither Gary nor the Lord God Jehovah Himself
could stop him from blowing the bitch to pieces.

In the tent, Katie stared into the darkness. She didn't
move, but her ears were strained to catch every word.
She heard Gary say in a low tone, "We gotta talk. Get
Dean."

"We'll use my tent," said Shorty, and she heard them
move away.

Katie's instincts told her that this meeting would be
about the weapons. Gary was going to pass along secret
information to his group. This might be the biggest missing piece of the puzzle so far. She had to be there to hear
it.

It mean risking everything twice in one night. It meant
getting out of the sack and putting on her clothes and
sneaking out of the tent and getting close enough to

overhear their conversation. Every nerve in Katie's body shrank with fear. Wasn't it enough that she'd been shot at already tonight, barely escaping with her skin? Did she have to risk it a second time, even within the same hour? Didn't she have any choice?

But this was not about choices. It was about duty, about loyalty, about Catherine Weaver's sworn calling. Katie willed herself to cut off her misgivings and her fear. She dragged her protesting body out of bed and put jeans and a shirt on it. Then, moving very quietly, she snuck around the line of tents until she came to Shorty's. Staying in the shadows as much as possible, Katie drew close enough to listen.

"Where?" Shorty was saying.

"New York, San Francisco, L.A., Miami, Chicago, Atlanta." That was Gary's voice.

"When?"

"Three days after the hit."

The hit? What hit? When?

"When's the hit?" asked Shorty, echoing Katie's silent questions.

"When I tell you," said Gary.

"Who is it?" Wes wanted to know. Ah, so then he wasn't in the innermost privileged circle of conspiracy. He was still on a "need-to-know" basis. But Gary knew. Gary was on the inside.

Katie tiptoed closer, trying to stifle even the sound of her breathing. This was the most vital piece of information of all. Somebody had been targeted for assassination, but who? Now she realized for the first time that Dan Kraus had not been murdered, he'd been assassinated. How many more before him? How many more after him? And who was the next victim to be?

But before she could hear Gary's answer, there was a rustle of sound nearby, and Katie froze in her tracks. Somebody was up and around. It was Lyle, coming out of his tent to use the latrine. Quickly, before she was seen, Katie made her way back to Gary's tent and stripped off her clothes.

It was true, then, horribly true. There *was* a conspiracy, and Gary Simmons was playing a leading role in it. He was privy to information the others in his group weren't authorized to know. Which meant that he was in on the planning stage, that he was meeting with those higher up in the chain of command. Who were those higher-ups? How would she be able to find out?

There was much, much more at stake here than a murder investigation. It had begun with murder, but the circles were widening, a lethal stone cast into a pool of blood. Katie Phillips was in deep danger. She felt suddenly, terribly vulnerable, even more vulnerable than when Wes was pursuing her through the woods with his killer fire. The only thing that stood between herself and death was the fragile trust Gary Simmons felt for her. A trust that was threatened by every clandestine move she made. And Gary wasn't anywhere near as naïve a man as she'd taken him for. He was smart and he was deadly.

He would be a lot harder to fool.

Chapter Twelve

Carpenter

Sunday morning. The last day of camp weekend. Time to strike the flags and load the vehicles and return to normal life. Or at least the semblance of normal life, because that's all it was, Katie decided, an outward show of normality. Underneath the happy, healthy Norman Rockwell–painting façade was a deep-running dark vein of ominous reality that made so-called normal life an ironic mockery.

Even the setting mocked her, a death's head in a bower of roses. Here, in some of the most beautiful countryside in the world, a blessed place of mountains and forests, clear air and blue heavens, hundreds of fresh-faced Americans, laughing and calling to one another in friendly voices, were stowing away in their cars and trucks their Nazi uniforms, KKK robes, guns, knives, grenades, automatic weapons, targets in the form of human beings, and other military and para-military matériel. Hannah Arendt's scholarly theory on the banality of evil was a true one, Katie decided.

It was like a nightmare Katie Phillips was having, only it was taking place in broad daylight, and she was all alone in finding such behavior psychotic. The others considered it patriotic, pro-American, and, most of all, righteous.

God was with them; these men and women believed

that implicitly. How many wars had been fought, how many people had died all through recorded history under that very banner, God With Us? The number was incalculable.

But if God was indeed with them, He was no benevolent, all-forgiving God. He was an angry God, an indignant God, a God who demanded human sacrifice, even the sacrifice of children's lifeblood.

An open-air church service had been held in the morning, in which the endeavors of these people—whatever endeavors they were, and most of them secret—were blessed. Now, a smaller, more sinister service was taking place under the temple roof of the sky, a service for the children. Rachel and Joey attended, Joey with some reluctance, but Rachel shining and eager.

Katie stood with Gary and the other parents on the sidelines, watching the Simmons children undergoing their "baptism" of rhetoric. The minister, tall, handsome in a paternal and distinguished way, with a thick head of hair that glistened like real silver in the sunlight, led his young congregation in a prayer that was more like an oath of loyalty given by a fourteenth-century serf to his master.

"If I must bleed, then I will bleed," he intoned.

"If I must bleed, then I will bleed," echoed the children.

"If I must die, then I will die."

"If I must die, then I will die."

"Praise the Lord."

"Praise the Lord," the children parroted, their indoctrination completed.

The minister raised his open Bible to the sky. "*This* is the Constitution of the United States!" he thundered, turning around so that everyone could see the Book. "*This* is what you're bound to obey, and don't let anybody tell you different! Hear me! Amen!"

"Amen!" cried the congregation with one voice, and the service was over.

Katie and Gary had nearly finished packing up the

Cherokee when they heard the sound of helicopter rotors. They looked up in time to see a small Sikorsky six-seater coming in to land in a nearby clearing. Who? wondered Katie, but she didn't have long to wonder. Within a few minutes, a group of men in business suits were walking into the campsite, engaging the campers in conversation. A couple of them looked mighty familiar.

"Isn't that—"

"Sure is," Gary answered, without waiting for Katie to finish her question. He grabbed her by the hand and the two of them walked over to the group of visitors.

Jack Carpenter, the candidate for his party's presidential nomination, was making an unscheduled appearance here, shaking hands, pressing the flesh, signing autographs, flashing his famous charismatic Carpenter grin. He was surrounded by aides who looked more like bodyguards and probably were bodyguards. A few steps away from this cadre stood Robert Flynn, the former National Security Council advisor who'd been terminated a few months before, and who was now spearheading Carpenter's campaign for the nomination.

"We gotta get organized," Carpenter was saying as Katie and Gary came up to the group. "Unless you want the Jews and the niggers and the faggots to keep on tellin' you what to do." Again the famous telegenic grin.

Support flowed toward him from all sides. "Hell, no!" "You sure are right, Mr. Carpenter!" "We're with you, Jack!"

"I know you are," Carpenter beamed. " 'Course, you know, a campaign like ours, it's gonna take some financin'. We ain't gonna get any help from the Jew media, that's for sure."

Katie marveled at how much Jack Carpenter could sound like a good ol' country boy when she knew he'd attended an Ivy League college, and his normal speech pattern was Ivy League lockjaw. What a con artist, and what a snow job he was giving these people, feeding right into their hates and fears! But what was he doing here?

This was a secret conclave, held behind locked gates; how did Carpenter learn about it? Unless he was involved . . . A new piece of the puzzle, and one even more difficult to fit into the pattern.

One of Carpenter's aides was taking a sheaf of printed cards out of his jacket pocket. "We've got donation pledge cards for you, if some of you want to sign and put it on your credit card," the aide told the assemblage.

But Jack Carpenter put up one restraining hand, although the people were already reaching for the cards. "Now, I don't want you to give me nothin' if you can't afford it. I mean that, now."

"No, you don't." Gary Simmons raised his voice so that all of them could hear it. Everyone turned to stare as Gary stalked up to Carpenter. "You don't give a shit whether they can afford it or not! All you care about is buyin' yourself another Cadillac, or another fancy suit, maybe." He grabbed at Carpenter's suit lapels, rubbing the luxurious fabric between his thumbs.

Jack Carpenter took a step backward, and his voice turned from folksy-genial to ice. "Who are you, mister? Whose side are you on?" he demanded.

Robert Flynn reached his hand out to Gary. "Come on, Gary. We're on the same side here," he said placatingly.

Gary! He called him Gary! Katie's eyes widened. Although she said nothing, her mind went racing through the possibilities. How do Flynn and Gary know each other?

"I ain't on *his* side," Gary said stubbornly, shaking his head. He wheeled on Carpenter, his brows contracting in anger. "You gonna win, Mr. Big Shot? You gonna get elected? You think votin' for you's gonna do any good? You ain't got a prayer, pal. You're just in it for the ride. Well, you ain't gonna ride on *my* back! All you're doin' is distractin' everybody," Gary continued, his face taking on a suspicious expression. "Maybe that's what you wanna do. Maybe you're on *their* side."

There were sharp intakes of breath all around him,
and Carpenter knew he'd lost ground here. He broke
into his famous smile. "A boy with your speakin' talents,
maybe *you* oughta be runnin' steada me." That brought
a few laughs. "I ain't real sure which one of us is the
politician, friend." More laughs; Jack Carpenter's old
savvy mojo was still working.

"Fuck you," spat Gary.

Now Carpenter was on more secure ground. A bump-
kin was never any match for a professional, and this
redneck Gary Somebody was no real threat. "You gotta
do somethin' about your speakin' style, though. Yes, sir,
you certainly do."

His dismissive words, uttered in contempt, brought a
wave of laughter from his audience, just as Carpenter
intended it should. The politician continued to move
through the crowd, shaking hands and signing autographs
while his aide handed out the pledge cards.

I don't get it, ran through Katie's head. If Carpenter is
a part of all this, then how come Gary went up against
him? Especially in public.

"Bobby!" Gary pushed through the crowd to get through
to Robert Flynn. Flynn stepped to one side so that, when
Gary Simmons caught up with him, the two men were
standing somewhat apart from the crowd around Carpenter.

Katie watched them from a distance. She wanted desperately to go over to them, at least move close enough
to hear what they were saying, but it was too risky. She
couldn't afford to take the chance of exciting Gary's
suspicions, not now, not when she already had so much
to report. If Gary had wanted her in on their conversation, he would have dragged her over by the hand, the
same way he'd dragged her all over the camp. The two of
them were speaking now in low voices; both wore ear-
nest expressions. Between their confidential tones and
the noise the crowd was making, Katie couldn't hear a
word they were saying. For the present, she would have
to be content with the knowledge that there seemed to

be a close connection between Robert Flynn and Gary Simmons.

"Jesus Christ, Bobby!" Gary's voice was husky with anger. "You hadda hitch your wagon to him? What the fuck did you do it for, Bobby? Why, man, why?"

Flynn lowered his voice even further. "Gary, what did I keep on tellin' you, back in Nam? I said to you, 'You're the best point man I ever saw. Stick to it, don't do nothin' else. Let *me* worry about the formation.' Didn't I say that, man? Didn't I?"

But Gary brushed Flynn's words aside. *"Take a look at him, man,"* he said intensely, staring contemptuously at Carpenter, who was patting little kids on the head now. "There ain't nothin' inside, don't you see? What are you gonna do when it hits the fan, when they get him for stealin' money or dickin' some jailbait or—"

"Come on, Gary—" Flynn laid a hand on the other man's arm, but Gary shook it off angrily.

"Take a good look at him, man! He can ruin everything we—"

Flynn scowled a silent warning, and Gary broke off. He reminded himself that they were out in the open and might be overheard by anybody standing nearby. But the rage still burned brightly in his face, and his mouth twisted bitterly.

"You think I'd ever let him do that?" Flynn spoke quietly, firmly, compelling Gary's attention. "I ain't never gonna let nobody do that. You hear me, point?"

Gary Simmons looked away, still not mollified, his rage a wall between them.

"You hear me?" Flynn asked again, more strongly.

At last, Flynn's words broke through Gary's anger. Gary grinned boyishly. "Hey, Bobby. I hear everything, Bobby. I'm the best point you ever saw, right?"

Flynn's expression changed, became distant. "This ain't the war no more. War's over, Gary."

"The fuck it is," answered Gary quietly.

Robert Flynn looked hard at Gary Simmons, then he broke into a smile. "The fuck it is," he agreed.

The last remnant of Gary's anger dried up and blew away. They were on the same side. That was all-important. The two men stood there smiling at each other, old buddies who had been through a dirty war together, who had ahead of them a dirty war still to fight.

Then Flynn grew serious again, and his eyes probed into Gary's. "I know what I'm doin', Gary," he told him. "I always did set up a helluva formation."

"Yeah, you always did, Bobby."

"Gotta go now." And Flynn melted back into the crowd around Jack Carpenter. Carpenter, his mind only on the impression he was making on this crowd, had never even noticed he was gone.

When Gary rejoined Katie, he found her kneeling on the ground beside Rachel, fussing with the little girl's hair where one braid had come loose. Rachel had one arm wrapped tightly around Katie's neck, and the two of them made such a pretty picture of female affection that Gary Simmons just had to smile.

It had been hard enough for Katie to get to a pay phone to place the call to set up the meet, but getting away from Gary to keep her appointment was even harder. It wasn't that he was suspicious of her. No, he was more in love with her than ever, and couldn't stand to let her out of his sight. Katie's superior marksmanship on the practice range had earned her big points with him. Also, the way the kids took to her, following her around, bringing her their little problems, had made a strong impression on his heart.

But at last she managed to make an excuse and slip away for a few hours.

The airport wasn't considered a safe meeting place by daylight. Katie had suggested the Holiday Inn motel on the outskirts of nearby Jefferson, a good hour's drive from Denison. It was there she found Michael, Al Sanders, and the junior agent, Donald Duffin.

On the long drive to the Holiday Inn, Katie went over

and over in her head the sequence of events—what she had witnessed when. She made mental lists of the weapons, tried to recall just how many had attended the camp from how many states—reconstructing license plates and regional accents.

When she got to Jefferson, the other three were already there waiting for her. Catherine Weaver's verbal report astonished her fellow FBI agents. She detailed every word that she had overheard, who'd said what. From the KKK and the burning cross to the army truck filled with stolen weapons to the appearance at the campsite of Jack Carpenter—each event of the two and a half days was chronicled. The only part of the story she omitted—and she wasn't sure why—was her desperate flight through the forest with Wes Bond and his Mac-10 in hot pursuit.

Michael Carnes grew more and more excited as Cathy's report unreeled. This case was the biggest yet! He could already read the national headlines.

"Carpenter's just a straw man. He's not into murder, he's into upward mobility. Gary's right," Michael said. "But New York, San Francisco, L.A., Miami, Chicago, and Atlanta! Jesus!"

" 'Three days after the hit,' that's all I heard," repeated Cathy.

"Yeah, but what hit? Jesus, what the fuck is this? Hits, mortars, rocket launchers, computers, enough machine guns to outfit a fucking division—" Michael's good-looking young face wore a look of perplexity as he tried to form a context for Cathy's information.

"What about Kraus?" asked Sanders.

Cathy's nerves were jangly enough already. "What do you want me to do, go up to him and ask if they killed Kraus?" she demanded, her voice shrill.

"No, I don't want you to do that, girl," Sanders said gently. "You know I don't."

Cathy nodded, too upset and strung out to speak. She had no idea how much fear and emotion she'd had pent up inside her until she'd been able to let out the whole story of the weekend at the camp. The strain she'd been under was considerable, and just to be herself for an hour or two, to reassume her name and identity, left her emotionally drained and physically exhausted. Every muscle in her body ached.

"Hell, yes, they killed Kraus," Michael said quietly. "That's what we gotta get 'em for. Conspiracy for all the other stuff—they'd be out in a year for good behavior." He glanced significantly at Cathy.

Oh, Christ, it's still not enough! she thought. They want to send me back in again. They're not gonna be satisfied until I'm dead and my bullet-riddled hide is stretched out on a barn door, or I'm lying in a wheat field like some damn scarecrow, blown to bits. Out loud, she said, "Wes knows."

Michael whirled on her immediately, his face tense. "What does he know?"

"About me."

"He can't. How could he know?"

"He *knows*, Michael." Cathy's face began to crumple, and she started to shake. "He's all over me!" She tried to light a cigarette, but she was so jittery she couldn't stop her hands from trembling. Al Sanders lit one and handed it to her.

"He's a nutcake," put in the grinning Duffin facetiously. "It's probably his way of showing affection."

"One of these days, friend, I'm going to hit you so hard you won't know what the fuck hit you," Michael grated, barely restraining himself.

"And I'm gonna be right there next to you when you do it," Sanders growled.

Duffin backed off, holding his hands up in a gesture of conciliation. "I'm sorry, I'm sorry. My parents were hippies. They made dumb jokes. It's not my fault."

Smoking furiously, Cathy walked over to the motel-room window and stood there staring out but seeing nothing. Fear had her by the throat. How long would she be able to continue the pretense? Especially with a man like Wes Bond already sniffing at her trail? How long could she continue to pull the wool over Gary Simmons's eyes? It seemed to her that if she went back in now, her exposure would be imminent, and so would be Katie Phillips's death.

Michael Carnes came up behind Cathy and moved the window curtain a fraction of an inch. He could see what Cathy hadn't noticed—the maid who was straightening the room on the opposite side of the motel courtyard.

"She's got to prove herself to them," Duffin insisted to Sanders.

"She has. They trust her."

Cathy turned bitterly on Duffin. "What do you want me to do, kill somebody?" she demanded.

"No," lied Michael, a beat too quickly.

"Not unless you got to," Sanders said. His words had the ring of truth.

Cathy's hand made a despairing gesture. "I didn't join up to kill anyone. You told me I wouldn't have to get . . . dirty. You were lying to me, weren't you? You were using me." Her voice faltered, went flat. "You're still using me," she accused, her eyes on Michael. She felt betrayed and utterly alone in the world.

Michael met her gaze evenly. "You're letting me use you."

The two of them stood face to face, their new antagonism blotting out the memory of their old love. Then Al Sanders spoke quietly, his authoritative voice breaking through the barrier of their confrontation.

"Everybody uses everybody, girl. It just depends what it is we're getting used for. *What it is*—that's all that counts."

Michael turned back to the window. The maid had left the motel room and was walking through the parking lot to the rooms on the other side of the "U," her arms filled with clean sheets. As she passed Katie's pickup truck, she gave it a sharp look, a look that disturbed Michael Carnes.

"Let's find a safe house," he said to Sanders in an undertone. "They could be anywhere."

Al Sanders nodded.

When Catherine Weaver drove off, Michael watched the pickup until he could no longer see it. Maybe he should have told her about the maid. No, a sharp look is hardly a piece of hard evidence. Besides, she was jumpy enough already.

Nobody was following her as Katie pulled out of the parking lot and started through the streets of Jefferson on her way back to Denison and Gary. She checked the rearview mirror a couple of times, but the road behind her was just about empty. She began to relax a little bit. But when she got past the second traffic light and was crossing the intersection, a county sheriff's black-and-white vehicle showed up in her mirror. A sheriff? What the hell? It couldn't be her he wanted.

Katie slowed down a little so the black-and-white could pass her. But the vehicle had no intention of passing. Instead, the siren started up, an electronic scream that shattered the silence, and the revolving lights on top of the car began to blink bright red as the police car speeded up, crowding Katie to the shoulder.

She pulled over and sat waiting, fear and suspicion worrying her insides like a dog chewing on a bone. The car door opened and a uniformed man in mirrored sunglasses came toward her, one hand on his leather holster. It was Gary's friend and cohort Dean.

He seemed to be surprised to see her. "What you doin' out here, Katie?"

Trying not to show her nervousness, Katie flashed him a smile. "Just some shoppin'. I gotta go, Dean. I gotta cook dinn—"

"There ain't no stores out here," Dean pointed out. "There ain't nothin' here 'cept the motel."

Katie thought fast. "I was down at the motel, Dean, screwin' my brains out with Lyle, okay?" she told him deadpan.

"Lyle?" Dean looked puzzled. It took a minute for the joke to sink in, but when he finally got it, he roared with laughter. "Lyle!"

Katie laughed, too, although to her ears the laughter was as phony as an eight-dollar bill. But thank the Lord for small favors, that dumb-ass Dean thought it was funny. Stepping on the gas, she got the hell out of there.

Still chuckling, Dean headed back to his black-and-white. As he did, the rental car with Sanders, Duffin, and Michael in it sped past him, the men looking grim-faced. Three strangers in suits; didn't see a lot of that in this part of the world. Dean looked after them curiously. Now what the hell?

Katie took the grocery bags out of the pickup and made her way with difficulty through the front door, propping it open with one knee. Gary was in the kitchen setting the big round table for dinner. "Where'd you go?" he asked her testily.

Katie hustled into the kitchen to put the bags down. She started pulling things out of the bags hastily, to mask her nervousness and give herself a chance to think of a cover story. "I went down to the mall over in Cloverdale," she said. "I told you I hadda go shoppin'."

Gary scowled. "You didn't tell me you was goin' to be out all day." It was clear that he was furious with her.

Careful, she warned herself. Don't let him sense your fear. She whirled on him, feigning anger. "I don't have to tell you how long I'm gonna be out! Don't crowd me, okay!" Katie glared at him, breathing hard.

"You're a fuckin' wildcat, that's what you are." Gary grinned, and the tension between them was broken.

"I got you a surprise," Katie said, pretending that her good humor was now restored. Outside, she was smiling; inside, she was trembling with relief.

"What'd you get me?"

Katie shook her head teasingly. "Uh-uh. Now you're not gonna get it."

Gary made an "awww" face and reached for her, but Katie slipped away and shook a mock-angry finger at him. "You put the forks in the wrong place!"

"Well, fuck me!" Gary reached out for Katie again, and again she evaded him.

"Later," she promised. "If you're good."

The children were in bed, asleep. The dinner dishes and pots and pans had been washed and scoured and returned to the kitchen shelves. The kitchen floor was just about swept clean. Katie put the broom and dustpan away, and went to take a shower.

When she emerged from the bathroom, clean and perfumed and wrapped in a bathrobe, Gary was sitting in front of his computer. Katie came and stood behind him, reading the screen over his shoulder. On it was a series of work commands and completion reports.

RECON SICKAGO TRAFFIC PATTERN.

—WILL DO.

ONSITE SURVEILLANCE CONTINUE.

—WILL DO.

LIAISON JEW ENGLAND REGIONAL.

—LIASION COMPLETED.

MANPOWER CENTRAL ASSIGNMENTS.

—ASSIGNMENTS COMPLETED.

"What are you doin'?" Katie asked.

Gary glanced up at her. "I ain't gonna tell you 'less you tell me what *you* were doin' . . . all afternoon."

THE WIND IS STARTING TO BLOW, the screen read. SUMMER LIGHTNING.

Suddenly frightened, Katie backed off, biting her lip. "I *told* you, I was—"

"I'm teasin' you, Katie," Gary interrupted, grinning at her affectionately. Her body was temptingly outlined under the thin robe. "You're sure lookin' pretty," he told her, his voice thick with passion.

"Do you wanna see your surprise?" Katie asked, cocking her eyebrow at him flirtatiously. She slipped the robe

off and struck a provocative pose. She was wearing a
black nightgown, lacy, bare, and clinging. It was the
epitome of female sexuality.

Gary took one sharp look at her and turned his head
away, scowling. Disapproval was written on every fea-
ture of his face.

"I thought you'd like it," said Katie, surprised.

"You don't have to dress up like a ten-dollar whoor,"
he told her sharply.

"What?" Katie gasped, astonished. She couldn't believe he'd said that to her. Nobody had ever spoken to
her that way in her life.

"You look like a whoor," replied Gary stubbornly. He
kept his face averted, as though one look at her would
turn him to stone. This was the man who couldn't get
enough of seeing her naked, but put a piece of black
lingerie on the same body, and it becomes suddenly
obscene. Katie had never encountered this mindset before, and she was surprised at the depth of the hurt it
caused her. Although it suited her purposes to *look* pained,
she actually *was* pained.

"I'm . . . not . . . a whoor," she stammered, her eyes
filling with tears.

"Then don't dress up like one," Gary said shortly, and
marched into the bathroom. When he came out, Katie
was dressed again in the old bathrobe she wore, and it
made him breathe easier. From the look on her face he
could tell she was still pretty upset.

Gary went over and put his arm around her, but Katie
held herself stiffly, not moving closer.

"I'm sorry," he murmured into her neck. "I got a lot
of pressure on me."

But Katie still kept her distance from him, saying
nothing.

"I got a job to do next week."

Still no reaction.

"I gotta stick up a bank."

That did it. Katie turned to stare at him. Was he

serious, or only joking? No, he was kidding around; just look at him laughing. Asshole. She turned away again, miffed.

Gary kissed Katie's shoulder. "You wanna come?" he asked.

Again she turned to look at him. He was still smiling at her, but in his dark blue eyes there was a look that told Katie Phillips that this was no joke. Gary Simmons meant every word of it. He was going to stick up a bank.

Chapter Thirteen

The Bank

As Gary Simmons unfolded the plan for the daring daylight robbery of the Union National Bank in Chicago, Katie sat astonished. She had to give him credit for the thoroughness of the preparations. This plan had to be weeks if not months in the making; Gary had the smallest detail figured out, and apparently all contingencies had been covered in advance. He knew the right time of day for the traffic pattern they needed for the getaway; he knew how many bank guards would be on duty and the kind of weapons they carried—Smith & Wesson .38 police specials.

The five of them were in Gary's living room. Shorty, Wes, Dean, and Katie listened carefully while Gary briefed them on the parts they'd be expected to play in the robbery. For the sake of security, Rachel and Joey had been sent over to Mrs. Simmons's house for the day.

"We park the van here, on DeKalb Street," said Gary, pointing to the location on the Chicago street map that lay spread out on the coffee table.

"What about the others?" Shorty Richards wanted to know.

"We'll meet 'em at the garage, they'll be ready." Gary walked over to the wall on which he'd pinned floor plans and glossy enlarged photographs of the bank's interior and exterior. "We go in here," Gary said, indicating the front door on one of the photos. "There's a guard here. Wes, you take him—I'll get this one." He broke into a confident smile, obviously enjoying this. Gary Simmons was a man of action, not talk, and it had chafed him to be sitting still all this time.

But now the winds of change were starting to blow. Operation Summer Lightning was past the planning stage and into the action phase. That's what made Gary smile.

"Nothin' to it," he continued. "We just go in like Wild Bill Hickok, stick 'em up, maybe we ain't gonna have to do no shootin'."

"What if we do?" Katie asked quietly.

"Then we do."

Wes Bond uttered a small snort of contempt. "She ain't gonna shoot nobody."

"She will if she has to," Gary replied. Everybody turned to look at Katie, who kept her face an impassive mask over a wildly beating pulse.

"You scared?" Gary asked her gently.

"What do you want *me* there for?" Katie demanded.

"You got a better eye 'n I do."

But Katie shook her head. "That ain't the reason." She knew the reason. This was to be Gary Simmons's ultimate test of Katie Phillips.

"It's reason enough," said Gary.

Katie stood up. "I'm gonna get the kids," she said.

"Mom's gonna bring 'em," Gary protested.

"I'll save her the trip," Katie said coldly, and walked out of the living room, out the kitchen door, and climbed into her pickup.

For a long moment nobody said anything. Wes's eyes narrowed; this was just what he'd been expecting. He looked at Gary questioningly. After hesitating a fraction of a second, Gary nodded his okay, and Wes left the room to follow Katie.

He took his pickup, driving slowly, searching both sides of the road. He kept well back, because he didn't want Katie to suspect she was being followed. After a few minutes, Wes found Katie's truck parked by a roadside phone booth, and Katie herself was inside, talking on the telephone.

Wes pulled off the road about a hundred yards away, in the shadow of a grove of trees, so that he could watch without being seen. A thin smile of triumph played around his lips and his pale blue eyes lit up with icy joy. He'd waited a long, long time for this moment. Caught her in the act, the bitch! He didn't know who she was talking to, but he knew what she must be saying. Passing along their secret plans to whatever Jew organization she was working for. So he'd been right about her all along. She *was* a grasshopper. She wouldn't think twice about betraying Gary and the rest of them, betraying the cause they were fighting for, a cause she only pretended to believe in.

Gary wasn't going to like hearing this, but it was time he took his head out of his ass where that cunt was concerned. Time he knew the score. If it was up to him, Wes, he'd have shot her down that first night in the woods, when they'd killed the nigger. But Gary hadn't let him; Gary hadn't believed him when he'd seen her spying on them in the camp. Should've killed her then, but the bitch was too damn fast for him. Well, now he had her cold.

Gary was sitting in front of the television set, a drink in his hand, when Katie walked in with Rachel and Joey. Rachel came running over for her kiss.

"Hi, Daddy!"

"Hi," he answered flatly, and there was no kiss. "Who'd you call?" he demanded of Katie.

Katie stood stock still, rooted to the spot. "When?"

"On the way to Mom's—who did you call?"

"You followed me? Is that what you did? You followed me?" She masked her sudden choking fear with the old pretense of indignation.

But this time her frontal attack didn't work. Gary got up from the couch, and his face was terrible in its anger. "Who the fuck did you call?" he roared.

Rachel and Joey came running out of the kitchen, wide-eyed with surprise and anxiety. Their father turned

on them, violence written across his features. "Go to
your room! Go!" he shouted, and the kids scattered like
terrified mice, scrambling for the stairs. Now he turned
back to Katie.

"Tell me!"

Katie stood looking at him, deeply afraid of his anger.
In the calmest voice she could muster, she said, "I called
your mom. I told her I was coming over."

Gary slammed his drink on the table and went to the
telephone to dial. Katie watched him, frozen, as he spoke
on the phone.

"Mom, did Katie call you before she picked the kids
up?" He listened for a few seconds, then, in a much
softer tone, said, "Thanks, Mom," and put the receiver
back on its cradle. His face, as he turned back to Katie,
was a mixture of relief and shame. He didn't know what
to say to her, how to apologize. He held his hand out,
but she ignored it and went running up the stairs.

God, he felt like shit, being so suspicious of her and
all. He'd break that goddamn Wes Bond's neck one of
these days. That bastard was always trashing Katie, just
because he hated women in general and Katie Phillips in
particular.

Meanwhile, in the bathroom upstairs with the door
closed, Katie Phillips was pulling herself together, washing her face with cold water and thanking God she'd had
the presence of mind to make the cover call to Gladys
Simmons after she'd gotten off the phone with Michael.
And she thanked God that Wes—she presumed it had
been Wes who'd followed her—hadn't been near enough
to her to see her make two calls. But that was a close
one.

The bank robbery would be a closer call, though.
Because the feds would be waiting for them when they
got there. Katie hoped that in all the excitement, she
could melt into the crowd and escape with her life. Then
and only then would this endless nightmare of violence
finally be over for her. She would have done her job, and
done it well. She would have handed over to the FBI a

group of armed robbers and conspirators, caught right in the damn act! They *couldn't* ask her for any more, not even Michael with all his ambition and his goddamned self-righteousness.

Yes, the nightmare would be over for her . . . *if* she could come out of it alive.

Downstairs, Gary Simmons could only sit and wait, hoping that Katie would come back down and forgive him. But he couldn't blame her if she didn't, if she never talked to him again. He'd acted like a real asshole. Glumly, Gary picked up his drink and slumped down in front of the TV set, only one eye on the CBS news. Dan Rather was talking about something or other.

". . . where a federal grand jury has been convened to investigate independent presidential candidate Jack Carpenter for alleged misappropriation of campaign funds."

Carpenter! Gary sat riveted to the screen. That mealy-mouthed hypocritical son-of-a-bitch! That puke-faced bastard! Gary *knew* this was going to happen, this or something exactly like it. Didn't he tell Bobby Flynn that, just a couple of days ago? Why the fuck wouldn't Bobby listen? Look, there was Flynn now, keeping to the background as that ass-kisser faced the cameras, still flashing that famous sixty-four-toothed smile.

"I think it shows that some people are being made very nervous by my candidacy," Carpenter was saying into a battery of microphones being thrust into his face. "I've done nothing wrong. They'll obviously do anything to stop me."

What a load of media-manipulating horseshit, Gary thought bitterly. Are they blind? Can't they see right through that fucker? There ain't one honest bone in that asshole's entire body. Well, the winds of change were starting to blow, and the summer lightning would soon be splitting the sky. And it would all come down. *Then* they'd see. *Then* they'd know. *Then* the eyes of the world would be opened for the first time in history. Shitheels like Jack Carpenter wouldn't be a part of it, while patri-

otic Americans like Gary Simmons would have their true
worth recognized at last.

They'd been driving on the toll road for hours, and
had already passed Iowa City. Road signs for Chicago
were starting to show up by the time they reached Mo-
line. Katie sat as far as possible from Gary on the front
seat of the Jeep. Her face showed her anger, and they'd
hardly spoken a word since they left Denison.

"You're still testing me, aren't you?" she demanded.

His eyes fixed on I-80, Gary didn't answer.

"Why can't you just believe that I love you?"

They'd had this argument over an early breakfast, and
Gary had other things on his mind. "Wes thinks they're
gonna be waiting for us inside that bank," he said shortly.

"What do *you* think, Gary?" asked Katie. She turned
to look at him, her eyes anxiously scanning his face.

"I think he's paranoid."

Katie settled back down in her seat, but she was far
from easy in her mind. Gary might trust her, but Wes
was still convinced that she was an informer, a plant, a
betrayer. And he was right. They *would* be waiting for
them inside that bank, and she knew that Wes Bond
would have his eye on Katie Phillips, and his trigger
finger would be goddamn itchy. Also, suppose Gary was
lying to her? Suppose he didn't trust her, either, and was
only going along with the pretense until he and Wes had
her in a pincer trap?

Don't think about it, she told herself. Just keep your
eyes and ears open and your ass covered. If you can.

They reached Chicago by midafternoon and drove to a
garage on the South Side. It was the agreed-upon meeting place. Wes, Dean, and Shorty were already there
waiting, along with two other men Katie had never seen
before. One of them, an older man, perhaps in his middle fifties, was wearing glasses. The other was in his
thirties, "with no distinguishing marks," according to the
language of law enforcement. They were dressed in full
suits of camos and combat boots.

In the garage was an unmarked van, large enough to carry them all. Shorty climbed into the driver's seat, and the others began to file in the back. There was a stack of automatic weapons on the floor of the van. Katie counted them silently. One Mac-10 for each of them, her included.

"You boys know Chicago?" asked Gary.

"I've been here once before," said the older man. "I'm from Boston." He pronounced it "BAH-ston."

"Hell, no, Ah'm from Tallahassee," the younger man said in a deep southern drawl.

Gary smiled. "Well, we been here once or twice, right, Shorty?"

Shorty Richards uttered a harsh, knowing laugh and Katie froze inside. Dan Kraus! It was Shorty with Gary, then. I would have sworn Wes. But Shorty! God, I've been so damn naïve. There's nobody you can trust, nobody. Every last man of them is a killer.

Traffic was heavy and the van moved slowly through the Chicago streets. Just as well, they didn't want suspicious cops nosing around them. The time for speed was the getaway. There were two benches along the sides of the van, and they sat facing each other, like skydivers waiting for the word to jump. Katie found herself sitting next to Wes, and it made her damn nervous. Was it just a coincidence, or was he bird-dogging her? He was already armed with his Mac-10; did he sleep with the goddamn thing?

"You know somethin'?" Gary asked suddenly. "My great-granddad, he used to rob stagecoaches."

The men laughed appreciatively, but Katie just sat there, her face a mask.

"*My* great-granddad was the town marshal," said Shorty, and this evoked an even bigger laugh.

"Mine was a banker," offered the middle-aged Bostonian. "Matter of fact, I manage a bank myself." And this drew the biggest laugh of all.

They were coming close to the Union National Bank now; it was only a couple of blocks away. Gary began handing out the Mac-10s and the stocking masks. They all pulled the stockings down over their heads, masking their faces, distorting their identifiable features, yet allowing them to breathe and see.

The unmarked van pulled up to the bank. Katie's shoulders were so tense that her stiff neck cried out for mercy.

"The wind is starting to blow," said the Tallahasseean quietly.

Katie snuck a look at Wes Bond. He was staring at her with those chilly pale blue eyes, and he had a rigid grin on his face that told her this would be make-or-break time for her. Katie said a quick silent prayer, which was odd, because Catherine Weaver wasn't the praying type.

"Let's do it to it," Gary said, and the van doors burst open. The men ran quickly out into the street, guns drawn, and charged into the bank at full speed. A fraction more slowly, Katie brought up the rear.

The bank was crowded with people, midday shoppers and office workers cashing checks. When the masked gang came hurtling through the door, immediate pandemonium followed. Screams tore the air as terrified men and women scrambled for the door. But the mild-mannered man from Boston had the front door covered. Grinning wolfishly, he menaced the shrieking customers with his Mac-10, and Katie could see he was just itching to use it.

Wes tackled the nearest guard, slamming him hard in the small of his back with the butt of his Mac-10 and bringing him crashing down to the floor. The second guard went for his gun, but before he could draw his weapon from its holster, Gary Simmons raced across the bank.

"You're dead!" he shouted.

The guard froze in fear, and in that split second, Gary was on him, knocking him down with a vicious blow from the barrel of his machine gun. The man slumped moaning to the floor, and lay still.

"Everybody down! Everybody down!" Gary yelled.

Like sheep when the sheepdog barks, the customers

obeyed, lying face down on the floor, praying silently that they wouldn't be killed. Many of them wept with fear, muffling their sobs in order not to irritate the robbers.

The whole invasion, including the downing of the two bank guards and the quelling of the customers, took no more than perhaps twenty seconds. But to Katie it was a nightmare scene played in slow motion; it was as though hours had gone by. She watched the scene unreel, standing numbly by a wall near the emergency door to the stairwell, her Mac-10 in her hands. She was playing her part, covering everyone, but she kept looking around for the FBI. She kept expecting to see Michael appear at any moment; where the hell were they? Near her Wes stood with his weapon poised to fire, and Katie was conscious of his suspicious eyes.

Suddenly the stairwell door behind Katie opened, and another uniformed bank guard appeared in it. He was armed; his gun was drawn, and it was pointing straight at Katie.

The guard's eyes locked onto Katie's, and she knew with the most awful certainty that he would shoot, and that in less than a moment she'd be lying dead with a bullet in her heart or her brain. Almost unthinkingly, she raised her weapon and aimed, pulled the trigger of the Mac-10, and fired a burst. At the sound of the sudden gunfire, the customers on the floor screamed in terror.

The bullets caught the guard full in the body; the impact flung him backward against a wall. He crumpled to the floor, bleeding. Katie froze to the spot, a look of disbelief on her face.

I killed a man! Oh, my God, I killed a man! The words ran over and over in her head. She couldn't think of anything else. She would never forget the look on the guard's face as the bullets tore into him. He looked surprised—no, amazed—as though this could not be happening. It was the way Katie felt. This couldn't be happening. Why was it happening? Where was the Bureau? Where was Michael?

Meanwhile, Wes and Gary had gone for the cash while

Dean and the two new men covered them, their guns trained on everybody who was lying on the floor. Gary and Wes leaped over the tellers' counter and began stuffing bank bags full of bills. Only a few seconds later, they hurled themselves back over the counter, the bags filled.

Now they all started backing toward the door, guns still aimed, ready for the getaway. All except Katie, who stood paralyzed, still staring numbly at the man she'd shot. Gary grabbed her hand, pulling hard, and she took a few stumbling steps backward with him.

"Git down!" Gary roared, firing a warning burst over the heads of the customers, making them press their faces even more tightly against the bank floor.

And then they were out in the street, all of them, and racing for the van, where Shorty had the motor running. The entire robbery from start to finish—including the pistol whipping of the two bank guards and Katie's gunning down the third—had taken less than three minutes.

They scrambled in—first the man from Tallahassee, then the Bostonian, next Dean. Gary pushed the still-trembling Katie into the vehicle and jumped in himself. Wes was the last to reach the van.

Suddenly, as though out of nowhere, a uniformed bank guard appeared on the bank steps, his pistol drawn, firing at Wes. The guard was a black man. Katie's eyes widened in astonishment as she recognized him. It was Al Sanders.

One of the bullets caught Wes in the neck, and he started to fall to the pavement, but Gary and Dean caught him, dragging him into the van as Shorty gunned the motor. The van sped away, hurtling through traffic.

Wes was bleeding copiously; Sanders's bullet had hit an artery. There was blood everywhere—on the floor and walls of the van, and down the front of Gary's camos as he cradled Wes in his arms. Some had splashed onto Katie's face and hair.

"Jesus fuckin' Christ!" yelled Dean, coming unglued as he looked at the dying man.

"Shut the fuck up!" Gary growled furiously. His best

friend was dying in his arms, dying without a last word, just like Nam. Somebody would have to pay.

It was over. Wes Bond was dead. Katie's thoughts went racing wildly. Why? Why hadn't the FBI stopped the robbery? They were there—Sanders was there. Why shoot one man and let the others get away? What went wrong? What's going on?

Gary looked up from the body of his friend. His face was white with sorrow and anger, and tears glistened unshed in his eyes.

"They was only supposed to have two guards!" he said, and Katie could see that this was a fact he wasn't going to let go of. She said nothing.

But Dean's eyes were narrowed in thought. "I know that nigger from someplace," he said with conviction. "I seen him somewhere. I seen him."

"They all look alike." The Boston bank manager dismissed Dean's words.

But Gary didn't. He looked hard at Dean, filing yet another fact away until later.

By now they'd reached the garage where their cars were waiting. Shorty and Dean carried Wes's lifeless, still-bleeding body out of the van toward Shorty's car. The two strangers had already driven off. Katie moved automatically toward Gary's Jeep Cherokee.

"Go!" he told her.

She stopped, confused.

"I'm gonna go with Shorty," Gary said gently. "I'll see you tomorrow. Drive out in the Jeep tomorrow." He came up to Katie and gave her a strong hug. "You did good. You're the best there is." Then he turned away, catching up with Shorty and Dean. Katie stood staring after him. This might be the last time she'd ever have to see him, at least until the trial. Oh, God, she hoped so.

Catherine Weaver let herself into her apartment near the marina. She stood inside the doorway, a stranger in her own home, a dirty, sweaty girl in faded khakis and jeans. It was a long time before she was able to leave the foyer and enter the living room, and then she moved slowly, like a sleepwalker, somebody in a dream. Did she ever actually live here, with these plants and these bright posters and this comfortable furniture? Was there really a Catherine Weaver who listened to music and read books in this pretty apartment?

Or was *that* the dream? Was the reality the bank guard bleeding on the floor?

Cathy roused herself; she had to get out of these clothes. She desperately needed to bathe. She needed a drink—several drinks, in fact.

She walked into her large, well-lighted bathroom, where dark green ferns grew profusely in the humidity. When she'd turned the shower on, adjusting the temperature of the water as hot as she could stand it, Cathy took a look at herself in the mirror. For the first time she noticed the blood on her face, the dried blood matting her hair. Wes's blood. He was dead and she was alive. And it was finished, finally and forever. Now she'd never have to go back there. Now all she had to do was to try and recover from the shock and the horror.

Cathy was sitting in a chair, smoking, her hair still wet from the shower, when she heard the key turn in the lock. The door opened and Michael Carnes walked in, his face creased with worry.

Lifting her glass, Cathy took a deep swallow of Jack Daniel's. Outside her window, the long dusk of a summer's evening was darkening into nightfall. She looked at Michael, said nothing.

"I've still got my key," Michael said.

"How is he?" asked Cathy in a dull voice.

"Who?"

"The guard. Is he dead?"

"He's okay. He made it through surgery."

Cathy stubbed her cigarette out with agitated fingers. "My God, Michael! I shot—"

"You had to," Michael interrupted, his voice hard and cold. "He was going to kill you. It was self-defense. You were protecting yourself. It was self-defense."

Self-defense. Isn't that what Gary kept telling her? You had to kill Jews and niggers because you had to defend yourself. Dear God, is that to become the excuse for every rotten thing in the world? That it's only in self-defense?

"He was an innocent," Cathy protested. "He was just a guard—"

"He got caught in the cross fire," Michael snapped. "I'm sorry, Cathy. It happens."

"Where *were* you, Michael? Where the hell *were* you?" Her voice rose despite her efforts to control it.

Michael looked at her for a minute, as though deciding what to tell her, how much she had the right to know. At last he said in a low voice, "We decided to let it happen."

At Cathy's gasp of disbelief, he added defensively, "We didn't want them for the bank robbery. We want them for whatever they're gonna do with the money. We've got to find out what they're gonna do with the money."

His words were like a blow to Cathy's solar plexus; they knocked the wind right out of her. So it wasn't over. So she was going to have to go back again, and again, and again, until finally it would end when she was dead. They were just going to turn their backs on her and let her hang there, twisting slowly in the wind.

"Goddamn you, Michael!" she shouted. "Goddamn you!"

Michael brought his face very near to Cathy's, to let her see his intensity up close. "Listen to me." He bit his words off one by one. "There were five other bank heists just like that one around the country today. New York. Miami. Atlanta. L.A. San Francisco. Just like you told us. We've got a total take of around three-point-two million dollars. Christ, they're putting together a war chest!"

Cathy stood up and walked away from him, going to stand by the window with her back to him. He could tell by the exhausted droop of her shoulders that she'd heard every word. He waited for her reaction.

"What about Wes?" she asked at last.

"What *about* Wes? You said he was on to you. I didn't want to risk it. The guy was a scumbag, Cathy. So we took him out, so what?"

"You killed him—for me." It wasn't a question.

"Yes, we did." Michael's chin lifted in defiance. "What the fuck does it matter? The world's a better place."

She turned around and stared at him as though she'd never seen him before. She didn't know this man, this callous man who looked like Michael, but whose attitude toward a death was that the world is a better place. That wasn't Michael. She'd once cared for Michael. But it was Michael, and he hadn't really changed. Cathy Weaver was the one who'd changed.

"I've had enough," she told him coldly. "I'm getting out, Michael."

"Great! Get out! Forget Kraus, forget their hunts. Forget the hit they're going to do. Forget whatever the hell it is they're planning. And, while you're at it, forget the bank guard you shot, Cathy."

It was the lowest possible blow, meant to bring Catherine Weaver to her knees. Cathy felt her knees buckling under her, and she forced herself not to sway or hold on to anything. She felt totally betrayed, betrayed and abandoned.

"What about *me*, Michael? What about *me*?" she cried out.

"You can put a stop to all of it."

"I said *me*!" Cathy's large hazel eyes were distraught, haunted.

Michael looked steadily at her. "I care a great deal about you. You know I do."

Cathy shook her head wildly. "I don't think you do. I don't think you ever did."

Now Michael was incensed. "You ended us, Cathy. I didn't."

"It was self-defense," said Cathy brutally, and it felt good to fling Michael's words back in his teeth. Just a small satisfaction, but it felt good.

Michael winced visibly, but he held his ground. Al Sanders, wearing street clothes and not the bank guard's uniform, walked into the apartment.

"How do you feel about dropping that piece of shit, Al?" Michael asked him with a tight smile, his eyes on Cathy.

"Terrific," Sanders answered. "Like cleanin' somethin' off my shoe."

The two men turned to Cathy, and she could read her destiny in the cold mirrors of their eyes. Katie was going in again.

Chapter Fourteen

Winds of Change

Early the next day, Katie pulled up to the Simmons farmhouse in Gary's Jeep Cherokee. Before she could get out, Rachel came running through the front door to throw herself on Katie, hugging hard.

"I missed you! I didn't think you were *ever* coming back!"

Katie leaned over the steering wheel to put her arms around the little girl's shoulders. "I always think about you," she told the child. "I'm always gonna think about you, Rachel. I love you."

"Bushels and barrels and stuff?" Rachel smiled, happy that Katie was home again.

"Bushels and barrels and stuff," Katie echoed solemnly.

It was true. What had begun as a pretense had turned to pity for the way the child's mind was being mercilessly manipulated. Pity had changed to attachment, and attachment to love.

With her hand in Rachel's, Katie got out of the Jeep and looked around at the farmyard. It was so hard to picture this place as harboring secret evil. Ronnie the German shepherd came running across the yard, barking happily at the sight of her. The sky was a deep blue, almost the color of the violets that grow shyly by the wayside. In the yard near the barn, the idle tractors were painted a cheerful red, some plump chickens and a couple of geese were pecking the ground, hopeful for a stray kernel of corn. The stable smelled sweetly of hay. The thought that the Simmons homestead was the epicenter of a murderous conspiracy was mind-blowing. Damn it, this was heartland America, not Nazi Germany! This farm was a place for children to play and grownups to do an honest day's labor. The situation now seemed to Katie totally unreal.

But it was real, really evil, really deadly. And, caught in the middle, two innocent children, already indoctrinated, their baby minds already filthy with the hatred and bigotry that had been drilled into them.

Rachel. Joey. Two kids Katie loved. As she held tight to Rachel, Katie's mind shied away from thinking about what she had to do to Rachel's father.

Gary didn't come home all day, nor did he turn up for supper. Katie fed Rachel and Joey and put them to bed, then sat up for a while watching television. The eleven o'clock news was electric with accounts of the daring robberies that had taken place the day before around the country. Some newscasters reported them as separate coincidences; others supposed that they were linked, the work of a large gang of professional bank robbers. Nobody was even close to the truth, and Katie knew that the FBI must have released a smoke screen to keep the media in the dark.

After the news, she went to bed. But she had no intention of falling asleep. She was waiting for Gary Simmons. There was a chance now that Katie might be in a position to force some more information out of Gary; her shooting the guard had given her that right. But she had to play it very smart. Katie had no illusions about her power over Gary. It was still a delicate matter, still touch and go, risky business. She'd have to be a very good actress to convince him.

When Gary returned, he found Katie lying in bed staring at the ceiling, a distant look on her lovely face. He tried to catch her eye with no success, so he went to sit beside her on the bed. With gentle fingers, he stroked her face, but Katie kept refusing to look at him. She wanted to show him how angry she was, how used she felt. If she could stimulate his sense of guilt, she might get something out of him. If he *had* a sense of guilt.

"It's rough the first time, I know it is," he told her softly, trying to get her to turn her face to him. But Katie resisted, looking stonily upward.

"You got a natural instinct for it," he told her.

"No."

"Yeah, you do."

"No, I don't." Agitated, Katie got out of bed, facing him from across the room, with the bed between them.

"I know you—"

"*No!* I *don't*!" There was no mistaking how upset she was, how jangled her emotions. "What did we do it for?" she demanded.

"What?" Gary stared at her blankly.

"What the hell did we do it for?" Katie was practically sobbing. "What did we rob a bank for? What did I shoot somebody for?"

Gary flinched under the barrage of Katie's questions and attempted to soothe her. "You're upset. It's natural—" he began, but Katie interrupted him. It sounded to Gary like she was on the verge of hysteria.

"*Tell me,* goddamn it, Gary. What did we do it for? Who's gonna get the money?"

"Friends of ours," Gary answered reluctantly. He understood that he owed her some kind of explanation, but he had to pick his words very carefully because she wasn't cleared to know anything vital.

"What friends?" Katie's tone brooked no denial.

"Friends." He walked around the bed and tried to embrace her, but she pulled away from him vehemently.

"What are they gonna do with it?" she demanded, and when Gary didn't answer, she yelled, *"Tell me!"*

Gary lost control of himself. "They're gonna rebuild this country," he shouted back. "This whole, dirty, shit-smeared country. We're gonna put the stars and stripes back into it. All we need is a leader. All we need is one man who—" He broke off, suddenly conscious that he'd already said too much.

Seeing Katie staring at him in disbelief, Gary brought himself back under control. "We did it for us, Katie," he told her in a much calmer voice. "For the kids. 'Cause we care about this country even if nobody else does." Now his grin broke out. "Shit, we're Americans. There's still a few of us good guys left, ridin' the range."

Katie didn't return Gary's smile. Sitting down on the edge of the bed, she kept her face turned away from him. It seemed to Gary that she was determined to give him a hard time, and he reckoned that she was entitled to it. But he needed her, didn't she see that? He'd just lost the best friend he had in the world, and he needed his woman for comfort. Damn it, men sometimes need some comfort, too.

"We buried Wes," he said quietly.

Katie said nothing. Alive or dead, Wes Bond was not her topic of choice. Hadn't he wanted to shoot her that night on the hunt? Gary read her thought from the stiff posture of her back, still turned to him.

"He was sure wrong about you," he acknowledged.

And now Katie Phillips turned to look him in the face, and he could read love in her eyes. "You got back early," she murmured.

Gary smiled. "I was in a hurry," he said, and took Katie in his arms to get the comfort she knew how to give.

Katie dressed up for the harvest dance. In that small suitcase she'd brought with her when she moved into Gary Simmons's house was one dress, a long prairie-skirted kind of calico, a real country dress, printed all over with flowers. With her long hair pulled back off her face and caught up in a ribbon, she looked like a sun-drenched farm girl from the turn of the century.

Gary was looking fine, too, in a fancy western shirt with embroidered yoke and mother-of-pearl snap buttons. Pushed back on his head was a broad-brimmed

Stetson. He was conscious of how good the two of them looked together, dancing close to the country-and-western music, Gary muscular and handsome, Katie slender and pretty.

Katie was also conscious of the way they must appear to others, two healthy and beautiful American young people, what a great couple they made! One of them was an undercover FBI agent, the other a bank robber, an assassin, a conspirator. If it weren't so horrible, it would be almost laughable. Almost.

Near them, dressed in their Sunday clothes and dancing together with the solemn formality of self-conscious children, were Rachel and Joey. A dance platform had been set up in the center of the Denison town square, and the local pickup band—guitar, fiddle, banjo, harmonica, and drums—played old favorite two-steps and waltzes.

Gary hummed happily along with the music and pulled Katie closer for a light kiss.

"No smooching!" yelled Rachel sternly.

"Gross!" Joey disapproved.

Katie and Gary laughed and went on dancing, with Gary's cheek pressed against the dark fragrance of Katie's hair.

"I love this place," he said into her ear. "It could be so good again for Rachel and Joey—just like it was for me when I was little. We're gonna make it good for them again, ain't we, Katie? Ain't we?"

"Yes," she lied.

"Yes!" Gary yelled happily. "Hell, yes! Yes we are. Marry me."

Stunned, Katie stopped dancing, pulling away from Gary and avoiding his eyes. This was a new development.

"Will you marry me?" Gary asked again, seriously.

Katie didn't know what to say; Gary's proposal had caught her completely off guard, and she didn't have anything prepared. What would Katie Phillips do? wondered Catherine Weaver.

"You don't have to tell me right away, Katie. Take your time and think about it. But say yes."

* * *

Once again, they assembled in Gary's house to be briefed on the next operation—the conspirators, Katie, Shorty, Dean. Only Wes was missing. This time, the job was bigger . . . much bigger. And a lot more dangerous.

Gary had spread out nearly everything on the table, the blueprints and the maps, while the glossies were again pinned to the wall. Katie drank in every word, because this was what she'd been waiting for. The winds of change starting to blow. Operation Summer Lightning. Everything was falling into place.

Outside, the children were playing some game noisily in the yard and Ronnie ran around them, barking loudly with hysterical joy. Summer was the dog's favorite time, when the Simmons kids were home from school and ready for games.

"This is the power plant here—" Gary pointed to the map. "They've got three guards, twenty-four hours a day. We knock this off, it kills all the lights in Jew York City."

"What the hell's *that* gonna prove?" demanded Dean.

But Gary didn't bother to answer; he continued with the agenda. "We're gonna have ten men go into Harlem, dressed up as cops, and start shootin' the niggers."

"Hot damn!" yelled Dean. "That's what *I* wanna do. That's fun."

Gary ignored the interruption. "The niggers are gonna riot. In L.A., we're gonna have guys torch the gasoline in the sewer lines. San Francisco, we're gonna blow the bridges. Detroit, we're gonna blow the school buses outta the yards. Chicago, we're gonna put four tanks of cyanide in the water supply."

Katie sat silent, aghast. This was the largest-scale terror operation ever conceived. If these conspirators were only one quarter as successful as they expected to be, America would be brought to her knees. The loss of life and destruction of property would be incalculable. Remembering the military precision with which the bank robbery had been executed, while at the same time duplicates of the same operation had taken place successfully all over the country, Katie's heart sank in her breast. Whoever was behind this plot had skill and cunning. And men and money and matériel, she added silently, recalling the hardware she'd seen at the camp.

Now she knew what they'd be doing with those automatic weapons, those rocket launchers and mortars. Taking over America. But who were they? Who was behind all this? Smart as he was, Gary Simmons couldn't set up a plan like this. It was too complicated, too ambitious. No, he was following orders from higher-ups, and Katie felt as far away from the answers as ever. Still, this was information she had to get to Michael Carnes and Al Sanders immediately. Things were already starting to happen.

The briefing over, they all walked out into the Simmons farmyard, where Shorty's pickup was parked.

"This country ain't gonna know what the hell happened." Dean laughed coarsely, impatient for the fun to begin.

"Mother of shit!" Shorty yelled suddenly, as something he'd forgotten, something important, occurred to him. "What about the hit?"

"We do the hit three days before, that's what's gonna set it off," answered Gary.

"Who's the target?" Shorty wanted to know.

But Gary merely smiled; that was top-secret information.

"Who's gonna do it?" Katie asked.

Gary stopped walking and looked at her. "You and me," he said softly.

The "safe house" that Michael and Sanders had set up for Katie was an abandoned farmhouse about three miles west of Denison. It stood at the end of a long dirt road that the county didn't bother to plow out anymore in the winter. The bank had foreclosed and the family had picked up and moved on. Nine generations of farmers and now they were living in a mobile home park somewhere outside of Sarasota.

Katie's meeting was a brief one. The three FBI agents listened in stunned silence while she unfolded the plot—the scheduled acts of violence, the riots, the killings, the poisoning of the water supply, the destruction of the bridges. The most important details—when it would go down, who would be the assassination target, who was behind the conspiracy—these were still hiding in the shadows.

"Well, we know what we're dealing with now," Michael said as the three men walked Katie to her pickup. "They're not looney tunes, these people. They're home-grown, red-blooded, all-American terrorists."

"We've gotta know who they're gonna hit," Katie said thoughtfully.

"You will. I know you will," Michael answered.

Katie made a small gesture of impatience. "You only know what you want to know, Michael. He wants me to marry him."

Michael stopped in his tracks as though he'd been poleaxed. His face was a study in conflicting emotions. Good. Let him suffer. Without another glance at him, Katie climbed into her pickup.

"Congratulations," put in Duffin dryly. "We'll send you a wedding present."

"Shut the fuck up!" Michael barked, wheeling angrily on the young agent.

"Listen"—Duffin smirked—"I know she can't marry him. A wife can't testify against her husband."

Fuck them all. Katie turned the key in the ignition, and the truck motor came to life with a cough, then a roar.

"It ain't a shotgun wedding, is it?" asked Al Sanders.

Michael whirled around to glare at Sanders, and Katie's eyes flashed angrily.

"Yeah. Good." The senior agent stepped up to the cab of the pickup and gave Katie a long, serious look. "You stay pissed, girl. You stay real pissed. You gonna need that edge. You gonna need it."

*   *   *

BETRAYED

When Katie came into the barn, Gary was busy muck-
ing out the chicken coops. He was bare to the waist,
sweating like hell. The chickens were squawking their
heads off, and the methane smell of the chickenshit made
Katie almost gag.

"I went for a drive," she said to Gary.

"I didn't ask you where you went."

"Yes," she said.

It took a minute for the word to sink in, for Gary to
get Katie's meaning. But the instant it did, he let out a
triumphant whoop and ran to her, lifting her high in his
arms and swinging her around joyously.

Of course there had to be a celebration. It wasn't your
everyday event, Katie and Gary getting hitched. Mrs.
Simmons drove over in the evening and Gary went out
for a few bottles of Cold Duck, Denison's answer to Dom
Perignon. By the time they'd killed the first bottle and
screwed the cap off the second one, Gary was high as a
soaring eagle. Katie, wearing her long party dress and
her hair swept up on top of her head, only sipped at her
drink, pretending it was too sweet for her taste, but she
made certain that her new fiancé's glass was kept filled
with the cold bubbly.

The party was a huge success. Rachel was ecstatic at
the news of the impending wedding, and even Joey seemed
to be coming out of his shell a bit. Gladys Simmons was
all smiles; at last she accepted Katie as one of the family.
As for Gary, he couldn't let go of Katie. He kept his arm
wrapped around her waist as though she would disappear
from his life if he didn't hold on extra tight.

"Can we have some champagne?" Rachel begged.

"Hell, yes!" Gary roared happily, filling her glass.

"Honestly, Gary, she's just a little girl!" Mrs. Simmons protested, but she said it with a smile, because this
was a very special occasion.

"You want some, Joey?" Gary waved the bottle over
his head.

"You're gettin' drunk," his mother chided him.

"Hell, yes, I'm gettin' drunk," Gary admitted cheerfully. "I'm gettin' married!"

Rachel smiled shyly at Katie. "Can I call you mommy after you get married?"

Katie looked down a little sadly at the child. "Sure you can. I'd like that." She bent to give Rachel a hug.

"Do I *have* to call you that?" Joey asked anxiously. He still had dreams about his mother.

"No, honey, you can call me anything you want."

"Hey," Gary yelled into her ear. "Speakin' of callin', you call your mom yet?"

Katie's breath caught in her throat and she shook her head mutely.

"Well, call 'er, what's the number?" Gary picked up the phone and looked at Katie expectantly.

Panic threatened to overwhelm Katie. That special number for her cover story, the mother in Texas with the gallbladder—was the telephone still being manned at the other end? She had no idea, but she had to take the chance.

"3125551701," she told him, and crossed her fingers mentally. She could hear the phone ringing at the other end of the line.

"Mrs. Phillips? Hold on." Gary handed the phone to Katie, who grinned in relief.

"Mama? Guess what? I'm gettin' married. No, I'm not kiddin'. . . ."

"Hey, I wanna talk to her, too. . . ." And Gary grabbed the receiver out of Katie's hands for a long happy conversation with the trained agent, Katie's "mama."

By the time the children were in bed and Gladys Simmons had retired to her own home, Gary had started on the third bottle of wine. His speech was slurred and his movements were a little fuzzy, but Katie couldn't make her move yet. She had no idea how much Cold Duck it would take before Gary Simmons's guard would drop.

They took a bottle up with them to the bedroom, Gary still hugging Katie so tightly he didn't want to let go long enough for them to go one at a time up the narrow stairs.

Once in the bedroom he pulled her to him again.

"When're we gonna do it?" he demanded.

"Do what?" asked Katie, her senses on full alert.

"Get married. I wanna get married!"

"Shhh," Katie warned, putting her fingers over Gary's lips. "You'll wake the kids."

Gary shook his head. "Naw, they're in bed drunk. I wanna get married tomorrow mornin'." He grabbed hold of Katie and pushed her down on the bed. The wine had made him clumsily amorous.

"My mama still ain't feelin' good—"

"To hell with your mama," roared Gary, brushing Katie's objection aside. "I wanna get married!" Burying his face in her throat, he nuzzled her, squeezing her breasts. Awkwardly he tried to climb on top of her on the bed, even though both of them were still fully dressed.

"What about that thing we gotta do?" Katie asked as casually as she could.

Gary stopped nuzzling her and stared into her face; his breath was heavy with wine. "Shit! There ain't nothin' to that!" Rolling off Katie, he stood up unsteadily. "That's so easy. You want me to show you how easy? I'll show you how easy."

With the bottle still in his hand, he made his way to the other side of the bedroom, stopped, and tapped on a floorboard. The board opened up; there was a secret space underneath the floor. Gary reached down and came up with a thick sheaf of white paper, a computer print-out. He carried it over to the bed and allowed one end of it to drop. The printout unfurled, and suddenly there was paper all over the place, closely printed with names and addresses.

Gary grinned lopsidedly. "All these names, here, look at 'em. They're all friends of ours. All kindsa friends all over, big places, little places." His voice was thick from the wine, and his words came out a little furry. "High-up friends, low-down friends. Helpin' us, lookin' out for us. We can hit a thousand people, there wouldn't be nothin' to it."

At last. Names. Names and addresses. Katie felt a rush of excitement that was very close to sexual.

With a rough laugh, Gary dropped the printout and threw himself on top of Katie again, kissing at her face and neck, missing her lips and getting the corner of her nose or her chin. "What are you gonna wear?" he asked her thickly.

"Wear?"

"What kinda wedding dress?"

Katie thought for a minute, then something from her childhood past came into her head and she began to recite.

" 'Marry in blue, your man's gonna be true . . .
Marry in brown, you'll live in town . . .
Marry in green . . .' "

She stopped, not remembering the rest of the line.

" 'Shamed to be seen,' " supplied Gary. " 'Marry in black, better turn back.' "

The memory was coming back to Katie now, becoming clearer. She used to jump rope to this rhyme, back in Dallas when she was a little girl, before her parents were killed in an automobile accident and Katie was sent to live in Chicago. " 'Marry in gray, you'll be sad some-day. . . .' "

" 'Marry in red, wish yourself dead,' " Gary chimed in.

" 'Marry in white, you'll do all right,' " Katie brought the rhyme to an end.

" 'Marry in white, you'll do all right,' " Gary repeated softly. He laid his hand gently over Katie's face, feeling the velvet softness of her skin. "You're so pretty," he murmured as he began making love to her.

The lovemaking was clumsy, because Gary's performance was hampered by the alcohol in his body. To Katie's great relief, it was soon over. Gary seemed satisfied, but he was probably too drunk to tell the difference.

His mood became somber as the alcohol in his bloodstream began to have its depressing effect. But that didn't stop his having another drink, then another.

"You ain't never gonna turn against me, are you?" he asked Katie, who lay beside him in the bed, her back turned.

"No," Katie answered.

"My wife . . . I used to *love* her. I *loved* her." Gary sat up on the side of the bed, naked. "She couldn't go along with me," he added sadly.

Katie stiffened, her instincts alerted. She listened hard.

"She got pregnant," Gary said slowly. He was having some difficulty speaking. "She went into Lincoln. She had . . . an abortion. She killed . . . my baby. She said she'd rather die first."

Katie turned slowly to look at Gary. But he was staring at the wall, looking down the long bitter road into his past.

"She tried to turn the kids against me. She ran away from me, writin' 'em letters, callin' 'em behind my back." He put one hand over his eyes, as if the memory was too visually painful and he could actually see the pain. Something like a sob tore itself out of his chest.

"I had to share my life with you," he said slowly, turning back to Katie. "All of it. I couldn't let it happen to me again." A deep budding suspicion took hold of Katie, making her feel a little sick. She held her breath, not daring to speak.

"I didn't have no choice," Gary said finally, and began to cry quietly.

The suspicion burst into a terrible, flame-colored flower.

"Did you kill her?" she whispered.

"Hell, no," Gary replied. And then, "Wes did."

Chapter Fifteen

The Lone Ranger

Katie believed she would never be able to go to sleep again lying next to Gary Simmons, but she was wrong. The emotional overload she experienced when Gary admitted his wife's murder was so great that it literally blew her circuits, and she burned out. With Gary weeping drunkenly beside her, Katie fell asleep almost at once, and slept on until the next afternoon.

Her dreams were monstrous. In them she was always armed, carrying a powerful automatic weapon through a dense forest on the track of . . . what? She didn't know, but her dream self was afraid that her quarry might be a helpless woman, or, worse, an innocent child. She also knew that while she was the hunter, she was also the hunted. Somebody or some . . . thing . . . with a hidden face was stalking her down. He . . . or it . . . was behind her, ahead of her, on all sides of her. She could sense, but she could not see. Her dream self was very afraid, yet more afraid of what she might be forced to do than what would be done to her. All throughout the night the dream recurred again and again, in variations of the basic nightmare. Katie was always both hunter and prey.

When she woke up at last, more exhausted than when she'd fallen asleep, early-afternoon sunshine was streaming in through the bedroom window. Beside her, the bed was empty; Gary had been up for many hours. Through the open window Katie could hear men's voices coming from the direction of the barn.

With a throbbing head, Katie made her way to the window in time to see Gary Simmons disappearing into the barn with Shorty Richards. Now was her chance. Moving swiftly, she crossed the bedroom to the floorboard Gary had shown her last night. She tapped the floor in exactly the same place, and once again the floorboard moved. The secret compartment lay open, and the thick computer printout, with the vital list of names and addresses, was lying where Gary had left it.

Glancing swiftly over her shoulder to make certain she wasn't being observed, Katie lifted out the precious printout. But that wasn't the only thing in the hole. Underneath it was a manila file folder that she hadn't seen before. She took it up and opened it. It was full of photographs—faces that Katie recognized, faces that anybody would recognize.

Henry Kissinger. Jesse Jackson. Ted Kennedy. Ed Koch. Mario Cuomo. Katie's fingers trembled as she riffled through the photos, seeing these faces and others equally famous, equally important. Although the pictures were large and glossy, they weren't studio portraits and hadn't been posed for. They were blowups of much smaller pictures. Some of them were fuzzy, some a little grainy, and all of them had been shot with a telephoto lens, by somebody who wanted to make sure that he himself wouldn't be spotted. These photographs showed their subjects caught unaware, getting in and out of limos, walking into office buildings, waving to crowds. These pictures had been taken by a person or persons who evidently had staked out his subjects and stalked them like a hunter, only with a camera instead of a gun.

On the bottom of the stack were two photographs of Dan Kraus. Somebody had taken a thick black marker and slashed a giant *X* over Kraus's Semitic features.

These are the targets, thought Katie in horror. Jesus Christ Almighty, these are the targets! First the camera, next the bullet! I've got to get to Michael!

She washed her face and quickly got into her clothes, braiding her long hair carelessly behind her as she watched anxiously out the window for signs that Gary Simmons was coming back to the house. But by the sound of it the two men appeared to be working pretty hard.

Once dressed, Katie grabbed up her leather purse and emptied it of its contents, sweeping it all—wallet, lipstick, hairbrush, and other paraphernalia—into a dresser drawer under her blouses. Her truck registration, driver's license, and keys she put into her jeans pocket.

Then, very careful not to wrinkle or dog-ear any of the pages, she placed the printout into the empty bag, laying the manila envelope on top of it. For the space of a heartbeat she stood looking at the last thing she'd taken out of her bag, the .22 pistol that Michael had given her. Then, with a decisive gesture, she threw the gun into the bag and pulled the zipper shut. There!

Kate made a critical inspection of her shoulder bag. Did it look too heavy? Would it excite Gary's suspicions? No, it might be a ticking time bomb inside, but on the outside the bag was just a woman's purse.

Clutching it tightly against her, Katie walked across the farmyard to her pickup, which was parked just outside the barn. Stripped to the waist and sweating like mules, Gary and Shorty were pitchforking hay into bales for winter feed. Joey was there helping them.

"Goddamn! Look at her!" Gary called out as Katie marched past them. "She don't even have a headache!" He himself was as hung over as a fat lady's ass on a soda-fountain stool, and nursing a headache the size of Mt. Rushmore.

"Congratulations, Katie," Shorty yelled, grabbing her and planting a sloppy wet kiss on her lips.

Katie forced herself to smile. "I'm goin' to the doctor," she told Gary casually.

"What the hell's wrong with *you*? *I'm* the one oughta be goin' to the doctor!" Gary grabbed comically for his throbbing forehead.

Katie put on a demure expression. "Women go to the doctor when they're gettin' married, Gary."

Gary poked Shorty in the ribs and gave him a leering wink. "Everything looked fine to me. Want me to give you another examination?" The two men laughed coarsely.

"Shut up," Katie retorted. " 'Bye, Joey."

When she left the phone booth on the road and climbed back into her pickup, Katie estimated the time she probably had left. It would take Michael and Sanders somewhere between two hours and two hours and fifteen minutes to reach the safe house. Say forty-five minutes for the meeting, no longer. Katie couldn't risk longer. Another hour or so to drive back to the farm. If she was lucky, Gary would still be baling hay. If she wasn't, he might be in the house for lunch. Either way, she had to get the incriminating documents back under the floorboards almost immediately. They'd have been in her possession for almost a day as it was, much too long.

She was cutting it very close. Too damn close for safety. Every minute the printout and the pictures were out of Gary's hiding place could mean a geometrically increased chance of danger for Katie. Maybe she shouldn't have risked it; maybe she should have only tried photographing the pages, even if she had the wrong camera for the job. Maybe she should have simply memorized the faces in the photos, and left the printout alone, for another, perhaps safer time.

Maybe, maybe, maybe. Katie had a lot of time to agonize over the maybes as she sat on the floor in the empty safe house waiting for the Bureau. By her calculations, Michael should have reached here only a little over an hour after she did. But two hours went by, then two and a half, and there was no sign of him. Katie began to panic. How long would her doctor excuse hold out? How many hours could a country doctor with a limited practice be expected to take to do a simple pelvic examination? Time was her enemy here, and it was a deadly enemy.

Surely Gary Simmons would be suspicious by now. Katie could picture him wondering where the hell she'd got to, phoning his doctor, then other doctors in the area around Denison; there couldn't be more than three or four. And Gary was no fool. Once his suspicions were aroused, he'd go straight to the floorboard. The biggest maybe off all: when Katie got back, maybe she'd be looking down the silencer of Gary's Mac-10.

She couldn't stand it another minute. Sitting here with her imagination running on overdrive was making Katie crazy. She had to stand up and move. Striding out to her pickup, she paced the yard, smoking furiously and trying to keep at bay the deadly mental images that crowded her brain.

At last, the sound of an automobile on the deserted road. Katie threw her cigarette away as the car nosed into the overgrown, weed-choked front yard and Al Sanders got out, followed by Michael Carnes. This time they'd left that asshole Duffin back in Chicago, thank God.

"Where the hell were you? I've been here three hours!" Cathy greeted them.

Michael could see how strung out she was. "We got held up, Cathy—" he began, but she interrupted him angrily.

"You don't get held up! It's my *life*!" She reached into her handbag and took out the printout and the folder of photographs, pushing them at Michael.

Michael opened the folder. With Al Sanders looking over his shoulder, the two men went silently through the photographs, looking at one face after another. When they came to the brutally crossed-out photos of Dan Kraus, they exchanged significant glances, but neither of them said a word to Cathy. Then Sanders took the printout away for photographing, while Michael took Cathy for a short walk around the deserted farm.

He knew what she was expecting to hear, that she had done her job and done it well, that she had furnished them with all the evidence they needed to bust the case wide open, that she was free to go back to Chicago. But it wasn't what he was going to tell her. He could see how close to the edge Cathy was, and he realized that what he was asking of her was beyond duty, even beyond dedication. There was no way he or the Bureau could minimize the danger or even protect her.

Michael's heart went out to Cathy as he looked at her sweet familiar face, at the new smudges of exhaustion under her eyes, the tenseness around her mouth and the hollows that had begun to appear under her cheekbones. He could see the physical evidence of her tension, of her knowledge of the fact that every breath she drew might be her last. But his sympathy and his affection would not win him this case; he understood that if he understood nothing else in his life.

Michael's silence and the look of pity on his face told Cathy everything she needed to know. It wasn't over yet. With a little moan, she shook her head vehemently. No. No. No.

"What've we got, Cathy?" Michael put the question bluntly. "So we've got some photos of Kraus with a black X over them. What does that prove? If we bust them for the bank robbery, what's gonna happen to *these* people?" He held the photos up for her to see, but Cathy turned her face away, refusing to look.

"Someone else will pull the trigger!" Michael's tone changed from matter-of-fact to pleading. "We're almost there. All we need is the name."

Opening the file folder, Michael went through the photographs, reading the names out loud. "Ted Kennedy. Jesse Jackson. Coleman Young. Howard Metzenbaum. Kissinger—" His intention was to make the roster into real people, people with significance for Cathy, but she didn't need to be reminded. Their names had already been imprinted on her soul.

"Maeroff is an investigative reporter in Louisville," Michael continued, turning over the next photograph. "Terry Sheridan is a linebacker for the Miami Dolphins. We couldn't effectively protect these people until God knows when. What are they supposed to do? Crawl into a room and stay there?"

It was a rhetorical question, and Cathy treated it that way. She already knew that nothing she could say would have an impact on Michael. In her entire life she had never felt quite so alone. Not when her parents died, not even when Gary Simmons took her into his arms and made love to her and she pretended to enjoy it.

She stared out across the broken fence to the acres beyond it, land in which no crop had been planted for years. Here and there among the weeds was a stalk of ripening corn that had grown up from a kernel dropped by a bird.

Like Gary, thought Cathy suddenly. An abandoned field where the good growing things have been choked off by the tangled weeds, so that nothing healthful grows anymore, only thorny vines and thistles. Long ago Gary must have been like a fertile piece of ground—worth cultivating, worth all the effort you put into it, strong and beautiful and productive. Long ago before the disappointments, before the rot of hatred set in. What a waste. What a goddamn tragic waste.

Apart from the handful of cornstalks, the meadow before her eyes was as strangulated and empty as the feeling in her chest.

"We need the name or the time and the place," emphasized Michael. "We'll monitor their schedules—then it's over." Even to his own ears, the promise sounded like a hollow mockery.

"I can't stand any more," Cathy burst out. Her nerves were stretched beyond taut to the breaking point; her emotions were so frazzled she couldn't think straight. She could only feel.

Michael put his arms around her and held her gently. "I wish I could do it instead of you," he whispered. "I'd give anything to do it for you. You know that, don't you?"

Cathy nodded mutely, holding tightly to Michael.

"You do, don't you?" he asked again, more insistently.

Again Cathy nodded, not trusting herself to speak. Burning tears were crowding behind her lashes, and she was determined not to break down. Crying wouldn't solve anything; crying wouldn't let her off the hook. She had to finish what she had been sent here to do, and tears were only a sign of weakness. Besides, in the long run, what had Michael given her worth crying over? A few crumbs of pity, perhaps, and a whole lot of useless words. Maybe he *did* love her, at least in his own way, but so what? Some pious words and a couple of hugs weren't what Cathy needed to save her life.

There was a sound behind them, and they turned. Al Sanders was coming back; he had photographed the print-out and was holding it in his hand, together with his written list of the targets. He handed the printout to Katie, his face grave.

"You'd better get this stuff back before he notices they're gone," said Michael.

Tell me about it, thought Katie bitterly, but she nodded. She felt numb. Her future, even her life, had been taken out of her own hands; she had almost no control over what was going to happen. She would have to follow where Gary led her, and wait for her next opportunity to act. The best she could hope for was to come out of it alive, but even that seemed problematical to Cathy now.

Screwed, blued, and tattooed. The phrase came back to Cathy from her college days; she didn't remember where she'd first heard it. Probably some dumb-ass fraternity party. Well, that was Catherine Weaver, all right. Screwed, both literally and figuratively. Any minute now, blued and tattooed. She felt soiled, she felt used, but most of all she felt numb with fear.

Silently, she put the damaging evidence back into her shoulder bag, walked to her pickup, opened the door on the driver's side, and slid in. She put the bag on the seat beside her and started the motor up.

Sanders came around to her side of the truck and the two of them looked at each other for a long time.

"You ain't half bad for a white woman, you know," he said at last softly.

Despite herself, Cathy was touched. From a man as brave and as experienced as Al Sanders, this was high praise. But she didn't want to show him how vulnerable his words made her feel, so she kept it flippant. "What are you gonna tell me, Sanders, 'Win one for the Gipper'?"

Sanders laughed, a rich, mellow sound. "Hell, no! He was just a dumb white jock boy with bad luck!" His smile faded and his eyes grew serious. "But *you* ain't."

"You're just sayin' that, Sanders."

"I sure am."

Katie nodded, and pulled the truck out of the driveway and onto the deserted road. Good for me, she thought. I finally got Al Sanders's respect, and I guess that's something. Now if only respect could stop a bullet.

The house appeared deserted and no lights were on when Katie came up the stairs to the bedroom an hour later. The long dusk of a July evening was still painting the sky purple and black, streaked with orange yellow where the sun was going down in a slow diminution.

"Gary?" she called, but there was no answer. Katie strained her ears to catch a sound. Everything was quiet. This was her chance to put the stuff back. Clutching her purse close to her, she started across the bedroom to the secret floorboard, and had just about reached it when the bathroom door opened suddenly behind her, and light came streaming out, catching her as if in a spotlight and freezing her where she stood.

Gary was standing in the bathroom doorway, a towel wrapped around his waist, shaving cream on his face.

Katie's hands clenched involuntarily, and her nails dug sharply into her palms. Had he seen her near the floorboard? Did he know what she was doing? Did he know his damning documents were missing and that she'd taken them?

"Doctor say everything okay?" Gary asked pleasantly.

Katie almost choked on her relief. "Yeah." She wanted

to move but she was still trembling so badly she'd better stay put until she was in control. "Where are the kids?" she asked casually.

"At Mom's. I gotta get dressed, we're goin' out." But instead of heading for his closet, Gary went down the stairs, still wearing only the towel.

"Where we goin'?" Katie called after him.

Gary didn't hear her. "You want a beer?" he yelled from the kitchen.

Katie thought fast. "Yeah. A real cold one. From the back of the refrigerator," she yelled back. As soon as she heard the fridge door opening, she tapped the floorboard and, with shaking hands, she put the printout and the photographs back.

When Gary came up the stairs with two Rolling Rocks, the bedroom lights were on and Katie was standing in front of the mirror, brushing her hair.

They'd been driving in the dark for what seemed to her to be hours. Katie didn't recognize this road; had they ever used it before? There was nothing on either side of the road but empty land, vast deserted fields. No houses, no barns. Gary had said very little during the drive; his mind was somewhere else.

What was he thinking about? Did he know anything? Had he somehow found out? Where was he taking her? For what purpose? Katie kept remembering the night of the hunt, the night Wes had threatened her with the Mac-10; and that night in the camp when he'd chased her through the woods, shooting at her. Katie's hands were sweating, but her mouth was dry, and she was having trouble swallowing.

"Where we goin'?" she asked nervously.

Gary swung the wheel around sharply. The Jeep Cherokee swerved off the road and onto a field that looked no different from any of the fields they'd passed. He switched the ignition off, and the car's headlights blinked out. Gary turned to her.

"Here," he said.

A jolt of fear set Katie's pulse racing. Here? Why here? The ass end of nowhere so they'd never find her body? He knew. He must know.

"What are we doin' here?" she asked in a low tone.

For a minute Gary didn't answer, and in that minute Katie became convinced that she was staring her death in the face. Then he cocked his head, listening, pointed upward, and said, "He's here."

For a second or two Katie didn't know what he was talking about, and then she heard it. The *thut-thut* sound of jet-powered chopper rotors, nearby overhead. The sound grew louder and louder until the helicopter came into view, settling down on the field about a hundred yards from the Cherokee.

"Stay here," Gary ordered sharply, getting out of the Jeep. He ran heavily through the down draft across the field toward the chopper. Katie tried to see who was in the copter, but the lights were on, obscuring the face of the man behind the stick. All she could see was that there was only one man. Gary ducked under the rotors, jumped into the chopper, and the two men began talking, but the noise of the engine and blades was deafening, and Katie didn't have a prayer at hearing even a single word. But she knew that something heavy was going down, and that the man in the chopper must be the one close to the top, the one giving the orders.

The man in the chopper was Robert Flynn. Bobby Flynn, Gary Simmons's old Nam buddy. Flynn, Jack Carpenter's shadow. The two men exchanged familiar greetings. But Flynn wasn't there to talk over old times. Reaching into his attaché, he extracted a large official-looking envelope and handed it to Gary.

"Brought you somethin'," he told him with a bright, cynical grin.

Gary didn't understand. What the hell was this? But he took the envelope from Flynn and turned it over in his hands, keeping his eyes on Bobby all the while, searching Bobby's face for clues. Flynn's expression remained deadpan, revealing nothing. Gary opened the envelope. There was a file folder in it. The contents took a minute to register on him. He stared at it in disbelief.

In big letters, the cover of the folder read

FEDERAL BUREAU OF INVESTIGATION
PERSONNEL
CONFIDENTIAL

Also on the cover was a photograph of a young woman named Catherine Weaver. Her name was right on the file, Catherine Weaver. But the woman wasn't Catherine Weaver.

It was Katie Phillips.

Katie.

His Katie. She was FBI. Just like Wes had warned him from Day One. The bitch was FBI. She'd been conning him all along, pretending to be straight, making out like she cared for him, while all the while . . . a fuckin' grasshopper.

Which meant they already knew; they had to know about everything. The hunt, the camp, the robbery, maybe even the kike Kraus. The FBI was on to them. They could even be watching right this minute.

And it was his fault, all of it. His own goddamn fault. Wes had seen through Katie from the git-go, Wes had warned him against her. Even the others hadn't trusted her right away. Dean, Lyle—they weren't too crazy about Katie Phillips. His own mother hadn't trusted Katie. But he'd been so fuckin' hung up on her he hadn't listened. He'd been in such a hurry to get into her pants that he'd taken her everywhere, shown her everything, told her all his secrets—all *their* secrets. All she'd had to do was open those legs and he'd turned into a braying jackass, telling her every goddamn thing she wanted to know. She'd never cared for him, never. Not for him, not for the kids. A lyin', cheatin' grasshopper whore, and he'd fallen for it like a horny sixteen-year-old kid.

And now Wes was dead, his best friend—dead. It was

her doing, it must have been. There were only supposed
to be two bank guards, not four. Katie's doing, but
Gary's fault. His own damn fault for being so trusting.
He should have known right after the robbery that something was wrong, but he was still too blind. He'd swallowed every lie she fed him. She must be laughing at him
behind his back. Well, he'd fix her so that she'd never
laugh again.

Ah, Katie, said Gary's heart. Why did you have to turn
out to be a grasshopper? I loved you, damn it! I really
thought we had something going, something good.

A deep surge of nausea shook Gary; for a minute
there he was sure he was going to throw up. He wanted
to look away, but he couldn't take his eyes off the picture
of this stranger, this Catherine Weaver. This woman he
knew and didn't know. This woman he'd loved and wanted
to marry. This cunt betrayer. Gary's eyes glazed over.
He looked as though he'd been hit over the head and led
to slaughter like a beef steer. The sense of loss was
overwhelming. He'd never hurt so much in his whole life.

At last he tore his eyes away and looked at Flynn, who
was still wearing that mocking grin. Silently, Gary leafed
through the folder, pretending to read a little here and
there, but actually seeing almost nothing. The paragraphs
were a blur, yet a few words jumped out at him: "Uni-
versity of Chicago." The cunt had gone to college, and
not only to college, but to that commie shithole. He
handed the folder back to Flynn, who accepted it without
a word, tucking it back into his monogrammed leather
attaché and spinning the complicated combination locks.

Gary may have barely comprehended a word he read,
but he understood enough. Just the familiar face on the
cover and the unfamiliar name attached to it—they were
enough.

"Brought you somethin' else," Robert Flynn said. Another envelope, considerably smaller, appeared out of
the inside breast pocket of his expensive jacket. Gary
took it, but hesitated before opening it. He'd already

been snakebit by one envelope tonight. But Bobby Flynn's eyes were on him, so he tore the damn thing open.

Inside, there was a map and two keys. What the hell?

"You got point, Gary," said Flynn, still smiling. "We're gonna win this war, man."

Katie watched Gary climb out of the chopper and back off as the rotors starting turning. He stood in the down draft, his hair whipping, his shirt billowing, looking up, watching the helicopter until it had disappeared from sight. Then he trudged slowly across the field toward the Cherokee, his head down.

As soon as he climbed into the Jeep, Katie felt it. Something had happened to change him. Gary was different. He walked different. The expression around his mouth was different. His eyes were hooded; they refused to look at her.

"Who was that?" she asked.

Gary switched the ignition on and spun the wheel around. The Cherokee bumped and bucked out of the rutted field and onto the road.

"The Lone Ranger," he said.

His voice was hoarse, without humor. His eyes still stared straight ahead.

"The Lone Ranger rides again," he added.

Katie felt a thrill of fear raising prickles along her spine and on the nape of her neck. Something was off; she sensed it. Even her limited experience as an agent, combined with her natural intuitive powers, was enough to tell her that something was definitely, terribly wrong.

But she couldn't show him that she suspected anything; she had to keep up the pretense. "Why won't you tell me?" she persisted.

"Who's crowdin' who now?" rasped Gary.

Katie subsided. He wasn't about to tell her anything, and pressing him would just make matters worse. They drove along in a heavy silence, each of them lost in thought, his black and bitter, hers anxious. For Gary, the loss he felt was beginning to subside; rage and loathing flooded in to take its place. As for Katie, she felt horribly insecure. Did he know about her or didn't he? Did she have some leeway in which to act, or was her death already determined? She kept playing over possible scenarios in her head—what if he . . . but suppose . . . maybe if I. . . .

"We're goin' to Denver tomorrow," Gary said suddenly.

Startled, Katie looked over at him. He was still staring at the road, his face set.

"Why?" she asked.

"You know why," he answered meaningfully.

The hit! So that's it! That's why he's so uptight! It's got nothing to do with me at all! Katie almost smiled in relief. Then, suddenly, her intuition and her heightened sense of danger gave her second thoughts. Easy, she cautioned herself. That could be only part of it. You're not out of the woods yet. But tomorrow! That's almost no warning at all. I've got to talk to Michael.

Later, Katie lay beside Gary in the big brass bed, waiting nervously for her opportunity to make the call. Gary had his arms wrapped around her, and she had her head on his shoulder. But neither of them was sleeping. Gary was lying on his back, staring up at the ceiling, and Katie could feel the tension in his body.

"What's the matter?" she whispered.

"I'm just tired, I guess," Gary said in a low voice. He pulled her closer to him and gave her a little hug. "Good night." And he kissed her on the lips, long and slow.

"Good night," Katie said shakily, and pulled out of Gary's arms, turning away to sleep on her side, her back to him. But she didn't close her eyes. She lay staring into the darkness, aware of Gary's body next to hers, aware of tomorrow.

Catherine Weaver had made her decision.

It seemed like hours before Katie was finally convinced that Gary was sleeping. Now was the only time she had to reach Michael Carnes. But she couldn't take the chance of waking Gary or exciting his suspicions.

Katie slipped quietly out of bed and went into the bathroom, staying there for a few minutes, flushing the toilet, running water into the sink. If Gary stirred and half woke, the familiar sounds would reassure him.

She came out into the darkened bedroom and stood in the bathroom doorway, her eyes on Gary. He was lying very still and breathing deeply and regularly. Asleep. Satisfied, she made her way quietly, downstairs, picked up the telephone, and dialed Michael's home number.

He was home. Thank God.

"I can't talk, Michael," she whispered into the receiver. "It's going down. Denver. Tomorrow."

"Are you sure?"

"Yes."

"It's over," said Michael, relieved. "We'll check who's in Denver tomorrow. We'll cover him with a task force. Get out—now!"

Katie hesitated a fraction, then she said, "I can't, Michael."

"It's too risky! I don't want you in Denver. Go! Now!" Michael sounded frantic.

But Catherine Weaver had made her decision.

"They'll stop everything. They'll do it some other time. I have to finish it. I *have* to finish it, Michael."

"You've done enough," he said desperately. "Cathy! Cathy? Cath—"

Katie put the telephone down quietly, and remained sitting, her pensive profile outlined in the light of the table lamp. Upstairs, pressed against the wall of the hallway out of sight, Gary Simmons stood watching her. When he saw her get up at last and turn out the light, he slipped silently back into the bed and shut his eyes.

He's still asleep. Good. Relieved, Katie got into bed and pulled the patchwork quilt over her shoulders, turning her back on Gary. She shut her eyes and longed for sleep to come and take her. Tomorrow, in Denver, she would need every ounce of her strength.

Suddenly, without warning, she felt hands on her neck, reaching from behind. Gary's hands. His fingers tightened. Katie lay paralyzed, wanting to scream, to fight him off, but found herself unable to move. Panic gripped her as tightly as Gary's iron fingers. His hands squeezed hard, harder. I can't breathe. He's going to kill me.

As unexpectedly as his grip had tightened, it loosened now. The hands went away. Katie felt Gary's lips on the nape of her neck, kissing, nuzzling. She slumped forward. Whatever had happened, it was over.

But was it? Katie turned in the bed, still shaking, to look at Gary. He appeared to be sleeping soundly. His eyes were shut; his cheek was pressed against his pillow. But was he really sleeping? Had he actually tried to strangle her in his sleep? Or was he awake, cruelly awake, enjoying Katie's panic? Was he tormenting her, as a hunting cat torments a captured sparrow, enjoying its helpless terrors, the shrill pipings, the panicked beating of its crippled wings, and its vain struggles to escape.

What did he know? For God's sake, what exactly did he know?

Chapter Sixteen

The Hit

Mrs. Simmons arrived early the next morning to look after the children while Katie and Gary were away. On the surface, everything seemed normal. The engaged couple was just taking a little pre-wedding trip together. They didn't say where they were going, but young people in love always value their privacy.

The skin under her eyes smudged black from lack of sleep, Katie walked numbly to the Jeep. She brought with her only her handbag. Gary was carrying a dark locked case, something like a briefcase. But Katie knew exactly what must be in there. The assassination weapon.

Rachel and Joey scampered along by their side, reluctant to say goodbye. Rachel, especially, didn't want to let Katie out of her sight.

"Goodbye, Katie. I'm gonna miss you. I'm gonna miss you so much!" She wound her little arms around Katie's legs and hips, holding on tightly and hugging.

Katie's heart swelled with love and pity. Every time she looked at Gary's children, she was reminded of what might have been, and of what she had to do instead. She reached down and threw her arms around Rachel, hugging her back. "Goodbye, Rachel," she said sadly. "Bushels and barrels and stuff, Rachel."

"Goodbye, Katie." Joey came forward to give her a quick, shy hug of his own. Katie's eyes filled with tears;

Joey's awkwardness compared with Rachel's outgoing openness was especially touching. Would she ever see Rachel and Joey again? She doubted it.

"Why can't we come?" Rachel begged plaintively. "Where are you going?"

"Let's go," Gary said coldly. He'd been watching the bitch's show of phony affection, and it nearly made him sick. His own kids! She was some piece of work.

Katie followed Gary into the Cherokee, but turned back for one last painful look and wave. The kids waved back until the Jeep was out of sight down the road.

Gary drove toward the interstate; Katie recognized the road they were taking. The morning was beautiful, but the day would soon be a scorcher; you could already see heat shimmers on the blacktop.

"Put some rock 'n' roll on," Gary said suddenly. Katie turned to him, surprised.

"You hate rock 'n' roll."

"You like it, don't you?" He smiled.

Nodding stiffly, Katie turned the radio on, searched the dial for music. Something's wrong somewhere. One minute he acts cold, the next friendly. Is it the hit or is it me? Or both?

Within the hour they had reached the interstate. As they approached the on-ramps, Katie saw the signs for WEST and DENVER. Without a word, Gary drove by the westbound lanes and swung onto the ramp leading east. The sign read EAST and CHICAGO.

Chicago! It wasn't Denver where it was going down, but Chicago! He'd lied to her. And she'd passed the misinformation along, to the Bureau. The FBI wouldn't be ready in Chicago; they'd be waiting in Denver. There'd be no backup for Catherine Weaver. Panic took hold of Katie, and she struggled to overcome it.

"I thought we were going to Denver," she said shakily.

"I changed my mind."

What was she going to do? That Gary was on to her was now terrifyingly evident. But maybe not. Maybe there was the thinnest possibility that he was only following some procedure he'd set up in his own head, a procedure in which nobody, not even Katie, was in his confidence. But one thing was sure. She had to get away from him long enough to alert the Bureau. They had to know it was Chicago, not Denver.

The Jeep was doing seventy, eating up the miles under its chubby tires.

"Can we stop somewhere and get some lunch? I'm hungry," Katie said.

Gary looked at her and smiled. He reached down under the dashboard and brought up a paper bag. With one hand on the wheel, he fished inside it, coming out with a wrapped sandwich and handing it to Katie.

"I made 'em myself." He cast a sidelong glance at Katie, who was sitting there holding the sandwich in dismay. "I thought you were hungry."

"I am." Katie took a bite of the sandwich, chewing on it slowly and painfully, afraid it would choke her. Her stomach was so knotted she doubted that she could get a bite of it to stay down.

They passed a sign reading:

REST STOP
2 MILES
BUSES WELCOME

Also on the sign were those little stylized outline drawings that universally stand for Toilets, Food and Drink, Telephones. A rest stop! Probably large enough and complex enough for her to maybe sneak in a phone call, Katie thought.

"I've got to go to the ladies' room, too," she said, through a mouthful of sandwich.

"Well, then I guess we gotta stop, don't we." Gary grinned. But he didn't wait until the rest stop. Instead, he pulled off into the next gas station. Katie's eyes scanned for a phone booth. There was a much smaller chance of making a phone call here than at a rest stop, but maybe if she really scurried . . . She didn't see a phone anywhere.

With a slam of brakes, the Jeep pulled up precisely in front of the door to the women's toilet. Katie's heart sank. She was trapped and she knew it. Unless there was a pay phone in the john, as there sometimes was.

"Be right back," she told Gary.

"I'll be here." Gary grinned, and now Katie read something vicious and cold in his boyish smile, and it made her quake inside.

Katie went into the bathroom. No phone. What do I do now? she thought. I've got to reach Michael. She stood for a few seconds, indecisive, then it occurred to her that she just might write a message in lipstick on the mirror, praying that the next woman into the john would be smart enough to deliver it. The chances were almost nonexistent, but doing even this was better than doing nothing at all. She reached into her bag for her lipstick, and had it in her hand when the door opened and Gary came in.

"Men's don't work," he said casually. "You don't mind, do you?"

Speechless, Katie shook her head. Gary pushed open the stall door and went inside. Katie sidled toward the door. If she hurried . . .

"Hey, wait for me!" Gary called pleasantly. "I don't want to get lonely in here."

Katie stopped, stayed put. Trapped again.

When they came out of the women's room together, Gary grabbed Katie and kissed her hard. She struggled, pretending to be embarrassed at a public display, and broke away from him.

"Gary!" she protested, but he grabbed her again, holding her close and running his hands over her body, feeling her thighs, her crotch, her ass, her breasts. If anybody had seen them, that person would have thought that here were just two kids hot for each other, but Katie knew different. Catherine Weaver knew a frisk when she felt one. Gary was searching for a weapon. Her panic deepened.

"Gary, stop it!"

"Sorry, honey. Just can't keep my hands offa you."

They climbed back into the Jeep, but instead of starting the motor, Gary made a dive for Katie's purse. He opened it, and pawed through its contents, finding nothing.

"What are you doing?" Katie demanded, although she knew damn well what he was doing. He was looking to see if she was carrying a gun.

"Lookin' for a dime for the candy machine."

Why are we both keeping up this pretense? Katie thought numbly, although she realized that this was how it was going to be until it was over for good. Gary Simmons was toying with her, like that sparrow-torturing feral cat. And she had to go along with it.

For the rest of the long journey they didn't exchange another word. It seemed like a year to Katie before they saw the signs reading DOWNTOWN CHICAGO, THE LOOP. Gary swung off the ramp and into the city.

They drove through a seedy part of town, a section that was undergoing rehab. Here and there, new buildings were under construction. Topped by tall cranes, their floors as yet uncurtained by concrete, steel, or glass, the unfinished structures stood like skeletons against the sky.

It was at one such unfinished building that Gary Simmons parked the Jeep. He got out and picked up the dark suitcase from the back seat of the Cherokee, jerking his head at Katie in a silent command. Numbly, she followed him.

The building was totally deserted; nobody in construction worked here on the weekends. The bottom floor stood open to the elements, and Gary led the way inside, across what would someday be a marble-faced lobby. The door to the stairs was locked, but somehow Gary managed to produce the key. It was one of the two keys given to him by Bobby Flynn, but Katie had no way of knowing that. Once the door was open, Gary pushed Katie ahead of him, and they began the long upward climb.

Where are we going? What are we doing here? Why here? Questions crowded through Katie's brain as her legs began to tire. When they'd reached the fourteenth level, Gary signaled her to stop. Once again, he took a key from his pocket and unlocked the stairwell door. Now they were on the fourteenth floor, inside.

They walked out into a vast, open space floored in concrete. The inner partitions had not yet been put up; and the glass windows weren't in. The huge open window space was covered in billowing sheets of plastic, blowing in the Chicago wind. There were holes in the plastic, vents to let the wind through so that it wouldn't shred the plastic to ribbons by its force.

Gary walked over to the window and peered through one of the holes. The building was designed to front the avenue. He could see, across the street, a low concrete block structure with a large roof transmitter. On the building was a sign: WCHL, CHANNEL 44.

Gary looked at his wristwatch and smiled. Perfect. "Sit down. We got a whole hour. You want another sandwich?"

Katie shook her head. Not if her life depended on it.

Carefully, Gary opened the locks on his case and threw back the cover, revealing its contents. In the case was what Katie expected to see, a world-class sniper's rifle. What made her eyes widen was that it was a gun reserved exclusively for the military—the M-21, a 7.62-caliber hand-finished rifle that can be fitted with a sound suppresser and a scope, a gun used by the army and the marines. Another piece of evidence of weapons-dealing in the armed services. Also in Gary's case was a Leatherwood automatic ranging telescope, and three clips of ammunition, each holding eight rounds.

Lovingly and with great care, Gary took the rifle out and fit the silencer and the scope to it, checking it out with his right eye first, then his left. He inserted a clip of ammo.

"Relax, Katie."

But it was impossible for Katie to relax; she was coiled as tight as a new bedspring. Here she was totally alone in Chicago, while the rest of her team was in Denver. How the hell could she relax? And how could she take a man bigger and stronger than she was, armed with a high-powered rifle? Think, Cathy, think!

The hour dragged by with agonizing slowness. Katie sat on the cold concrete floor, her back against a wall, her arms wrapped around her legs. She smoked cigarette after cigarette, but her eyes never left Gary Simmons. Gary seemed content to sit by the window, peering out through the hole in the plastic, just smoking and waiting. He didn't appear to be nervous at all, just a man with a job to do who knew he could do it well.

The sun went down and the long summer dusk held Chicago in its gold-tipped purple fingers.

"Ten minutes," Gary announced, checking his watch. Katie felt a powerful jolt of anxiety; only ten more minutes to zero hour, and she still didn't have a workable plan!

"You nervous, Cathy?" he asked. His back was still turned to her.

Cathy? Startled, she stared at Gary in a panic. Had she heard him correctly? Did he call her Cathy, not Katie?

As if she'd spoken the questions out loud, Gary faced her and answered them, a sneer in his voice. "It ain't Phillips, either. It's Weaver. Your mom ain't sick, and your dad never taught you to shoot. The grasshoppers did. You don't even have any family—your parents died in a car crash when you was a kid."

He turned away from her in disgust and checked out the window again. When he turned back, he had the M-21 aimed directly at Catherine Weaver's heart.

And Cathy was staring right back at him, holding a .22 revolver pointed at Gary Simmons.

Oddly enough, she no longer felt afraid. The fear had vanished the minute Cathy knew for certain that Gary was going to kill her, that he knew she was FBI. It was uncertainty that gave Cathy the jitters. Now she was very calm.

"You're under arrest, Gary, put it down," she commanded.

As if in reply, Gary's finger touched the trigger, and the rifle never wavered. "Where'd you hide it?" he asked, meaning the gun.

"The Jeep, under the seat. Why did you bring me up here if you knew?"

Gary smiled. "I wanted 'em to find a dead shooter, a dead FBI agent shooter. That's pretty good, ain't it?"

Cathy cocked back the hammer of her gun.

The smile disappeared from Gary's face, and a look of real anguish took its place. He had to ask, had to know!

"You were their whoor all along, weren't you?"

Cathy didn't flinch. She met his eyes steadily. "Not in the beginning. I thought I was falling in love with you."

But Gary didn't buy it. "You laid down with me to get what they wanted!" he cried out passionately.

"I didn't think there was anything to get," Cathy answered sadly.

There was nothing left to say. The past was over, whatever they meant to each other or might have meant to each other was history, and now there was only the present. A now in which a man and a woman faced each other down with loaded guns, an invisible line drawn between them as impassable as a steel wall.

"Put it down, Gary. Please."

"What for?" Gary whispered raggedly. "What the hell for?" He checked his watch again, then looked hard at Cathy, looked out through the plastic sheeting, then at Cathy again. It was impossible to know what he was thinking, but he was obviously coming to some decision. All the while, she kept her .22 trained on him; it was a standoff.

"It's time," Gary said quietly.

"Don't. Please," Cathy begged softly. Inwardly, she prayed: Don't make me do this, Gary. I don't want to do this. I'm not even sure that I can.

Gary Simmons raised the rifle stock to his cheek in the sniper's position. He took a careful aim at Cathy, at the space over her breastbone, just above the heart. For several seconds he stood like that, killing her with every breath she took, then he wheeled around and pointed the gun out the window, down at the television station.

"Don't!" cried Cathy.

"You gonna shoot me in the back, Katie?" Gary drawled, without looking around.

In the same instant, both of them remembered the hunt, her trembling hand that couldn't pull the trigger on a man already marked for certain death. Not even to save her own life.

"Put it *down*, Gary!" cried Katie Phillips, agonized.

"I loved you," said Gary in a low tone.

He lifted the rifle and brought the scope up to his eye, sighting down the barrel, searching through the scope for the designated target. As his finger curled around the trigger, Catherine Weaver fired her pistol.

The bullet slammed into Gary Simmons's back, the impact twisting his body around and sending him sprawling face up on the concrete floor. His eyes were staring into hers, his lips curled back slightly into . . . what? A grimace? A last mocking smile? It looked to Katie like Gary's old grin, almost as though, dying, he gave her his approval. Good shot. I knew you had the guts. You're my baby.

"I could have loved you so much," Katie whispered to Gary, but he was already dead.

Catherine Weaver stepped over the shooter's body and went to the window. Through the hole she could see the TV studio across the street. Two limousines had just pulled up to the curb. Out of the first one stepped presidential hopeful Jack Carpenter, the charisma kid, and his aides, along with Robert Flynn. Carpenter was about to make yet one more television appearance to sell his campaign as an independent candidate.

Carpenter. The target was Jack Carpenter.

And then, just as he was about to enter the station,

Cathy saw Carpenter stagger and spin. She saw blood appear on the back of his jacket, blood seeping from a bullet hole. He was hit! Again, and now again! The people in the street screamed and ran, the aides scattered like bowling pins after a strike as a hail of silenced bullets caught Jack Carpenter's falling body and punched it full of holes.

Oh, my God! Cathy thought in disbelief. There's another shooter!

Chapter Seventeen

After

After she had used deadly force in the course of duty to prevent an assassination, after she'd shot Gary Simmons in the back and killed him, what was left for Catherine Weaver to do? It was over for her, finally over. And what had she accomplished? The hit had gone down anyway. Jack Carpenter, the target, was dead. The assassin was unknown, had escaped in the mass hysteria and the confusion. He could be anybody, anywhere.

Cathy put the safety back on the .22, shoved it into the waistband of her jeans, picked up her handbag, and left the building without a backward look at the body of Gary Simmons. She made her way down fourteen flights of stairs, out into the street, and started walking. There appeared to be no direction to her movements; she just kept going. As long as her feet carried her, she kept moving.

The enormity of what had happened was still sinking in. She'd killed Gary. But Jack Carpenter was dead anyway. Gary wasn't the only shooter. Slowly, Cathy began to realize the complexities of the Summer Lightning plot. It occurred to her that once her cover had been blown and her real identity had been revealed, it wasn't only Catherine Weaver whose life was in danger. Who was it who loved her? Who was it who believed in her? Who was it who trusted her? Who was it who had

confided in her, had invited her inside the movement and
shown her its secrets?

Gary Simmons. And so Gary Simmons had to die. It
was really very simple. If you designate him as the shooter,
and send him off to an assassination in the company of
an agent of the FBI, weren't there only a limited number
of possible scenarios? If Gary killed Cathy, well and
good. But what if Cathy were to kill Gary? Also good.
He was no longer to be trusted. Once he'd killed the
grasshopper, then "they," whoever "they" were, would
kill him. Oh, they'd probably make it look like an accident, but Gary Simmons was no longer useful to the
cause, and he knew too much. And they had to punish
him, to make an example of him—of the man who
betrayed them by falling in love with a grasshopper. He'd
betrayed them, so they would betray him.

That's why there was another designated assassin. They
didn't trust Gary Simmons anymore. He'd lost his credi-
bility and he was good for only one thing. To kill the FBI
agent. They were using Gary to dispose of Catherine
Weaver, and *using Catherine Weaver to dispose of Gary
Simmons*. Either way, "they" couldn't lose. Either way,
"they" came up winners.

She'd used Gary; he'd used her; "they'd" used them
both. The Bureau had used them both. They never had a
chance, Katie and Gary. Not a prayer.

When the reality finally sank in, Cathy stopped walking, engulfed by a swell of nausea. Stumbling into a
garbage-filled alley, she spewed up, her slim body racked
again and again by spasms of vomiting. And when she
thought of how she'd pulled the trigger, how she'd been
the instrument used to gun a man down, she threw up
again.

Then, remembering Gary Simmons's last words to her,
his last smile, she wept.

It seemed hours later that Cathy found herself at Michael Carnes's apartment building. Unconsciously, she
must have been headed there all along. After all, she still
had one last report to give. And she couldn't go home;

she knew that. "They" were waiting to kill her. "They" wanted both of them dead—Gary and Katie. One down, one to go.

Michael had kept the key to her place; well, she still had the key to his. She let herself in and placed a call to the Bureau in Denver, identified herself, told them that it was an emergency, that Michael had to phone her at once in Chicago. Then she poured herself a large Jack Daniels and sat down to wait. She was hollowed out, drained. Completely empty. She had even lost track of who she really was. Katie or Cathy? Cathy or Katie?

It was several hours before Michael let himself into his apartment. He found Cathy sitting in the dark, watching the news on his huge rear-projection television screen. He snapped on the overhead light, but Cathy didn't even turn around.

She looked terrible; burned out. Her eyes were staring, her hair was wild and uncombed, and she seemed to Michael suddenly very young and very small, sunk into his down-filled oversized couch, and in her dirty jeans and worn boots she appeared out of place in Michael Carnes's expensively furnished decorator apartment of chrome and glass.

On the screen, the familiar figure of Robert Flynn was addressing the public through the media. His eyes, looking straight into his audience's, flashed fire, his jaw was firm and strong, and he seemed to be suddenly possessed of a charisma he hadn't displayed before, as though the persona of Jack Carpenter had descended on him, like a mantle over his shoulders.

"You tell me where this country's going if a man can be gunned down in the street because of what he stands for," Flynn was saying in sonorous tones. "The saddest part is that's exactly what Jack was always saying—that we have to return this country to the kind of country we grew up in. America, he said over and over again, mustn't be a lawless society. We're going to continue this crusade, and if I have to run in Jack Carpenter's stead, then that's what I'll do. Nothing is going to stop us!"

Something in Flynn's words rang a distant bell in Cathy's memory. She reached for the thought to grab it and pin it down, but then Michael spoke and the formless wisp of memory vanished out of her grasp.

"I got here as soon as I could," said Michael. It was plain that he was elated, on a high. His voice was close to shaking with suppressed excitement.

"We're busting people all over the country. That print-out you got was a gold mine! We're getting weapons, money—Washington's going to make a statement in an hour. We did it! We got 'em!"

Cathy kept staring at the TV screen as though she hadn't heard him. Now the news program was showing film clips of Jack Carpenter at his last press conference.

"Some people are being made very nervous by my candidacy," said Carpenter. "They'll obviously do anything to stop me."

Cathy smiled bitterly. "It's the best thing that ever happened to them. Now they've got their own martyr." She shook her head wearily. What the hell had they really gained? These people grew like mushrooms on a lawn after a rain. Cut a few off and others sprang up instantly to take their place. And you couldn't pull them out by the roots, because mushrooms don't have any roots.

But Michael's fire wasn't easily dampened. He actually didn't hear what Cathy was telling him. "We got 'em, Cathy!" he went on enthusiastically. "Don't you get it? We're bustin' 'em all over the country!"

Cathy put her drink down and stood up. She ached all over. What she needed was a long soak in very hot water. But not yet. Not yet. She walked over to the large living-room window and looked out. Michael lived on the thirtieth floor of a high rise overlooking Lake Michigan, and his view of the city's skyline was spectacular, especially at night after the lights came on.

But Cathy didn't even notice it. "He knew who I was, Michael. Gary knew who I was."

"He couldn't have!" Michael gasped.

"They've got someone inside."

"They can't!"

Cathy turned to face him. Didn't he understand anything? Didn't he know how things worked? "They've got friends all over, Michael."

"We'll get him," Michael replied confidently. "Whoever he is, we'll get him."

No, he didn't understand. He was so full of today's success it was impossible to make him understand. But *Cathy* understood. Michael hadn't been there; Michael hadn't seen what she'd seen.

"No, we won't. We *won't* get him. We'll *never* get all of them," she said blackly.

It was over; time to go. Catherine Weaver looked around the room as though she'd never seen it before, as though she hadn't spent many nights in this apartment. She looked at Michael Carnes as though she'd never seen him before, as though she hadn't spent many nights in his arms.

Slowly, Cathy pulled the gun from the waistband of her jeans and dropped it on Michael's gray tweed couch. Only one bullet had been fired. Only one bullet had been needed. Because a man had turned his back to her, believing that she'd never shoot him in the back. What a goddamn fool! She walked toward the door.

"Where are you going?" asked Michael, startled.

Cathy stopped and turned around. Her face was empty of all expression, her eyes were dead.

"I had to kill him," she said hoarsely.

"Of course you did!" Michael cried.

A look of pain slashed across Cathy's features. "I didn't have any choice, did I?" Her tortured eyes begged him.

"No."

Her voice dropped to a near whisper. And now, the confession. The horror of it, the guilt. "I shot him in the back, Michael."

Michael met her guilty eyes defiantly. "So what?"

Those two words hit Cathy like a blow to the chest.

She turned and started for the door. She had to get out of here.

"Where are you going?" Michael asked again, this time more nervously.

"What do you care?" she retorted wearily.

"I care! You're going to need protection! Cathy, they know who you are!"

Cathy smiled wearily, giving her head a little shake. What did it matter? Michael almost ran to her, took her into his arms, holding her gently.

"Cathy, listen to me—"

"Don't. Please don't. Please," she said, holding her body stiffly, refusing to yield herself to his embrace. After a moment, he released her, knowing that she didn't want him to touch her.

But Cathy had felt something in his touch. A reaching out. A memory of what they'd had. He deserved better than her silence. He deserved to know how she felt. How she felt about all of it, the whole stinking, shitty business. Yes, he deserved it.

"I never had a family, Michael," she began haltingly, her words choked with emotion. "You were my family. The Bureau was my family. I trusted you. You used me. The Bureau used me. And then you betrayed me. And then, finally, up there, I betrayed myself." She paused, to give herself a chance to force back the tears. "I don't have a family anymore. I don't have anything anymore. I got too dirty. I just got . . . too dirty."

Looking at Cathy, Michael could see she was hurting bad. Her eyes were huge, filled with anguish, and her lips were trembling. He knew she'd been through hell today, but it was worth it. It was worth it! If he could only make her understand what was *really* important, then maybe she wouldn't hurt quite so much.

"Jesus, Cathy, we won," he told her softly. "We won."

Cathy shook her head. "What did *I* win, Michael?"

There was no answer to that one. She'd lost, and she'd be forever changed because of it. Michael couldn't deny what Cathy was accusing him of, him and the Bureau.

He *had* pushed her, he *had* sent her back in time and again, even after she pleaded to be allowed to walk away while she was still clean. To Michael, killing your first perp was like making your bones. To Cathy, it was the death of innocence. These two lived in two different worlds, possessing two very different sets of priorities.

Al Sanders came in the door to find Michael and Cathy confronting each other with a tension between them so palpable you could almost see it hanging in the air.

At the sight of Sanders, Cathy turned away from Michael and walked purposefully to the door.

"Where you goin'?" asked the black agent.

Cathy thought about it. She didn't know. "Away," was all she said.

"You can't."

"Yes, I can."

"There ain't no goin' away, don't you know that, girl?" Sanders's strong face softened with affection and concern. "There ain't no goin' away."

"Goodbye," Cathy said quietly. For her, there was no turning back. Not now. Not until she understood fully what had happened to her, how she had changed, what her future could be.

"Take care, girl," Sanders said softly. "Take good care. You hear?"

Catherine Weaver nodded. She heard. And then she was gone.

Catherine Weaver left Chicago to save not her body, but her soul. She went in search of America, of an America she remembered from her childhood and understood. She went looking for survival, for simplicity, for roots, for honesty, for comprehension of how the world—which sometimes was too soul-sickening to endure—might function if hate were absent.

It didn't matter where she went, really. But Texas was as good a place as any to begin her search. It was where she herself had started, twenty-five years ago.

It wasn't to the Texas of the ranches or the oil fields, or Neiman-Marcus, or the air-conditioned Mercedes limousines that she went. Cathy was sick to the heart and tired of talk, fed up with specious arguments, grimy rationalizations, pathetic excuses. She wanted dignified silence and good, hard, physical work. To hell with her goddamn college degree. She wanted to get her hands into the soil, to feel the sun hot on her skin, burning her face and arms, baking her brains. She wanted to be so goddamn tired that she could sleep at night without dreaming that she was shooting Gary Simmons in the back.

She picked onions in a field, down on her hands and knees, surrounded by incurious migrant workers, who spoke to one another only in soft, limpid Spanish, ignoring the *gringa* who so obviously wanted only to be left alone.

Even if she *was* left alone, Catherine Weaver knew she was being watched. It wasn't always the same man—the face changed almost from day to day, as though they were taking shifts, but it was always the same expression on the face. Just watching her from a distance, close enough to let her see it was happening. Often they smiled.

She wasn't afraid. She had learned that there were worse things than death, and fear was one of them. She was never going to let them scare her again.

At night, she'd drink beer in a local bar, mingling with nobody, talking to nobody, dancing with nobody. She sat and she smoked and she drank Dos Equis or Lone Star, and she listened to the juke. She was kind of getting to like country music, how about that? And she thought. Catherine Weaver thought.

Then she'd go back to her cot in the migrant workers' shack, and she'd lie on her back, smoking and looking up at the ceiling, and thinking. One night, months after she'd begun migrant labor, it all fell into place. She knew what that wisp of memory had been that night in Michael's apartment, the night she'd shot Gary Simmons. She knew who the man in the chopper was, and who'd laid out the hit and given the order to shoot.

Flynn. Robert Flynn. Had to be. The first rule of law enforcement: look for the motive. Who benefits? In this case, Bobby Flynn benefited. His campaign was really rolling now, gathering momentum. Who else but Flynn would have fingered Carpenter as the target? Picked Gary, "the best damn point man in the world"? Who had stood close to the seat of power for many years, quietly taking the pulse of an angry minority, feeding hatreds, building up an organization of influence and strength, an organization well funded and well armed, uniting every splinter hate group into one rabid militia just waiting for the command to unholster their guns? Who but a former officer of the National Security Council could penetrate so many hidden chambers, put a mole even into the FBI?

It all fit. It even made perfect sense. Flynn sets Jack Carpenter up as a straw man, to test the wind. To see if an independent candidacy based on America's deepest hidden fears could get up the vote. Then, when it looks as though Carpenter has some chance of going all the way, Flynn steps out of the shadow and gives the order.

Bang, bang, instant martyr. Jack Carpenter dead is worth a hundred of Jack Carpenter alive. The grieving Flynn dips his mantle in the spilled blood and comes up a hero. Now he can go all the way.

And Carpenter? Why, he was nothing more than the scarecrow they were using as a target. Just a scarecrow to be blown to pieces, like the one that Katie had found that day in the wheat field, a million years ago next Wednesday.

Could they touch him? Could the Bureau get Flynn? Cathy lit another cigarette and pondered the question. Probably not. On what grounds? Where was the evidence? No, he was too goddamn smart, making sure that there was too much distance between himself and the hand on the trigger. Flynn would probably go on to greater glory. He wouldn't be the first in history to follow a trail of blood to the highest seat. He wouldn't be the last, either.

And then Catherine Weaver knew with certainty that

it was time to go back. Time to pick up her old skills, only with a new way of looking at things. She'd hardened, sure, but she was smarter now. More together, less vulnerable maybe. And no longer afraid.

But before she went back, there was something she still had to do. Cathy made up her mind to leave at daybreak.

It's a long drive from southern Texas to the Midwest plains especially if what you're driving is kissing cousin to a junk heap. The further north she drove, the colder it got. Her clothes weren't warm enough, and the car had no heater. There was deep snow on the ground in Denison, and the old Pontiac didn't have snow chains or even radial tires, so it was pretty heavy going. More than once, Katie had to fight to keep the car from skidding off the road.

The Simmons house looked different with its roof covered in snow—like a picture postcard of Christmas. The last time she'd seen it had been high summer, when she'd left it with Gary. She got out of her car in the farmyard and looked around. Nobody. No sign of life at all.

"Rachel? Joey?" Katie yelled, but there was no answer. "Rachel?" she yelled again.

Then she remembered. Sunday. Of course. It was Sunday, and she knew where they all were. Shit. If there was anyplace Katie Phillips didn't want to be, it was in that hate-filled hellhole of a "church." Maybe she'd just wait here for them to come back. She'd sit in the car and try to keep from freezing.

As Katie turned back to her car she noticed for the first time a large snowman the children had built in the yard. It had coals for eyes and a carrot for a pipe. On its head was a battered old hat, and pinned to its breast was a yellow Star of David. Nothing had changed. Gary was dead, but the hatred continued, the ignorance flourished.

Katie took a deep breath and squared her shoulders. Reaching up, she pulled the yellow badge off the snowman, crumpled it up, and threw it onto the frozen ground.

Then she got into her car with determination written all over her face, and drove to the church.

Service was over and people were just streaming out of the Christian Reality Church as Katie drove up. The Reverend Johnson, hellfire preacher, was out there saying goodbye to his congregation. She recognized them—Lyle, Dean and Toby, Buster. They looked somehow different, then Cathy realized that they were all bundled up for winter. Heavy boots, down jackets, denim coats lined with artificial fur, woolen caps with earflaps. And there was Gladys Simmons with Rachel and Joey.

Katie sat in the car and with trembling hands lit a cigarette and put it out again. She didn't want to get out of the car, didn't want to run the gamut of these hostile and angry men and women, Gary's friends. After all, she'd betrayed him.

But Katie remembered what Cathy already knew—that she was never going to be afraid of these people again. Or of anybody else. She climbed out of her car and started toward them slowly.

There was a gasp, followed by a shocked silence as every eye was focused on her. The anger emanating from them was a living thing, a ferocious slap in Katie's face.

"Katie!" Rachel saw her. The little girl's face lit up brightly and she started to run forward, but Mrs. Simmons grabbed the child and held on tight.

Katie had eyes only for Rachel; she ignored the others. "Hi, Rachel. I missed you very much."

"I missed you, too, Katie."

Now the Reverend Johnson stepped out of the crowd, his face angry and accusing under its mane of white hair. "What are you doing here, Jezebel?" he thundered in biblical rhetoric.

"I came to see the children," Katie answered evenly.

"You're a whoor! You're a Jew whoor!" Joey's voice was a shrill scream, and his small hands were balled into tight fists. He began to run wildly at Katie, yelling, but Lyle kept a tight hold on the boy's shoulder. "You killed my dad! You killed my dad!"

"I bet she didn't," said Rachel. Gladys Simmons raised her gloved hand and slapped Rachel hard. The child began to cry, and Katie instinctively went to her.

At once, the reverend and several of the men formed a block in front of Katie, keeping her from Rachel.

"Get out of my way, Reverend," Katie told him without fear.

For a long moment, the two of them were eyeball to eyeball, but Katie didn't back down an inch. At last, with a grudging grunt, the preacher stepped aside, just enough for little Rachel to duck through the space and into Katie's arms. She was still crying, but as Katie held her, rocking and soothing her, her sobs began to tail off, and she began to calm down a little.

"She's a whoor! She's a whoor!" Joey yelled. He was crying now, too.

"We know what she is. We know *who* she is. She'll get her just rewards."

Katie looked him straight in the eye. "So will you, Reverend."

"Get away from here, Jezebel!" boomed the preacher. "This is the House of God!"

"This is America, Reverend. I'm staying right here."

A murmur of rage rose from the congregation, and they looked at Katie with hate. A few of them started forward, their hands forming fists, but nobody wanted to be the first. Something *had* changed after all. There was no Gary Simmons to lead them now. One by one they dropped back, or their wives pulled them away, and they went to their cars. Soon, the only ones left were the preacher, Mrs. Simmons, Rachel and Joey, and Katie.

Then the Reverend Johnson, still glaring balefully at Katie, retreated back into the safety of his church, banging the large wooden door hard.

Katie Phillips and Gladys Simmons stood fifty feet apart, looking at each other. The woman who had given Gary life, and the woman who had taken it from him. Between them could be nothing but bitterness.

Mrs. Simmons put her hand out for Rachel. She said

nothing, but her expression was very plain to the little girl. It said, "Come." Rachel looked uncertainly from her grandmother to Katie, then back to her grandmother. Slowly, she began backing away, obeying Mrs. Simmons. Her eyes, though, were still on Katie, who gave her a tremulous, loving smile.

With a little cry, Rachel stopped and ran back to Katie, throwing her arms around her in a big hug, burying her face in Katie's neck.

"Bushels and barrels and stuff," Katie whispered.

"Bushels and barrels and stuff," Rachel whispered back. And then she was gone, walking back to her grandmother, ignoring Mrs. Simmons's outstretched hand, ready to obey but not to be subdued.

Katie Phillips stood looking after her in the growing darkness of a winter afternoon. She shivered a little, but inside, she was warm. She'd be all right, Rachel Simmons. It might take her some time, but she'd be all right. They both would. Two orphan girls with only themselves to depend on, but with a little luck it ought to be enough.

Catherine Weaver opened the door to her ancient car and slid behind the wheel. She was ready to go back now.